The Deadly Caress

O. N. Stefan

Editing by Kyle Sharpe and Christine Day

Manuscript assessment by Victoria Chie

Cover design by akira007 and David Broom

Payella Pty. Ltd.

First published on Kindle 2014

ASIN: B00I0DI0MY

ISBN-13: 978-0994293206

Dedications:

This book is dedicated to:

Max for supporting my writing efforts.

Chris for listening.

Nicole for helping me when I was stuck with too many choices.

Victoria Chie for helping me make this story better than it was and allowing me to pick her brains when I couldn't find a solution.

Fay Weldon for her encouraging comments on my rough manuscript.

On Seeing A Sheep About To Be Slaughtered.

Ill fated sheep, so innocent and mild,

So harmless, timid—gentle as a child,

Thy dying hour is come:

The slaughtering knife is raised above thy head,

To lay thy panting, spotless carcass dead,

And seal thy hapless doom.

Ah! Cease to bleat, there's no retreat,

Those anxious looks are vain;

One moment more, 'twill then be o'er,

And thou released from pain; —

But ere 'tis done for pity's sake I'll fly —

I cannot, will not stay to see thee die!

By J.W. King published London. 1850

CHAPTER 1

Amanda Blake opened the door of the silver Rolls Royce and nervously sucked in the Monterey sea air. Oh God, she was terrified that this wasn't going to go well.

She shouldn't have accepted the invitation. She could've been in Tasmania taking photos of Tasmanian devils for National Geographic instead. The knot in her stomach tightened as she climbed out and hoped that she was up for whatever would happen.

The chauffeur hurried around to help her.

"Thanks, but I can manage," she said. "Ricardo, isn't it?"

He nodded and straightened his cap that partly covered his short black hair.

She fumbled in her purse for some notes, which were all the same color. Unlike home, she had to remember to tip everyone here. She pulled out ten dollars.

Ricardo he shook his head when he saw it.

Was the bill too much or too little?

"Mrs. Campbell pay me good. I work for Mrs. Campbell for many years. She ask me to look after you," Ricardo said with a heavy Mexican accent.

Amanda bit her upper lip. Her first blunder and she'd just arrived.

She shaded her eyes from the afternoon sun and stared at the modern brick, concrete and glass mansion perched on about an acre of prime California real estate. This house must have a dozen bedrooms from the size of it. It screamed of money and privilege…something she'd never experienced.

The contents of the letter that had shattered the illusion of her world and lured her half way round the world remained branded in her memory.

Dear Amanda,

It is hard to know where to begin. I regret that I never made contact with you before, but this was the agreement I made with your parents. Even now, I am writing to you now with the permission of your father, Samuel.

I wish there were a gentler way to break this news to you. Elaine is not the woman who gave birth to you, I am. Nor is Samuel your biological father. He can verify this. I know your life has been reasonably happy from the annual letters Samuel sends me.

I know you must have many questions you want answered. Please direct them to me, since I am the only one who can answer the circumstances of your birth.

I hope you can forgive me for this sudden intrusion.

Please come and stay with me as soon as you can. I have enclosed an open-ended ticket to California for you.

I want so much to see you.

Yours sincerely,

Jean Campbell.

Amanda had traveled from her home in Sydney to meet the woman who had given her up at birth. Now Amanda hoped her trip wouldn't be in vain.

Google had provided a reasonable amount of information, but not the things she really wanted to know. What was *this* mother really like? And why did this woman feel compelled to break this news to her *now?* Twice, she picked up the phone to call this woman named Jean but stopped short. She'd been too nervous and didn't know what to say to a stranger who was her mother. At least if she'd called, she'd have gotten to know her a little.

One of the double-fronted doors swung open. A short woman wearing a maid's garb, with her black hair pulled back into a bun, hurried down the granite steps.

"Welcome. My name is Estella," the woman said.

Startled, Amanda took a half step back. Chauffeurs, maids …what next? She heard the Rolls start forward. "Oh! My bags, my camera. He's forgotten about them." She swung around and waved, trying to attract Ricardo's attention.

"Please do not worry, Miss Amanda. He will take your luggage to your room." The maid spoke English quite well but her Mexican accent was still evident. "Mrs. Campbell is please you have come. She is waiting for you inside."

***

"Jean, have you heard anything I've said?" Lionel Cohen, her balding and overweight lawyer asked, seated beside her on the cream damask sofa.

"I hope Amanda likes me." Jean Campbell pressed her manicured hands to her temples. "Oh she'll probably hate me, despise me. Be upset that no one's told her. That I hadn't contacted her years ago."

"I did suggest it would have been better to leave it."

Jean looked suddenly towards the door. "Is that Ricardo?"

She jumped up and straightened her silk skirt. "I should be out there to greet her."

"Come back and sit down. We're not done. Estella will bring her in."

"But-" Jean began.

"You want to look calm, don't you?" Lionel interrupted. "She doesn't need to know how desperate you are for her acceptance."

But I am, she thought. "And her love, Lionel… the child must feel abandoned by me. I have only one chance for a good impression."

He put his glasses into his suit pocket and then picked up some documents from the coffee table. "I can't say that I agree with the changes, but I'll get them done and back to you tomorrow." His tone was grudging. Lionel was a good lawyer, Jean mused, but he was an extremely old-fashioned man, with outdated ideas; he didn't like that she'd gone against his advice. Though, she couldn't divulge to him what she knew yet until it was confirmed. If all went as planned, tomorrow would be the day.

Jean pulled out a knitted baby's bootie from her suit pocket. "I slipped it off Amanda's foot the last time I saw her." She shook her head as the memory of that heart-wrenching moment assaulted her. "You can't imagine..."

"No, I guess not," he said, giving her a blank stare.

Twice she'd managed to sneak into the nursery to see Amanda. It was during the second time that she'd taken the bootie off that tiny pink foot.

For many months afterwards, she'd cried herself to sleep. Every year, on Amanda's birthday, she sank into the shadows where there was no hope, only alcohol, and lately prescription medications from any doctor whom her money could still convince. The melancholy took many weeks to lift and the supply of pills always dried up. Her daughter's birthday was tomorrow. Now, for the first time in thirty years, she hoped they would celebrate it together.

"Is there anything else you want to add to this draft?" Lionel said holding up the pages in his hand. "I'm advising you not to leave-"

Jean held up her hand. "Lionel, I've agonized over this, you know that." After staring at the bootie again, she put it back into her pocket along with the years of guilty memories. "Somehow, I have to try to make it up to her." *Something I should have done long before this*, she said to herself.

"I'm tired of people telling me what I should do." She lifted her head to look at Lionel. "I lived with that when Murray was alive. You know what it was like—he told me who I should see, who I could

4

speak to, what I should wear. No one will dictate my life again. I'm sorry, Lionel, not even my closest friend."

***

The sound of Amanda's low heels on the stairs announced her arrival and with each step, she grew more apprehensive.

The white dress she wore, was it too casual? Perhaps she should have changed into a suit? However, the only one she owned was past its expiration date. She paused in her stride and tried to gain some strength from the confident woman she'd worked so hard to become. Well, at least, her workmates often told her she was fearless. Forget the dingoes and snakes, they'd been easy compared to what she was facing now. She'd even Googled a few places to stay just in case things didn't work out today.

Did it really matter what Jean thought of her? She hated to admit it, but her opinion did matter. For all the reasons she had to dislike Jean and what she'd done, there was one reason to like her that outweighed them all. She would have a mother again. It had been a long, lonely eighteen years without one.

To still her nerves, she stared at anything and everything, from the ceiling-to-floor water cascade on colored glass, to the huge Andy Warhol by the wood and glass-paneled staircase.

What would her mother think of her? What if she didn't like what she saw? Her breath caught. The thought made her turn to run outside.

"This way, Senorita," Estella held open the door to the living room.

Too late for escape now, she thought.

A balding man carrying a briefcase and wearing a tight-lipped smile came towards her. "It's a pleasure to meet you, Ms. Blake." He pumped her hand. "Lionel Cohen, I'm Jean's lawyer. I'm the reason Jean couldn't meet you at the airport."

Amanda found herself staring incredulously at an older copy of herself. A slim blonde, dressed in a white and navy suit, crossed the expanse of beige carpet towards her. *This woman had given her up at birth. What sort of a mother would do that?*

"Pleased to meet you," Amanda finally said to the lawyer.

"Tomorrow around noon, Jean?" he asked.

"I'll be here." Jean said.

"No one would mistake you for anything other than mother and daughter. The resemblance is striking," he said before he left.

"Amanda?" The name hung hesitantly between them.

"I can't believe it." It stunned Amanda to see what looked like her own, deep-blue eyes staring back; unlike her own, they seemed to be brimming with welcome and acceptance.

"I knew there was a likeness from the photo you sent me, but seeing you here now…well it's wonderful," Jean said.

"I'm surprised you still have a bit of an Aussie accent."

"That's what people tell me, but I can't hear it myself." The older woman drew her into a warm embrace. Nonplussed, Amanda stiffened at the unexpected display of warmth. She bent down a little to let her mother kiss first one cheek then the other. The scent of wildflowers and sandalwood lingered in the air as her mother withdrew.

"It's so good to meet you at last," Jean said. "I'm sorry I wasn't able to be there at the airport. I hope Ricardo looked after you in my place."

"Thank you for the invitation and the first class ticket, Mrs. Campbell." Amanda was pleased how calmly she answered this woman even though her heart was drumming so hard against her ribs that she felt certain this woman could hear it.

"It was my pleasure. Please…call me Jean."

The urge to call someone mum again, maybe this someone, was there inside her.

"I've left a smudge of lipstick. Let me wipe it off."

The intimacy of Jean's touch stirred an unexpected response from within, elation and something else that she couldn't identify, like being atop the crest of a wave, and the feeling was so new. She worked hard to stop tears from surfacing.

"Make yourself comfortable." Jean buzzed the intercom beside the marble fireplace and asked for two cafe au lattes.

"That's just the way I like it." How did she find out? Who had told her? Amanda drew in a deep steadying breath, and took in the quiet ambience that she'd been too preoccupied to notice until now. She recognized two Picassos, a Degas, and a Monet among the paintings on the walls. Everything fitted together; everything was carefully matched, and mismatched. She sank into a wing-backed chair and stared the expansive view of the ocean that she only enjoyed on occasion, but for Jean it was a normal everyday outlook.

Jean smiled as she settled into the chair nearby. "How was your flight?"

"Good." Amanda couldn't return her smile; she couldn't relax. "Thanks for the first class ticket." My God, she'd thanked the woman again. Get a grip, she told herself as she suppressed a yawn, her coping mechanism. This woman would think her bored.

"I know it's a long journey from Sydney. If you'd prefer, you can go upstairs to your room and rest? We can talk later."

So she'd caught her yawn. "I came here to find out so many things that I hardly know where to begin?"

"Ask and I will try to answer," Jean said.

Amanda steeled herself. "Why did you wait so long?" When she saw the puzzled look on Jean's face, she realized what she'd said. Jean must think her an idiot. She swallowed and began again. "Sorry. What I meant was…why contact me now? Why not years ago? Why contact me at all? I'd have probably not found out until Dad died, and found the adoption papers among his documents."

Estella carried in a tray of petite-fours and hot drinks and set them down on the low table in front of them.

Jean watched the maid leave and then said, "I still remember your birth as if it was yesterday. I was only seventeen at the time. No money, no job."

This woman recalled what…that she'd given birth to an unwanted child. "What about the father, my real father? Wouldn't he support you?" Why didn't her mother address Amanda's first question?

Jean's hand trembled as she sugared her coffee. "He moved away before I'd summoned up the courage to tell him I was pregnant."

"I hoped that I would have a chance to find him." He may have been a victim like her. It had been hell as a child not knowing from one day to the next what mood her mother, Elaine, would be in. "Did you know that Elaine, well I still think of her as my mother, was a manic-depressive? Dad told me when he thought I was old enough to understand. And…" She paused to get a lid on the sadness that welled up from somewhere deep inside. "Not long after that…I'm not good at this…I guess you know my mother committed suicide."

"Samuel did write to me. I am sorry things worked out that way for you."

"Sorry doesn't cover it." Was that all this woman could say! Amanda picked at the edge of a napkin as her eyes smarted with tears. "It wasn't easy living with a mother like that."

At times, it was terrifying. That was past and she'd done her best to bury it but it didn't always stay that way. "Why did you give me up for adoption? Your family, wouldn't they support you?" She wanted more justification for why Jean hadn't been able to raise her. Furthermore, that Jean had *really* wanted her.

"My father's business was bankrupt. My parents were in no position to help me. It was just about impossible in those days in a country town to keep your baby as a single mother. Orange, where I grew up, was no different."

"Adoption was encouraged by everyone from the doctor to the hospital staff. Also, I thought you'd have a better chance at a normal life with a mother and father to care for you."

How she wished her family had been normal. Amanda went to sugar her coffee but stopped herself.

She sipped her drink in an effort to suppress the urge to say what she really thought. *I missed out on a mother because you gave me away. Elaine wasn't a real mother to me.*

"Who's my real father?"

"I can't remember." Jean's face colored, she would not meet Amanda's gaze.

"I don't care if he's good, bad, single, or married; I just want a chance to meet him." Amanda stirred her coffee as she battled to keep a calm exterior.

"I don't know where you'd even begin to look for him. He was someone I knew for a brief period in my life. I'm sorry. I can't remember his last name."

"Record of birth at the hospital?"

"You were registered under my maiden name," Jean sipped her coffee.

"I'd like to try and find him."

Her mother's face drained of color. "Don't."

"Why not?"

"He was...a married man."

She was determined to go to the hospital when she got back home to see if she could somehow trace her father.

"If I could wind back the clock I'd have done things differently," Jean said.

Agitated, Amanda pushed her fingers through her hair. "I can't believe that mum and dad kept this secret from me for nearly thirty years." She'd come home for a weekend's break from her latest assignment, and Jean's letter had been waiting for her.

"I agreed to this when I was too young to know better. I know this doesn't excuse it but it's a decision that I've bitterly regretted," Jean said.

"Why didn't you do something about it before?"

Jean's eyes looked glassy. Was she holding back tears?

"Please, help yourself. They're fresh from the French bakery." Her mother gestured to the tray of petite-fours.

"You think I want cake? What about my father?" She swallowed nervously, uncomfortable with Jean's display of emotion.

"You can't be watching your weight? You have a lovely trim figure."

"Why are you changing the subject? Okay…I'll have one." *You won't want to know about that*, she thought.

"You look a little flushed. Are you okay?"

"I'm still trying to adjust. Finding out you're my mother and Elaine…not being. Meeting you." Had this trip been a big mistake? For her own peace of mind, she'd known she had no other possible choice. Cool down, she told herself, give this woman a chance.

Jean selected a pastry. "My father died about ten years ago and about four years ago I brought my mom over here to live. But after mom was diagnosed with dementia, I had to put her in a nursing home. We can go there another day."

Amanda leaned forward momentarily. "I'd like to visit her."

"I'll arrange it. Some fresh air might do us good." Jean rose, crossed the room to the glass bi-fold doors, and opened them onto a wrap-around veranda. The distant sound of seagulls seemed to dispel some of the tension in the room.

Jean's steps began to falter as she walked back to the wing-backed chair. Amanda wondered if she had an injury.

"My husband, Murray, passed away last year."

"Your husband, he wasn't my father, was he?" A stab in the dark to see what response it provoked.

Jean blinked. "No. I met Murray in my mid-twenties when I was on a working holiday in California. We fell in love…and eventually married."

"Why should I believe anything you say when you've done your best to evade my questions?"

"I wouldn't lie to you," Jean said.

"Then answer my questions."

CHAPTER 2

The Campbell home was perched on a cliff that jutted out to meet the ocean. From his vantage point on the beach, Brian McMahon saw the prearranged signal. Jean had opened the veranda doors.

He raced across the coarse gray sand, and past large boulders that seemed like some giant had strewn handfuls of them at the bottom of the cliff. His fingers skimmed the handrail as he bounded up the steps carved into the cliff's rocky face.

Slow down, he told himself when he reached the top; Jean needs time alone with her. Allow them both some time. However, he was dying to meet Amanda.

Borders of scented lilies and irises were just splashes of color as he hurried along the path that led to the covered courtyard. He felt the eagerness of a young schoolboy, the schoolboy he'd never been. It took all his self-control to pause at the back door. These boyish thoughts took him back to when he was fourteen and living on that run-down acre with that alcoholic he called a father.

He'd never known the carefree life of a teenager: to enjoy going to the local movie theater in the school holidays like the other boys did. He'd been too busy surviving.

***

Jean closed her eyes momentarily. "Give me a chance. That's all I ask."

"I've come all this way not because I'm just curious but to find out what I can and you keep putting me off. That's so infuriating. You're starting to sound like Samuel who won't tell me anything no matter how many times I ask."

"Your father was a sales representative for a large company that sold machinery and parts. It would be impossible to trace him."

"Thank you." Finally, she was getting somewhere.

"I know I must be repeating myself, but it's wonderful to have you here at last. I can't tell you how much this means to me." Jean turned away. Not before Amanda saw a tear roll down Jean's cheek.

Amanda suppressed the sudden kindling of similar emotion. "If it hadn't been for the photo shoot I was doing on dolphins in Western Australia, I'd have been here weeks ago. Right now, I should be in Tasmania doing a piece with a writer for the Australian Geographic."

"Your job sounds demanding."

"I've been taking photos ever since I can remember. Mostly since the part-time job at a photographic studio while I was in high school. Why I chose to do accountancy at university I don't know."

"What happened?"

"One year was all I managed before I threw it in. Then I was back at the studio. That's where I learnt my trade." The hobby that became her passion had kept her sane when the darkness in her mind seemed to overwhelm her, and she thought she would go down the same path as her mother. Well, the woman she'd believed to be her mother.

Jean picked up a ring-bound folder from the coffee table and handed it to Amanda. "I've kept a scrapbook of your work."

Amanda leafed through it. "How did…that's from Geo, and that spread, the National Geographic? Even the one I did for Black and White. That one shot. You've no idea. I had to hang upside down under a bridge."

"Wasn't that dangerous? You could've been killed."

Amanda laughed, and couldn't believe she had. "I had so many harnesses on me, I could hardly move." Jean cared…she really cared. A welling of heartfelt feeling expanded in her chest, it was so unfamiliar that it threatened to overwhelm her. She took a deep steadying breath. "I'm surprised that you've collected all these."

For more years than she could remember, she'd yearned for some small sign of interest in her work from Samuel. She'd driven herself harder and harder to win any show of pride from him. However, it was never enough.

"Mum...oh I mean Elaine-"

"It's okay," Jean said.

"Mum gave me my first camera for my twelfth birthday." It was one of the few presents she'd ever received. After the Christmas holidays, her school friends would talk about their presents and Christmas parties. Not to feel left out, she'd invented grand parties, and extravagant presents.

"It was soon after that that she...she'd..." The guilt still hung over her even now. Psychologists had tried to convince her it wasn't her fault. They'd told her that if she'd stayed home that day it wouldn't have made any difference. But she thought somehow, some way, she could have stopped her mum from killing herself.

"It must have been hard. How did you cope?"

"Dad got someone to cook and clean for us." That was what this woman wanted to hear. Not that she was in her early twenties and sought help because she still blamed herself for her mother's suicide.

"You have a boyfriend. Any long term plans in that direction?"

"I called off our engagement ages ago. Charles wanted me barefoot and pregnant right after we were married. Can you believe that?" Also, there had been another reason, one that she'd barely acknowledged until now: the fear that she would be the same type of mother Elaine had been. "How did you find out about him?"

"Samuel." Jean said.

"Dad told you everything? How dare he!" Did he tell Jean about the anorexia? He couldn't have. He'd never acknowledged that she'd had a problem. Her pent-up anger against him flared anew.

"He only told me of the milestones in your life. My letter must have come as a surprise to you."

"You can't imagine how it feels to suddenly find out that your mother wasn't your mother. No explanation from Dad or from you in your letter. My whole life was suddenly a lie."

Jean drew in a long breath. "I'm so sorry. I regretted giving you away from the moment I signed the contract. And the agreement...that I was not to have any contact with you." She shook her head. "I was too young to know any different then. I wanted to call you, to hear your voice, so many times."

Many times…her mother actually said that? One brick, from the wall around her heart, fell. "Really?"

Jean reached over and touched her hand. "Yes."

Amanda shrank back, hesitant to accept what her mother said.

"I meant what I said," Jean whispered. Tears welled in her eyes.

Amanda's emotions were in the verge of spilling over. "Don't cry. You're making me cry too." Amanda dabbed her eyes.

"I can't help it." Jean blew her nose.

"It's okay."

They sat in silence for a while until they had composed themselves. Embarrassing as it was, she had to acknowledge that Jean had done her a favor.

And, she wasn't comfortable about Jean prying to her private affairs. "Thank you for paying my bills. I made a few bad investments-"

Jean held up her hand. "No need to explain. I'm glad I could help."

"How did you find out?"

"I have my sources."

Amanda reminded herself that there were still plenty of unanswered questions and this was why she'd come, so she ploughed on.

"After all these years of keeping secrets with Samuel…why…why now?"

Jean stared at the floor. "I wish I had contacted you sooner."

Just when she thought that their relationship had grown a little, again her mother evaded the question.

"I have a twenty-two year old stepson, Dorian."

"Your husband's son?"

"Yes. Murray's first wife died long before I met him."

"What's your stepson like?"

"Dorian's studying entertainment law at Berkeley. He usually stays

14

there through the week, but tonight he's coming home for dinner. You'll meet him then."

"Anyone else I should know about? Any more brothers or sisters?"

"Only one and he's outside waiting to meet you."

"Are you serious?" Then she saw the look on her mother's face. She glanced toward the door and started to rise. "My brother? My real brother?"

The mantelpiece clock chimed the hour as Jean nervously smoothed down her skirt. The stillness in the room seemed suddenly suffocating.

Long moments passed before Jean answered. "He's your twin."

"What?" Stunned, Amanda sat down again. Jesus, were there any more secrets?

"Did you raise him?"

"Brian was adopted as well."

Amanda noticed Jean's eyes were momentarily shadowed with what could have been pain. Was it for Brian? Why?

A thousand questions vied for primacy in Amanda's head. "Tell me about him. What's he like?"

"Brian works somewhere near Darwin as a stock hand on a large station, yes station. I'm sure he called it that."

Amanda heard the front door slam and footsteps echoed down the hall.

"He arrived from the Northern Territory twelve days ago," Jean said. "That should be him now. You both received an identical letter from me."

Amanda's heart pounded as a tall man strode in. His hair, a darker blond than hers, looked like it had been hurriedly combed into place.

She half rose, sat down, and then rose again, uncertain how to greet him as he crossed the carpet to her.

"My God, you do look like a younger version. You've got to be Amanda, I'm Brian."

"Hi." This man: her twin...had no hint of the typical Aussie outback drawl she'd expected after hearing that he was a stock hand. She drank in the sight of him with disbelief. The resemblance, although definitely male, was there. His eyes were deep green with hints of gold.

"Hard to take all this in, isn't it, Sis?"

A full head taller than she, and she wasn't short, he had to bend over to kiss her cheek.

She didn't like the liberty he took by calling her "Sis." Her mind was in turmoil. She supposed she should embrace him but couldn't.

He was still staring at her; she recalled he'd asked a question. "I'm still adjusting," she said.

"Me too. It's weird isn't it?"

What had his life been like? Had it been as lonely as hers, longing for a sibling to grow up with, to share secrets with; and she had plenty of those.

"You're looking lovely." He leaned over, lightly pressed his lips to Jean's cheek, and then made for an armchair. His suntanned frame seemed to slide into it in one lithe movement.

"How long have you known about me?" Amanda asked as she sat down again. He looked too well dressed for a country boy in slim-fit chinos and Ralph Lauren polo shirt.

Brian shrugged. "Almost a week now, Sis. So I've had a little more time to get used to all this."

"Don't call me Sis. I'm not sure if I like it," she said. He was taking liberties, albeit not large ones, and it didn't sit well with her.

"Oh, for God's sake, I can't see a problem. You're not going to get all strange about this, are you?"

"You're being pushy. You've had the advantage over me. You knew I was coming but I didn't know that I had a brother, let alone a twin brother." Amanda gritted her teeth to stop herself from snapping at him any further.

"Where did you grow up?" she asked.

He blinked. "We moved a lot. But, Wollongong mostly."

"I grew up in Ryde."

"Upper class, huh?"

She bristled. "No. Working class."

"You haven't met Dorian yet, have you?"

She shook her head.

"I wonder what you'll think of him when you do."

"Why?" Was Dorian handicapped or was it something else entirely?

Brian smiled. "Wait and see."

She didn't know what he was on about but she couldn't think straight. It was as if a fog was settling on her brain and her eyelids were heavy. "I don't know what's wrong with me but I think I'll have to lie down."

"Pleasant dreams, Sis."

CHAPTER 3

Amanda stifled a scream, and jerked herself upright in bed, her skin slippery with perspiration. Her heart felt like it was bursting through her chest. It was the same nightmare she'd had with startling regularity for the past month since she'd received Jean's letter.

Her hand trembled as she switched on the bedside lamp. 8:00 p.m. How had she managed to sleep the afternoon away? No way would she sleep later tonight after the nightmare she'd just had.

The creepy part was that she could picture it as if it she were still there. The strange bedroom with hardly a stick of furniture from which she was desperately trying to escape, but her legs wouldn't move. She stared at her hands smeared with blood. She was terrified of something or someone. Suddenly the dream had moved on, and she was in a little tiled room and she could hear running water. Then, as usual, she saw a woman lying on the floor, her blue dressing gown flung open. Somehow, she knew the woman was dead. Every time she tried to peer at the face, she woke drenched with sweat. However, this time, she knew why she did not dare see that face: she feared it was her own.

Now every dark corner seemed threatening. She flicked on the overhead lights, and ran to the ensuite bathroom. She locked the door behind her, and slumped against the wood. Breathe, she told herself. When her gasps returned to something more normal, she turned on the shower, undressed, and stepped under the stinging hot stream. The spray cascaded down her skin and relaxed her limbs as she lathered up. She stood there until her skin was wrinkled before she stepped out.

Amanda returned to the bedroom feeling refreshed and hungry. She dressed and made her way downstairs.

They might have eaten by now, she guessed. Leftovers might be all she'd be offered. When she was working late editing shots, dinner was whatever was in the fridge that still looked edible. Or she'd get take-away.

She picked up her digital camera—the professional equipment she'd left at home—from the French dresser and went into the hallway.

She passed Brian and Dorian's rooms, which were opposite each other, as she continued to the staircase.

As she came down the stairs, someone burst in the front door and strode down the hallway.

Estella emerged from the living room carrying a tray of empty glasses and nearly collided with a reed-thin male. "Lo siento, Dorian. I did not see you."

"Martini, Estella. You know how I like it." He strutted into the lounge in his distressed designer jeans and t-shirt.

Amanda was a few steps behind him. "Hi everyone. Sorry I overslept. I guess you've had dinner?

"Just about to," Brian said.

"What's this, a party?" Dorian said.

"Dorian. You knew Amanda was coming today." Jean clasped her hands together. "Are you feeling better now, Amanda?"

'I had a nightmare,' Amanda said.

"How awful. I hope it wasn't the room."

Her mother showed real concern. Well, it seemed real enough but she'd rather not had that horrible dream at all. "The room's lovely. I've had this dream before. I don't know why."

"They're only dreams," Brian said.

"You never had a nightmare?" she asked.

He hesitated for a moment. "It's not like they mean anything."

Although he was not admitting to this, she noted the pause before he spoke and thought he didn't like to confess to any weaknesses.

"A beer," Brian said.

"Nothing for me, thanks," Jean said.

Amanda had guessed that her mother would refuse. How did she know what this woman liked? Was it some sort of mother-daughter thing?

"Would you like a beer, Miss Amanda?" Estella asked.

"I know I'm letting the side down but I can't drink the stuff. Water," Amanda said.

"Lo siento." Estella apologized. "I thought all Australians liked it. I visited your country last year. My cousin drinks beer. She lives in Wollon...something."

"It could be Wollongong if it's down the coast from Sydney," Amanda said.

"Do you eat fish, Amanda?" Jean asked.

"Love it."

"Good. Estella, get Rosa to cook another serving, please."

Dorian stopped beside a side-table pushed up against a wall and stared at her. His untidy brown hair fell to one side across his forehead; his features had no softness, from his hollowed cheeks to an angular jaw. "Oh yes. The only children to come from your womb are all finally here. Isn't that just so Brady Bunch."

"Dorian, stop that," Jean said.

"So what. Half of the Brady Bunch were step-children, Dorian," Brian said.

Dorian ignored him and plucked one of the white lilies from the crystal vase on the table. He watched the water drip onto the carpet.

Amanda was surprised that her mother didn't reprimand Dorian further. He certainly deserved it.

Understandable that he should feel like the two of them were muscling in on his turf, Amanda thought. However, it was not of her doing. She would have to tolerate his rudeness for the moment, she didn't plan on making him a regular part of her life. Who was he to her, anyway?

Brian glared at the other man. "Cut that out. You're going to ruin mum's carpet."

Jean blinked when Brian called her mum. Maybe she was still getting used to him calling her by that name. Amanda couldn't bring herself to do so yet.

Dorian jabbed the flower back in its place. "So you're Amanda then?"

Amanda sat back. "In the skin."

"How long are you staying?"

"I'm not sure yet."

"Music?" He strode to the stereo, and scanned the list for tunes.

Brian drummed his fingers on the armrest when the deafening voice of a singer and his backing band—which Amanda had never heard before— filled the room.

"Please, turn down the volume," Jean said.

Thank goodness, her mother had spoken up.

"Can you play something softer not that crazy thump, thump stuff?" Now Amanda was showing her age.

"Only trying to get into party mode," Dorian said.

"This is not that sort of a party, mate. Some of us don't want to compete with that," Brian said.

"Dorian!" Jean yelled.

Her stepson turned down the sound. "I couldn't wait to meet my dear half-sister. Although she isn't quite that, is she?'

Jean's mouth was set in a firm line. She looked angry, which made Amanda more annoyed at Dorian's behavior.

'Now what is she? Half stepsister. What a nice mouthful." He flounced to Amanda's side, bent over and kissed her cheek. "You must tell me what color eye shadow you're wearing. I love it."

Stunned by his behaviour and his question, it took her a moment to answer. He was trying to provoke her and it was working. "Straight-brown. I don't know if it would suit you."

Estella brought their drinks. "Dinner is ready. I can carry the drinks to the dining room."

"Thank you, Estella," Jean said as she rose.

They all made their way to the next room where a long walnut and fir table was dressed with a low centerpiece of hothouse orchids and silver candlesticks. "Could you sit there, Amanda, and you opposite, Brian." Jean said.

Dorian's sat at one end and Jean at the other.

The surrounding walls held artworks from old masters. "Isn't that a Degas, and that one a Claude Monet? I love his work. His country scenes always remind me of summer."

"You know something of art?" Jean said.

"I discovered Monet when I studied art in high school. I could rave on about him all day."

"I buy what I like and I like his work." Jean took a tiny sip of her drink.

Dorian rolled his eyes and yawned.

"Would you like some white wine, Amanda?" Brian asked.

She nodded and he poured a glass for her. "Do you mind if I take photos?"

"Go ahead," Jean smiled as Amanda focused.

Brian pulled a face, and flung up his hands as she clicked.

"I hate photos," he said.

"It's for an album I'm starting for us," Amanda said as she took more shots.

"Didn't you hear me?" Brian said.

"Please. What's wrong with a few family pics?"

"Too ugly, huh?" Dorian smirked.

"Drop it, Dorian. I don't like to have my picture taken." He turned his head away. "Put the camera away, Sis."

Not wanting to upset him further, she put her camera down.

"I'll put them all on CD and you can all have a copy." She intended to put them onto her phone as well so she could remind herself that these people were her real family. For years, she'd wanted a sibling with whom to laugh and to hang out. Now this happening, she had an urge to pinch herself and make sure she wasn't imagining it.

As she took her place next to Brian, she noticed two gift boxes on the table. One slightly large box was in front of her seat and the smaller one in front of Brian. "My birthday's not till tomorrow."

Jean smiled. "I couldn't wait. Go on. Both of you."

"Thank you," she said.

Brian lifted the lid on his present. "Thanks for the gold pen." He scribbled on the paper napkin. "Well, it works."

"I'd be very surprised if it didn't."

As Amanda slipped off the red ribbon, her eyes moistened. Many birthdays and Christmases had come and gone with hardly a gift from her parents...and now this... Sadness welled up in her throat and she felt like she was choking. She couldn't bring herself to open the box.

She coughed. That somehow relieved the intensity of that emotion, and she glanced up. Her mother smiled a wistful smile. Could she read her thoughts? She hoped not.

"Go ahead and open it," Jean said.

When she saw the gift, she sucked in a breath. "Pink pearls. I love them." She put them back onto their bed of velvet. "I'm sorry. I didn't bring you anything."

A gift for a mother-come-lately wasn't even a consideration when she'd booked this visit. She'd been too busy trying to come to terms with having a mother again. Now that she'd met this woman, and had been given a gift, she felt guilty. "I can't possibly accept them."

"Murray gave me those South Sea pearls for our first anniversary. Please, I want you to have them. I hope they'll be as special for you now as they were for me then."

"Thank you." Amanda pulled her blonde bob aside and tried to put them on but she was so nervous that she couldn't secure the diamond-encrusted clasp.

"Let me," Brian said. Then he drew back. "They look nice."

She fingered them. "They're beautiful."

A silver-haired white-aproned woman carried in a tray with their meals of grilled salmon with sautéed potato, asparagus, and salad.

"Thank you, Rosa," Jean said.

The cook busied herself with offering each of them condiments.

"Got any ideas what you'd like to do tomorrow?" Brian asked.

Amanda picked up her wine glass. "No. What have you got in mind?"

"What about we catch the tourist spots around Monterey and

Carmel, then we can lunch at a little café that I found in Carmel," Brian said.

"Perfect." She tasted her wine. "Nice."

"Can I get a rain check on that? Lionel Cohen, the man you met earlier, is coming over. We have some urgent legal matters to attend to," Jean said.

She shrugged. "I guess we can do something together another day."

Jean must have sensed her disappointment because she reached over and touched her hand. "How about this Saturday the two of us go to Ano Nuevo State Reserve. It's famous for its elephant seals and sea lions. And I know a great little Italian place where we can stop for lunch. Afterwards we can go visit your grandmother."

"Sounds great and I can't wait to see my gran." Her spirits lifted at the thought. Amanda tucked into the salmon, which was delicious.

"Don't get your hopes up. Half the time, she doesn't recognize me when I visit," Jean said sadly.

Dorian ate another mouthful of fish and suddenly pushed the plate away. "I'm going out."

"Hot date?" Brian asked.

"None of your goddammed business."

"Will it kill you to be civil, Dorian? You haven't finished your food," Jean said.

"I can't see a reason why I should be nice to anyone here." He stormed from the room.

From somewhere in the house, the ringing of a phone intruded until it suddenly stopped.

Estella put her head in. "Sorry to interrupt but there is a call for you, Mrs. Campbell."

"Please take a message, Estella," Jean said

"It's Horace Beare."

"I'll take it in the library. Get Rosa to bring the coffee and cake when she's ready. Please excuse me. I have to take this call."

"What have you been doing, Brian?"

"You know the usual stuff, sightseeing, A bit of shopping but I'm not much of a shopper. I think it's a girl thing," he said as he polished off his meal.

"I can't do that day trip thing that some women do. A couple of hours and I've had enough. I must be letting the side down but I've never liked walking around looking at stuff for hours on end," Amanda said.

Rosa walked in carrying a tray of chocolate cake and their coffee.

"The salmon was cooked perfectly," Amanda said to the cook. "No cake for me, thanks."

"Thank you, Senorita," she said as she served Brian.

He spooned some sugar into his coffee and then fiddled with the teaspoon.

There was a tension in the room, which hadn't been so evident to her before. It wasn't what he was saying, it was the way he'd lifted his shoulders and clunked the spoon on the table as if something was worrying him. Perhaps he didn't like her. Now from where had that thought come? He hardly knew her, so he surely would not have formed such an opinion. Whatever it was, it was irritating. She glanced at him, and finished off her glass of wine.

Brian reached for the slice of chocolate cake beside him. "So you like art."

"I would've thought that obvious," she said.

"I've never had an interest in that stuff." Brian said. "You've demolished that fish."

"I haven't had a decent meal since I left Sydney yesterday. I'm not a good traveler so I don't eat much on planes. I just take a couple of those little travel sickness pills, which make me drowsy and spaced out." She rose. "I need the loo. Back soon," she said and left.

Amanda walked into the hallway; she could hear Dorian and Jean's voices in the room across the hall.

"Why can't I have the money? It'll be mine someday anyway."

"I'm not having your father's hard-earned money wasted on some Metropolitan Community Church in San Francisco," Jean said.

"It's mine and I want at least part of it now."

"I'll tell you what I told you last week when you asked. No! You get more than enough to live on. Give them some of that. With $400,000 a year from the trust fund to play with, surely you can spare some."

"On that pittance." Dorian forced out an ugly laugh. "I should have had it all when Dad died. But you had to come along and make him crazy for you. And you weren't satisfied till you had a wedding ring on your finger."

Amanda hesitated. She shouldn't have been listening. She was not used to family arguing. Her parents hardly spoke.

The door flew open.

"You," Dorian said. "I'll bet she didn't tell you why she hadn't contacted either of you before this."

"No, please don't." Jean rasped.

"You're so rude," Amanda said.

He didn't even acknowledge that she'd spoken. "Dad didn't know she'd had children. I didn't know myself until a month ago."

"What?" Amanda said.

Jean whispered. "He'd said when we had just married, he didn't want any more children. And he ran down unmarried mothers. I didn't know how he'd take it if he'd found out I'd had twins when I was seventeen."

"You couldn't even tell him. Here I was thinking it was some other reason that you hadn't invited me before this." Her mother's words were like wire barbs twisting in Amanda's chest. Jean hadn't had the courage to speak the truth to Murray. Amanda wanted to turn and run as far away as possible but couldn't. "I wish I hadn't come."

"I've made a mess of things. I'm sorry. I'm so sorry, Amanda. I wish-"

"Liar." Dorian interrupted. "You didn't want your children. I don't know why you bothered to contact them now."

"What I said about Murray is the truth. Dorian, please," Jean said.

Amanda gasped. This was tearing her apart. What sort of mother was Jean really? She would have been far better off not knowing that she indeed had a mother such as Jean. The woman who had raised her had been worse, but this…it was killing her.

Brian joined them. "I heard the shouting. What is going on here?"

"It doesn't concern you," Dorian said.

"Don't speak like that to Brian," Jean said. "Are you okay, Amanda?"

She nodded and told herself to breathe. She needed a dose of Ventolin but the puffer was upstairs.

Jean put her arm around her. Amanda shrugged her off. "Don't, please. I need time."

"I was going to tell you, but not like this," Jean said as she blinked away tears.

"What's between the three of you has nothing to do with me." Dorian said. "I still need the money. I'll get Lionel Cohen to sign more of my trust fund over."

Jean expelled a long breath. "He won't. He knows how impulsive you are, and; you know what a stickler he is for rules. Besides, the terms of your father's will make it very difficult to do that. You'll have to wait till you're thirty to get the rest."

"You just want to keep your hold over me. Make me come to you for any extra. I'll get it somehow."

Dorian pushed past Amanda. He took a few steps then swung around. "I don't know why you came. If it's money you want: don't bother. She's so goddamned tight you won't get a cent till she's in her grave."

CHAPTER 4

Amanda zipped up her raspberry-colored dress, and then stepped into her sandals, her thoughts centered on Dorian's argument with Jean last night.

She recalled her mother's words before Dorian strode away. "I'm sorry. I was going to tell you."

Still wounded by Jean's confession that she hadn't been able to tell Murray she'd had twins, Amanda pulled aside the silk drapes, and the weak morning sun streamed in.

More than half of last night, she'd mulled over how it must have been for Jean faced with that decision. How could she begin to understand when she'd never had children?

That she blamed herself for the loss of her own unborn child at the age of twenty had been more than enough guilt for her to carry. It had been a horrific way to wake up to what she was doing to her body and start eating properly again.

From her bedroom, she could see a path curving from the veranda, past a winding narrow garden of mauve irises and white lilies; and at the cliff face, steps that disappeared downwards to the beach. Near the steps grew two Cypress pines that clung precariously to the rocky cliff face and leaned towards the restless, churning, water.

Even after last night's incident, and the conflicting emotions that had brought her here, she was glad she'd come and been given the chance to meet her twin. Being part of a family again made her feel whole. She opened the window and heard the ocean crashing angrily against the rocks and the wind wooing as it skidded past the house.

No matter what the weather brought, she was looking forward to spending time with Brian.

A glance at the clock told her it was seven-thirty. She picked up her earrings from the French provincial dresser, had pushed one hoop in her lobe when she heard a scream.

The woman screamed again. Amanda opened the door and hurried toward the sound, which seemed to be coming from a room at the far end of the hallway.

She stopped in the doorway to Jean's room. Estella stood sobbing beside a writing bureau, her face buried in her hands. A broken cup lay at her feet. She looked up as Amanda entered.

"She's…." Her voice trailed off.

Amanda couldn't understand her, but she noticed the stricken woman staring towards the ensuite bathroom, its door half-open.

Heart hammering, she pushed the door open as far as it would go.

"No," she gasped. "No."

Jean was sprawled on the tiled floor, her eyes open, staring at nothing, her mouth agape as if wanting to say one last word. Her blue satin dressing gown had fallen open, revealing her negligee.

A sense of unreality gripped Amanda.

"Is she?" Amanda couldn't say the word but she knew the answer to her question. There was no life left in her mother's body.

A toothbrush lay beside Jean's outstretched fingers. Amanda stared hard at them, wanting them to curl around the handle, to show some small sign of life.

Finally, she moved her gaze to the marble vanity. There lay the mundane necessities of the living—a half-drunk glass of water, an open bottle of mouthwash, toothpaste, an open bottle of pills, perfume, lipstick and a compact.

The blue dressing gown…

Was it still a dream…her dream? She opened her mouth to scream but no sound came out. The tap was running, and the sound echoed through her thoughts.

The scene swam out of focus. Her head felt light, and the room seemed suddenly darker. She could smell the soft scent of wildflowers and sandalwood as she felt herself sink to the floor.

***

"Drink this."

Brian's voice commanded her attention. Amanda felt woozy and limp. Somebody touched her cheek.

"You fainted," Dorian said.

She sipped the cool water pressed to her lips, and then opened her eyes.

A worried trio of Brian, Estella and Dorian bent over her.

"You want more water?" Estella said, hovering nearby.

"You look pale," her stepbrother said. He was dressed in pink jeans and a t-shirt.

Someone had closed the bathroom door. "Is she still there?" Amanda asked. "Tell me it's a dream. Please, it's a dream, isn't it?"

She wanted desperately to cling to the thought that Jean was alive. This was not supposed to happen. She had to put right the argument last night with Jean, Dorian and herself. How was she going to do that now? It was supposed to be happy families and laughter.

It was as if someone had ripped her heart out. She was dizzy again and hoped that she would pass out. It was better than this pain. She tried to breathe normally but it was as if she was suffocating.

Brian, in pyjamas and bathrobe, knelt beside her. "I wish I could say it wasn't real but it is."

"What happened? Was she sick? Did she have a heart attack or something?"

"We don't know," Dorian said as he retreated to the threshold of the bedroom.

Brian squeezed her hand reassuringly. "The police have been called and they said that no one is to touch anything in there."

Something in her memory niggled at her, just out of reach.

"P...police. Good." Damn, that stutter had returned. The first time it had happened was at the wake for Elaine. She'd tried to ask Samuel about how her mother had died and found she couldn't get the words out. The problem returned only when she was super stressed.

"Let me help you up," Brian said.

She reached out her hand to him and then she remembered.

"N…no!" She cried. "It…it's my nightmare." She stood on shaky legs. "Th…thanks. Can you get my puffer? It…it's on the bedside-"

"I will." Estella hurried out.

She half expected her palms to be bloody just like in her nightmare. She stared at them and saw Brian watching her doing this. He must think she was going mad. Maybe she was. She wanted to cry but that would have to wait until she was alone.

"What's this about a bad dream?" Dorian shifted his weight against the door jamb, and folded his arms. She didn't know what upset her more, the stutter or Dorian's casual stance when his step-mother was lying there in the next room.

The maid returned.

"Th…thanks…Estella." She took the puffer and inhaled. "Th…this is exactly my nightmare. Oh God, it's not fair. I…just wanted more time with her. Now it's too late."

"Poor Mrs. Campbell." Estella started to cry and searched her apron pockets for a tissue.

Dorian said, "Best you help Rosa with breakfast."

The maid wiped her eyes, and let another sob burst forth as she left.

"Estella's still in shock," Brian said.

"Sh…she probably needs something to settle her. I…think I need a strong drink myself." Amanda took a few deep breaths, and folded her arms.

Dorian glanced at his watch. "I'll be back in a while."

"You can't go." Brian said. "The police are coming."

"Don't tell me what I can or can't do. You can handle the cops," Dorian said.

Amanda felt uneasy under Dorian's sudden scrutiny. What was he trying to tell her? "Th…they might want to question you."

"What about? What are you suggesting?" He paused. "You look like shit."

"I don't care how I look." The stutter had stopped. Did he not see how upset she was?

"Get some breakfast. I'll call Lionel before I leave." Dorian strode away.

Amanda hardly remembered returning to her room, nor punching in numbers on her phone until a female voice answered.

"It better be good." Anna quipped. "Do you know what time it is? It's the middle of the night."

Amanda stared at the mobile expecting it to explain to her best friend how she was feeling. "S…sorry. It's me."

"Oh, hell. It's your birthday. Happy birthday, Funny Face."

"M…my mother's…gone." Someone was sobbing hard, and she looked around to see who was in the room with her. Then she realized she was making that noise.

She tried to stem the flood of tears, and she blew her nose. "S…sorry."

"Your mother's been gone a while hasn't she? Wait, you don't mean to say the one you just met? You're saying she's…"

"Yup." Amanda couldn't say the word.

"Oh, hell. Don't apologize. It should be me telling you sorry. You poor thing. Are you okay? Obviously, you aren't if you're calling me. I wish I could fly over to be with you. You know that I'm working on-"

"I just wanted to hear your voice and share," Amanda said.

"Shit. There I go again."

"I…I'm a mess. I…didn't get time to know her."

"She wanted you in her life again. I'm sure of it. Otherwise she wouldn't have contacted you."

"I…don't know. I just…keep seeing her…on the floor."

"It must've been awful."

Amanda sobbed. "I…I don't know if I can take this."

"Just be strong. I'll ring you back in a few hours? Then I'll be awake and more human," Anna said.

"Please." She called off and sank to the carpet sobbing.

CHAPTER 5

A sergeant from the Monterey City Police Department entered the living room with Estella.

"I'm Sergeant White. Are you Brian McMahon?" He stared at Brian.

"Yes."

"You reported a fatality?"

"Yes," Brian said. He introduced Amanda and Rosa to the sergeant.

"I am sorry for your loss. Where's the deceased?" White asked.

That word was so final. Amanda's intake of breath caused the sergeant to glance at her. Estella joined Rosa on the sofa.

"Upstairs. I can take you there," Brian said.

"Sure." They both left the room. Amanda opened the glass bi-fold doors and went out onto the balcony. She sucked in the sea air to try to gain some strength to face what was ahead. Her mobile played the Pink Panther opening credits. "Hi, Anna."

"I'm awake now. You are made of stronger stuff than me. Hear me, Funny Face. You can get through this."

"The maid found her. We still don't know anything. Why did this have to happen now? My mother's on the floor upstairs. She's been there since I rang you, lying on the cold tiles."

"You know that she can't feel anything now."

Amanda felt tears slide down her cheeks. "Maybe I should get a blanket for her."

"Listen to me. You mother doesn't need anything."

"We argued last night and now I can't even make up with her." She explained briefly what it was all about.

"You weren't to know. I'm sure she had her reasons."

"The guilt is eating me up." She ignored the wetness on her cheeks.

"You did what anyone would do. By the way, my bill for

33

counseling is going to be huge."

"Thanks." Amanda smiled for the first time today. "You're the worst counselor I know."

"Ha, but I made you smile, didn't I," Anna said.

"You did." Amanda heard Brian's voice. "Speak soon. Thanks for the support." She called off, blew her nose, then returned to the living room as Sergeant White and Brian walked back in.

"First of all, I need to establish who was home at the time the body…er the deceased was discovered," the sergeant said.

The body. *No*, thought Amanda as she sat on the sofa. "Her name is Jean Campbell. I would appreciate it if you could refer to her by that name."

"Sorry, ma'am. Now, who was here this morning?"

Amanda crossed her legs, pulled her black jacket around her and folded her arms in anger. She wished she could tell the sergeant to go away. That it was all a mistake.

"Rmm." Brian cleared his throat. "There were five of us. The only one not here is Dorian."

"Where is he now?"

"I don't think any of us know where he went." he glanced at Rosa and Estella.

"No one?" the Sergeant asked.

"No," Amanda said. Estella and Rosa both shook their heads.

"Why did he hafta leave?"

Brian shrugged. "You'll need to ask him that yourself when he returns. He said he wouldn't be too long."

"Who's related to Mrs. Campbell?"

Amanda's temples began to ache, which she did her best to ignore as she thought about the plans she'd made with Jean last night. There were so many questions she'd wanted to ask her mother.

"…and Amanda and I are Jean's children. We're twins. Both of us were adopted out," Brian said.

"And Dorian, Rosa and Estella?" White asked.

"Dorian is her stepson and the other two are employees. Why all these questions?" Brian asked.

So caught up in her own thoughts, Amanda had hardly listened to Brian's answers until now. Her twin was getting snappy. Possibly he was not handling this as well as she thought.

"Because I gotta be prepared for Detective Hart from homicide. Everyone will hafta make sure they're available for questioning when he comes. There's a photographer and more police coming."

"You suspect murder?" Brian, hands in pockets, stood rigid.

He seemed as alarmed and stunned as Amanda was to hear that they were sending someone from that department.

"The homicide office had an anonymous call just before we left the station."

Murder? It didn't make sense. "What did this person say?" Amanda leant forward as she asked the question, barely able to wait for the sergeant's reply.

He snapped his notebook shut. "That's classified."

"I have a right to know. Jean's my mother."

"I'm not at liberty to discuss it. Anyone else?"

"Dorian Campbell, as I said before." Brian glanced at Amanda. His smile didn't succeed in comforting her even for a fleeting moment. Why would anyone think someone had murdered Jean; and what could have been the motive?

The Sergeant scribbled something in his notebook. "Anyone else who's been here in the last few days? Workers? Visitors?"

"I'm not sure if I'm correct but…Joe DeAngelo the gardener, and Ricardo Periuz, the chauffeur. And there are the two cleaners from some agency. They came two days ago. And Lionel Cohen dropped in yesterday."

The sergeant noted that in his pad too. "Is Mr. Cohen part of the family?"

"Family lawyer," Amanda said.

"One more thing, Mr. McMahon, where's Periuz and DeAngelo now?"

"Ricardo's coming soon to wash and polish the cars," Estella said.

"Dorian's the person to ask about the other staff," Brian added.

"Hart'll hafta sort that out when he comes. Nobody is to touch anything in that room. Nobody is to go near that room. I'll go and check on what's keeping Hart," the sergeant said.

Rosa glanced at Estella then spoke. "Ms. Amanda, you like cup of coffee? Waffles? I make for you?"

"No waffles. Just the thought of eating makes me feel sick." She hadn't touched the hash browns and eggs Rosa had prepared earlier. That fried stuff would make her fat. God, she had to stop thinking about calories.

"Sorry. I get you something for stomach ache, yes?" Rosa asked.

"No. It's a bad headache. Just let me sit for a while. If I get hungry I'll let you know," Amanda said. She watched Estella and Rosa leave.

Brian sighed. "You okay?" He sat into the wing-backed chair beside the sofa.

"I just can't get my head around what's happened." Amanda stared at the glass bi-fold doors. "I remember her hugging me and I didn't really hug her back. But I should have." She choked up and had to stop.

"I'll always remember that perfume she wore." She touched her cheek. "You know, she kissed me and then wiped away the lipstick she'd left on my cheek." She could feel her eyes tearing again and she blinked the moisture away.

CHAPTER 6

Dorian parked his red Audi sports car near the five-car garage. Two policemen were at the front entrance to the house. One had been leaning against the patrol car; now he turned to stare as Dorian slammed his door. He nodded and waved, in a rare display of politeness.

A dark sedan had pulled up behind him. The wind billowed Dorian's shirt as he walked towards Lionel's car.

The lawyer stepped out. His gesture seemed sympathetic as his pudgy hand touched Dorian's arm. "I received the message you left with my assistant. What can I say, except, I'm so sorry. Her passing dreadfully saddens me. Jean will be missed by all of us." Lionel Cohen's balding head glistened with perspiration as he stared up at Campbell.

Dorian shrugged. Missed? He'd been too busy hating his stepmother until now.

"I'm sorry I couldn't come sooner," the lawyer said.

"I've been out for a couple of hours and just got back myself." Visiting his lover, Garth, in that run-down apartment had been gut-wrenching. Garth's condition was getting worse. His skin was a mass of crusty, red weeping sores and he'd developed a hacking cough.

"Lionel, I know it's bad timing to ask you this now but I have no choice. I need an advance against my trust fund. Could you arrange it?" He couldn't wait for any inheritance to be released. Garth needed the money for medical treatment as soon as possible.

"How can you think about money *now*?" Cohen glared. The wind made his suit jacket flap.

"It won't bring her back no matter how I feel." How did he feel about his stepmother? He hadn't shed a single tear.

"Your father." The lawyer shook his head. "He spoiled you. And Jean-"

"All I want is an advance. Can I have an answer?" Campbell

asked.

"Then it's no."

"You're in charge of the fund," Dorian said. "It can't be that difficult."

"I can only follow the instructions your father left. And they forbade the releasing of extra money except in extraordinary circumstances and as far as I can tell this is isn't one."

"You asshole! You know what I really want the money for, don't you!"

Cohen reddened. "Why should I? It's of no importance to me."

"You know it's for Garth. I told you weeks ago he's got AIDS. Jean thought I wanted the money for the Metropolitan Community Church. I couldn't tell her the truth."

"She would have been horrified had she known, as I am," Cohen said.

"Both of you blamed Garth for leading me astray. Gay bars and-"

"Spare me the details."

"But Garth's been the only one."

"Have you at least had the sense to have some tests?"

"I've been given the all clear for now."

"Thank God," Cohen said.

"I'll have to go back to have regular checkups for a while yet." Dorian stared at him.

Lionel wouldn't meet Campbell's gaze. "How can you continue to see… this…this…man? It's unnatural."

"Unnatural? Open your eyes. They even have gay TV shows. Damned hypocrite. I'll bet you've lost count of how many partners you've had. You've had more women than…" Dorian hesitated, not wanting to say what he really meant. Even though his parent had been dead a year, it still hurt, "my father."

"How dare you! All that finished five years ago."

"Yeah. Because your investments nearly bankrupted you. And your health couldn't take it. You didn't even care if the women were married or not. Nothing was sacred."

"Shut up. If your father were alive today he'd-"

"Don't give me that crap. Is Felicity Beare a good fuck?"

"Don't you speak about her like that!"

"I'll bet that husband of hers would like to know what she does in her spare time." It had been only by chance he'd stumbled upon them a while ago having an intimate tête-à-tête at some restaurant. He'd passed quite close to their table. They'd been so engrossed in each other that they hadn't seen him. The rest had been guesswork.

Lionel grabbed Dorian by the front of his shirt. "How did you find out?"

"Hey, you okay?" the officer shouted to Dorian.

"We're fine," Dorian said.

"How would it look in the society columns? Wife of major stockholder of Campbell-Beare Pharmaceuticals has affair with the Campbell family lawyer," Dorian said.

Cohen let go. "If you think you've got me by the balls then you're wrong. I'm going to ask Felicity to marry me."

"You're not serious are you, after all these years of smorgasbord?"

"Yes I am." Lionel suddenly seemed very tired and troubled.

He didn't look like a man who was going to ask the woman he loved to marry him, thought Dorian. "So how about the money for Garth's medical treatment?"

"I can't help you. Please...stop seeing him."

"I should have known it was just too much to ask you to be compassionate. Don't tell me who I can see. You're not my father. It's *my* life." He could see a deep pain in Lionel's eyes, and guessed it was for Jean.

"I just don't understand. Why can't you pursue what normal men pursue?"

"I'm different. I can't help it." This man had always been like an uncle to him; but since Garth, their relationship had deteriorated.

Cohen touched his elbow. "I know a very good psychoanalyst."

Dorian jerked away. "Oh sure! What's he going to do for me? Help me understand myself?"

"A few months of therapy and you'll-"

"What did you get that idea from, the dark ages!"

"It is possible there were negative influences that made you-"

He cut in. "People are homosexual because they're born that way. Anyway, I don't need your help. I don't need anyone's help. I'm very happy the way I am." He turned away from Cohen, tormented. "It took me years to admit to myself that I was gay."

"You never dated any girls?"

Campbell turned back. "Once, but it was a total disaster. " The knowledge of what he was had made him miserable for too many years and he'd finally come out of his hermit-like existence and found a man who loved him.

"I can give you the number-"

"Shut up." He needed that money now.

Dorian saw, in his peripheral vision, the officer making his way to them. "I'm going in."

CHAPTER 7

The front door slammed. The sudden noise made Amanda jump and set down her empty cup with a clatter.

Moments later Dorian strode into the living room, his usually pale complexion flushed, his jaw clenched. With him was Lionel Cohen.

Dorian nodded to Brian seated beside Amanda, and then said "Amanda, have you met Lionel?" He forced the man's name out as if it were repulsive to him.

"Yesterday." Amanda rose from the sofa as the lawyer crossed the room to her.

He wrapped his fleshy fingers around her small hand, pumped it. "I'm sorry for you loss. It must be very hard for you."

"I hardly knew her." She slumped back into the sofa. "I didn't get the chance."

The lawyer moved on to Brian. "Will you please accept my condolences?"

"Thank you."

Dorian sat near Amanda. "There's two cops outside. One started asking me questions but I couldn't tell him much."

He was making conversation with her. It had taken *this* for him to be polite. "Where did you go before?"

"Gym. Then I just drove." Dorian nervously bit off skin at the edges of his fingernails.

So, this was where he'd rushed off to earlier? "Why?"

"To think."

Had Jean's death been a turning point for him? Why couldn't this have happened while Jean was still alive?

"Lionel, can you tell us why the police think it necessary to send someone from Homicide?"

"We'll have to wait for the detective to inform us when he arrives."

"I feel like I've been here longer than just one day. You did

41

mention something about coming to visit Jean today, didn't you? What was that all about?" Amanda asked.

"I planned to bring a new will for her final approval and signature." He paused to pull out a handkerchief and mopped his brow. "Unfortunately, I can't do that now."

"Will?" she said, surprised.

"What was in it?" Campbell asked. He crossed his right leg, and swung it out like a tension driven pendulum. He looked agitated.

"Well, it is rather irregular for this to be discussed now. This new will remains unsigned. So it cannot be enforced."

"Cut the crap and just tell us," Brian said.

"Well, since it remains unsigned I guess it won't do any harm. In brief…Jean continued Dorian's trust fund and the shares left to him by his father, he would still have received when he turned thirty, which are a substantial holding in some of the top companies. Except for the $10,000 left to each of her staff—Estella, Rosa and Ricardo— Amanda would have received the bulk of the estate, including about $450 million.

Amanda sat back. "Are you…serious?" That was a scary amount. She pushed her blonde hair from her face.

Brian looked at her. "You would have become a very wealthy woman."

"That bitch was going to pull a stunt like that," Dorian said.

"It was no stunt and it was not signed," Cohen said.

The very idea that she could have inherited such a sum stunned her. "I…I didn't…know about the money. A…any of it. Why me? Why now?"

She could only guess that her mother had altered her will to try to make it up to her for abandoning her as a baby. But Amanda hadn't wanted money, she'd wanted a mother.

"What do you mean?" Brian leaned toward Amanda.

She shook her head, not wanting to attempt to speak with that stutter. How could this mother make up for the years she had endured without her? Where was she when she needed someone who really cared for her? Perhaps she wouldn't have become anorexic. Perhaps she wouldn't have been so desperate for love that she'd sought it in the arms of the first boy that noticed her. If only she'd known Jean then.

What was she doing thinking about this? She couldn't get a breath. She tried, but she felt as if she was suffocating.

She pulled out her puffer and inhaled.

"Asthma?" Dorian stared at her.

"Do you need a doctor?" Cohen asked.

"N…no. I'll be fine in…a minute,' she said.

"Are you sure?" Brian asked.

She nodded not trusting herself to speak. Amanda concentrated on taking a slow breath in and out.

"What about Brian? He's her flesh and blood too," Amanda said.

"I don't understand why my mother would do this." Brian said to Cohen.

"She asked me to draw up the will and I did. Sometimes she'd take me into her confidence over a matter but this time she didn't."

"What did the rest consist of?" Dorian snapped.

"The $450 million? Some of that would have been in shares, bonds, and various other investments. There's a home in Boston, one in Denver, this one, and a couple of houses in Europe and London."

Dorian stilled his swinging leg. His lips were set in a thin line. and he looked angry. Was she the source of his agitation? He sprang up, crossed to the glass doors, and stared out. His back and shoulders formed a barrier between him and everyone else.

Brian broke the uneasy silence. "So you are telling us there's an existing will and it's still current."

Lionel nodded. "It was drawn up a year and a half ago. The reading will be after-" he paused and took a long breath as if it were too difficult for him to say the words, "after the funeral."

At that last word, Amanda tensed. How would she endure it…the endless stream of questions, of who she was and why she was there. Or would they even notice her? She doubted Jean would have been eager to tell any of her society friends of her illegitimate children.

CHAPTER 8

Detective Melvin Hart, or Mel as he liked to be called, only his mother called him Melvin now, switched off the mike in his early model dark-blue Buick as he continued driving. He couldn't stand listening to the broken dispatches for more than a few minutes at a time. Police news interrupted his train of thought, especially when he was on a case.

Jean Campbell's death had all the makings of something that could be big. The little research he'd done this morning had told him the Campbell woman was loaded and the major stockholder in a multi-national company, Campbell-Beare Pharmaceuticals. There were people out there who would kill for a lot less.

A speeding Jaguar shot out from a side street and careened in the path of his car. He slammed on the brakes, and skidded to a halt with only inches to spare.

Holy baloney. Where did some people learn to drive? Who did they pay to get a license?

The car swerved past Hart to the other side of the road. Mel caught a glimpse of the man's black hair through the partly-down tinted window. The car disappeared around the bend before Mel caught any more than a fleeting glance at the license plate.

Definitely not the sort of crazy driver you would expect in this neighborhood. But he guessed that money couldn't buy you brains.

He rubbed his forehead as if he'd bumped it, but he knew he hadn't. A reflex action from the accident he'd had twelve months ago in his classic Ford Galaxie. His head had slammed against the steering wheel then and the result had been concussion. He moved off cautiously.

A few minutes later, he arrived at the gates to the Campbell residence. After showing his badge to a duty officer at the gate, Hart drove past a hedge in spring bloom—a sea of purples, pinks—to the two-story mansion.

A sergeant and an officer stood talking beside a patrol car.

Hart eased his bulk out of his Buick and lumbered against the wind towards them.

They exchanged greetings. Hart pushed back his wavy brown hair from his forehead.

"You're the new guy that transferred from San Francisco. Settled in okay?" Sergeant Gabotsky said.

"Don't you remember me? I headed the case on the Master's Company warehouse fire. I've been here eight months now."

"That was you? Anyhow, you're still considered new to these parts," Gabotsky said.

"What's the story?" Hart asked.

"No signs of forced entry. Security cameras everywhere. No one gets in or our without the security company knowing. And there were no uninvited guests today or yesterday."

"Where's the body?"

The officer, who had been silent until now, said, "Upstairs bathroom."

The sergeant filled him in on who had been home.

Hart searched his jacket pockets for some gum. It kept him thinking. As he pulled it out, a movie ticket fluttered to the ground; he picked up the keepsake from some movie he'd seen before he'd moved from San Francisco. He popped the gum in his mouth.

"Something else," the sergeant said. "The lawyer said he called the deceased yesterday. When they'd finished talking about this new will he'd drawn up for her he was almost sure that when she'd hung up there was a second click on the line, like someone else had been listening."

CHAPTER 9

A melon-shaped man, ushered into the Campbell's living room by Estella, trudged towards Dorian who had been aimlessly pacing the room.

The man nodded a greeting. He flipped his badge. "Detective Mel Hart from Homicide Division, Monterey City Police Department. I am sorry for your loss."

"Thank you," Amanda said.

Hart's brown hair had a permanent windblown look. At first glance, he seemed too soft for the job, but one look into his eyes and Amanda knew she'd misjudged him. They were sharp and watchful.

"Is everyone here?" Hart asked.

"Rosa Estivariz is in the kitchen. I'll call her. I'm Dorian Campbell, Jean's stepson." He buzzed the cook on the intercom.

"I'm Amanda, her daughter." She turned to her stepbrother. "Dorian, could you ask her to bring something for my headache?" Churned up over the news that someone from homicide was coming, Amanda had paced outside for a while.

Hart produced a notepad from his sagging jacket pocket then stared at the painting opposite. "I don't know why people spend money on artwork."

"Picasso? You must be joking," Lionel leaned forward from one of the wing-backed chairs. He introduced himself to the detective.

"Cohen." Hart's eyebrows furrowed. "Can I speak with you later?"

"Yes," the lawyer said.

"We believe you got a call about Jean," Brian said. "What did the caller say?"

"I'm surprised you even know this. Right now I have a few preliminary questions to ask all of you. Then I'll speak to each of you privately. I need to establish the last person to see Mrs. Campbell alive."

A sudden stillness settled in the room.

Estella remained silent, her lips turned downward.

"I saw her last night before she went to bed," Brian said.

"I didn't see her after I had an er...discussion with her in the hallway last night," Dorian said.

"After Dorian left, I spoke to her for a moment. Then I went to my room," Amanda said.

"Okay then. Ms. Periuz, you found her. Why did you go to her room this morning?"

Estella shut her eyes for a moment. "Poor Mrs. Campbell." Then the words she'd probably been holding inside tumbled out. "She's good to me. She was too young to die...Jes, I go to her every morning."

"Why?" Hart asked.

"I bring her hot milk. Wake up her if she is asleep and get medicine ready."

The words collared Amanda's attention. Had her mother been seriously ill?

The detective glanced up from his notes. "What was the medicine for? You can answer now, or if you prefer, later in private."

Estella shrugged. "The doctor knows why she takes tablets. He always visits on Friday." She paused as if suddenly remembering something. "I must call the doctor or he will come, today, one o'clock."

"I'll call him. I want to talk to him anyway."

The maid gave him the number.

Amanda had to know. "But Estella, you must have an idea what those pills were for."

The maid's cheeks colored as she shook her head.

Amanda stared at Estella. It was obvious this woman knew.

"Listen, Ms. Blake, I'm asking the questions. Is that clear?" Hart said.

"I'm her daughter. Is that clear!" Amanda's throat tightened. Daughter? It could have meant so much, but now the same emptiness she'd felt as a young girl on the brink of puberty when Elaine died engulfed her.

"So, where were you this morning when Mrs. Campbell was found?" His gaze was watchful.

"I was in my room. Estella was screaming, so I went to see what had upset her."

"What about last night?"

"I went upstairs about nine and stayed there 'till I went to bed."

"Someone must know Mrs. Campbell's movements last night." He studied each of them in turn. "What about you?" He gestured to Brian, who had gone to stand beside the side table, which held a vase of red roses.

"After Dorian left and Amanda went upstairs..." As he spoke, he ran his fingers nervously, along each of the dethorned rose stems. "I stayed with Jean till about ten I guess. I wasn't watching the time." He jerked his hand away. "Damn thorns." He sucked his thumb. "Then I went to bed soon after."

"It should not have thorns." Estella hurried over. "Let me see."

"You should have checked all of the stupid flowers before you arranged them." He jerked his thumb away.

She'd thought that Brian was coping well; now she could tell he wasn't.

Dorian folded his arms then began to tap his foot impatiently.

"Lo siento, sorry, Mr. McMahon," Estella said.

"Ten," Dorian spat. "Well, I saw her at eleven. That clock over there chimed the hour as I passed the study on my way to my room. The door was ajar and I saw Jean reading something. I wondered why she was still awake when she was normally in bed well before then."

Amanda glanced up and saw Rosa in front of her. She hadn't noticed her come in.

The cook held a tray with a glass of water and a bottle of aspirin. "Thank you, Rosa."

Hart looked up from the notes he'd been taking. "Mr. Campbell, did anyone see you return to your room?"

49

"Now that I think of it, I passed Estella coming down as I climbed the stairs."

"I got a drink from kitchen then I went to my room," the maid said.

"Anyone see you?"

"I did see Mrs. Campbell." Estella seemed distressed to admit this. "She was putting some papers in safe. I told her not to forget her medication. She said she'd taken it in very, jes, angry way. She never spoke to me this way before. Except, one time last week. Someone called her and afterwards, she was very...very upset. Looked worried when she thought no one see. But I see."

"Who called her?"

"I do not know."

"Thank you Ms. Periuz." As he chewed his gum, Hart studied each of their faces again as if searching for an answer and then wrote in the note pad.

Estella excused herself and left.

Dorian sauntered over to Amanda and settled next to her. "You're very pale. Aching, is it?" His tone seemed to be sympathetic, as he leaned towards her.

She nodded, still waiting for the pills she'd downed to take effect. For the second time today, he was being civil to her. Why couldn't this have happened while Jean was alive?

"And you Ms. Estivariz? When did you go to bed?" Hart asked.

"I go after I clean up kitchen."

The cook looked frightened, Amanda thought. What was she hiding?

"What time was that?"

"I think nine-thirty, maybe a little later."

"I see. I'll question each of you separately when I return. I must insist that no one is to leave until I've had a look at the deceased upstairs." Hart pocketed his pad and left.

Deceased. The word echoed in Amanda's head. She suddenly realized Rosa had asked a question. "Sandwiches? I suppose somebody might be hungry. Thank you."

"Music?" Brian asked.

"I don't feel it's right to play music now," she said.

"Come on, lighten up a bit."

A moment later, some jazz singer's voice floated in the air.

If someone had asked Amanda what the others had talked about while the detective was gone, she couldn't have given them an answer. She was mulling over what could have upset and worried Jean so much and why Rosa seemed so scared.

She'd barely been aware of the food and hot beverages arriving or that the others were eating the sandwiches until Brian's urging forced her to take one. She'd taken a small bite and pushed the plate aside. It was her birthday today and she'd totally forgotten about it 'till now. "Happy birthday, Brian," she said dully.

He stared at her, and then it must have suddenly registered. "Oh, hell. I completely forgot. Happy birthday, Sis." He went over and kissed her cheek.

"Thanks. It's one birthday that I'll never forget," she said.

***

Hart started up the staircase.

"Mr. Hart," Estella called, from the foot of the stairs.

He swung round, "Yes?"

Estella's gaze took in the surrounding area as he descended. "I did not want someone to hear. Upset everyone too much. Mrs. Campbell was sick with cancer. Slow growing. She told me there was no possible operation for this. She did not want family to know."

"Thank you." He watched the maid hurry along, past the living and other rooms to the kitchen at the end of the hallway.

Hart went outside to ask the sergeant to contact the doctor. That done, he went upstairs. As he passed the officer guarding the entrance to the main bedroom, he spoke a greeting and continued in.

Hart stopped at the threshold to the bathroom, and stared at the cadaver as the photographer worked.

The medical examiner, behind them, coughed. "Horrible weather outside."

"Mmm." Hart's gaze spanned the room. He saw a stain on the carpet beside the bureau. He bent down and touched it. It was still wet. He sniffed at the substance on his fingers. Milk? Beside the stain was part of a broken cup: the maid's morning wake-you-up for her employer? Otherwise, nothing had been disturbed, and no evidence of a struggle.

He went into the bathroom and mentally catalogued the perfume and other things on the vanity, then called out to the officer. "Bag all this stuff around the sink, and that piece of broken china over there, and anything else that's lying around. And, that stain there. Get a swab of that too."

When the photographer was finished, the medical examiner put on his gloves and bent over the body. "Looks like she was gasping for air."

"Strangulation?"

The medical examiner studied her neck and moved her head to one side and then the other. "No obvious sign of it. But I can't say anything for sure. I'll know more after the autopsy."

"Then let me have your report as soon-"

"That's what you guys always say. You'll have it when it's done and no sooner," the medical examiner said.

Hart went outside and saw another three police vehicles parked beside his Buick.

He plodded over to the first patrol car. "Did you contact the doctor yet?"

"Yep. He's coming in to make a statement. I asked about the slow growing cancer the Campbell woman was supposed to have. He said something about patient confidentiality, but he half admitted I was on the right track."

"Did you ask him if this could have been the reason for her death?"

"He didn't indicate that, but he did say that he would talk to you. Give him a call."

"Then I'd better see who most wanted her money, or wanted her dead," Hart said.

CHAPTER 10

After lunch when Hart finally summoned everyone back to the living room.

"The doc's been and the people from the coroner's office have taken Mrs. Campbell. We've also collected some of Mrs. Campbell's things. Mainly it's the stuff in the bathroom," he said.

Lionel coughed. "Would all of you join me in the library? Perhaps you should come too, Mr. Hart," Cohen said.

Before the detective had a chance to speak, Amanda asked, "What's going on?"

"It was Jean's wish, one that she made only a week ago. She made me promise that I would open the safe in the event of her death. Though I'm certain she didn't anticipate it would be so soon," Cohen said.

"Does it have to be now? Haven't we been through enough?" Brian's smile didn't reach the corners of his mouth.

"I understand you may not feel up to this now. However, another day will not make it any easier. I have her handwritten note with specific instructions that every family member must be present when the safe is opened. This will ensure no one can dispute its contents." Lionel reached into his jacket pocket and produced the note. "She writes that inside is one letter for Amanda and one for Brian."

"Nothing for me?" Dorian jumped up. "So, Jean still just wants to boss us around. She couldn't have wanted me present."

Cohen intercepted Dorian's path to the door. "She asked that all the family be present."

Rosa crossed herself with a shaking hand. "It bad luck to read letter from dead person."

Dorian, breathing hard, returned Cohen's glare. "Fine!"

Cohen turned and strode from the room with Dorian in his wake.

They were strange people, strange family. She didn't really know any of them.

What had motivated Jean to do this?

One by one, Amanda watched each person follow until the only ones left were Hart and herself. Did the letters contain information about Jean's family, or something concerning Brian's and her births? Whatever the contents, it must have been something that Jean couldn't face telling either of them in person.

Hart was watching her and she grew even more uneasy. Finally, he said. "Are you joining us?"

Amanda's stomach churned. She couldn't avoid the inevitable any longer and she had to admit to herself that she wanted to know the contents of those letters. "I'm coming."

CHAPTER 11

When Amanda entered the library, the others were either sitting or standing around the desk.

Lionel nodded to her in acknowledgment. "Now that we are all present, let's proceed. Jean gave me the combination to the safe in this sealed envelope." He tore it open.

Amanda could hardly breathe, she was so nervous. She forced her gaze to the wall of books in an effort to distract herself. She saw a well-worn copy of Jane Eyre. Had it belonged to her mother? Perhaps it'd been her favorite book. It certainly looked old enough.

Cohen skirted the cedar desk, and pressed a button behind the Ansel Adams photograph. The picture swung open to reveal a wall safe. He put on his glasses, and proceeded to spin the dial, partly hidden from view by his frame.

Amanda watched Lionel, unaware that Brian had come to stand beside her until he touched her sleeve. She glanced up as he mouthed a word.

"Excited?"

She gritted her teeth then shook her head in an emphatic *no*. How could anyone be excited at this point? She was so wound up that she felt jittery. Why did he have to stand so close to her? She stepped back to give herself some room.

Cohen opened the safe.

Amanda stared at the cavity, which contained a small mother-of-pearl inlay box, what looked like two envelopes and a folded document.

"Are you going to read them?" Brian's eyebrows furrowed.

Lionel took out the document. "It is a copy of the signed will. This was drawn up immediately after Murray died." He pocketed the document and pulled out the envelopes. His face drained of color.

"Opened? I don't understand. These were supposed to be sealed."

Cohen stared at them as if they would somehow supply him with an answer. "Both addressed to Jean. Not to Brian or Amanda. I don't understand," he said again as he slapped the envelopes onto the desk. He withdrew a handkerchief from his trouser pocket and mopped the moisture from his balding head.

"What's going on?" Hart asked.

"I wish I knew." He grabbed the box, and opened it. "That's the antique gold locket Murray gave Jean early last year. There should have been…." He closed the lid and shook his head. "I don't know…"

"Anyone know what happened to the letters that were meant for Amanda and Brian?" Hart asked.

"How would we know what happened to them? The safe was locked, wasn't it?" Amanda said.

"What would anyone want with some stupid letters that Jean supposedly left in the safe?" Dorian looked flustered. "Maybe they weren't there in the first place."

"Are you sure that Jean left them? Maybe she took them out herself." Brian said.

"I am certain." Cohen let out a tense breath. "I saw Jean put them there myself only a week ago. Do you think I would have asked you to witness this otherwise?"

Amanda's shoulders slumped at the anti-climax. Was this a trick of Jean's? She rejected the thought outright. Surely, her mother couldn't have been so cruel.

"What's in those envelopes?" Hart asked.

Lionel extracted the contents of one. "Photos." He turned each one over. "They're baby photos of Amanda and Brian. In their hospital bassinets, I think."

"Who cares?" Dorian said.

"I do." Amanda leaned forward to get a better view.

"Jean told me about these a month ago, but I'd never seen them till today," Cohen said. "She said they were the only ones she had of her twins."

"Didn't Samuel send her any more of me?" Amanda asked.

"I asked her the same question myself. She told me the adoption agreement stated that she would receive only one annual letter from the parents. That in itself was unusual. Most agreements in those days did not allow any contact whatsoever with the birth mother."

"Can I have a closer look?" Amanda stepped forward, her earlier disappointment momentarily forgotten.

"No one touch them." Hart lumbered past the desk. "I want them dusted for fingerprints just in case."

Amanda drank in the black and white images of the newborn infants wrapped in their bunny rugs. The corners of the snapshots were bent from constant handling.

"She loved both of you very much," Lionel said.

Amanda stared into his brown eyes for any sign that he was lying. "How do you know?"

"She told me many times." Lionel's deep voice seemed sincere.

Her eyes misted over. She'd wanted to hear this so badly, and hadn't realized until now. Her mother had never forgotten her, not even for a single moment. A building of an emotion swelled inside. She didn't know if it was love as she'd never experienced this intensity before, but thought it might be. Eyes closed, she hugged herself.

Brian went to put an arm around her but she shook her head.

Hart withdrew a bag from his pocket, and slipped the snapshots into it.

Lionel's glance fell on the forgotten open envelope. He sighed as if all this had become a pointless exercise and picked it up. "No surprises here. It's empty!"

Dorian straightened his thin frame. "What a total waste of time. I'm out of here."

"I know her feelings for you were very deep."

"Lies. Goddamned lies," Dorian said.

"It's the truth," Cohen said as Dorian stormed from the room. He flipped over the envelope.

"It's from…Scott McMahon, Wollongong, Australia…your

brother?"

Brian hesitated before he answered. "Yes."

"Can you offer any explanation for this?"

"Blowed if I could tell you why he'd contact Jean. We were never close. Once our parents died, we lost touch. "

The lawyer raised an eyebrow.

Amanda's thoughts were racing. "Is he my brother too?"

"We were both adopted," Brian said.

"You never mentioned him."

"He's the black sheep in our family. Why would I want to talk about him?"

"Brian, why don't you ring him, and find out what he sent to Jean?" Could there have been some connection between the missing information and Jean's death?

"That's a stupid idea." Brian said.

She glared at him. "I don't think it's stupid. It's worth a shot. No one has any other suggestions," she said.

"Scott wouldn't give me the time of day," Brian said.

"You'll contact him, won't you," she said to Hart.

"In due course."

It didn't sound like he intended to. What was wrong with the stupid man? Couldn't he see that he should follow every lead, no matter how small? Either way she wanted to find out, even if it came to nothing. There were already too many unanswered questions.

Hart, as if sensing what she was thinking, added. "We don't know if this is definitely a homicide case yet. The death could be from natural causes or even suicide."

Shocked at his suggestion, Amanda blurted, "I can't believe Jean would kill herself. Why did she invite us to her home if she planned that? It's not possible." Please God, she thought, it couldn't be that. Not again. Not for the second time. Just when she thought she'd been released from the fear that suicide ran in her family, and that she too might take her own life.

"I can't dismiss anything at this time," Hart said.

"Natural causes." Brian offered

Amanda shrugged. "It just can't be suicide. What about the pills Jean took every day that Estella had talked about earlier? Maybe she was very sick."

"It could be an overdose," Brian said.

"How can you say that," she snapped. "Sorry. I don't know what's got into me. Our mother could have died from a heart attack or something." She rubbed her forehead; her headache had returned.

Perhaps that mystery envelope from Scott McMahon held the answer.

Brian touched her arm. She was about to snap at him again when she saw the sympathetic look in his eyes.

"Whatever it is, I'm sure the detective will sort it out," Brian said.

"Lionel, you're sure there were supposed to be two letters in the safe for the twins?" Hart queried.

"Here, read it yourself."

"What about the will you pocketed?"

"I'm just following Jean's instructions. Here, if you want to read them."

Hart examined the letter. "It's there as you said... right...interviews. If there are no objections, I would like to conduct the interviews in the dining room."

"I can see no problem," Lionel said.

"No one is to leave until I've seen them. I've asked my colleague, Detective Stephan, to sit in on the interviews. Let me check outside and see if he's arrived." He turned to the maid. "I'd like to start with you, Ms. Periuz. Please wait for me in the dining room."

CHAPTER 12

Amanda went out the side door to the back terrace. When she saw Brian waiting for her on the path that led to the cliff face, she waved. The wind flattened his t-shirt against his chest, and tossed strands of his dark blond hair onto his face.

She bypassed a couple of easy chairs and exotic palms in urns as she made her way to him. It had been Brian's suggestion as they left the library that they meet outside in about ten minutes, to get some air. She'd taken little more than that time to pull her hair into a ponytail and change into jeans, jacket and joggers.

Brian smiled as she neared. "How's the headache?"

"Getting better finally," she said as she stared at the gray sky that reflected her bleak mood. Clouds scudded and seagulls sat with feathers fluffed on sheltered rocks.

He led the way along a path of irregular shaped flat stones. "Well, Lionel's reveal was a complete fiasco."

"What do you think happened to those letters?" Amanda had to take long strides to keep up with him.

"Perhaps Jean changed her mind and destroyed them. Perhaps Lionel did. He's the one with the combination. How do we know he hadn't had a peek before, Sis?"

"But it would have been stupid of him to drag us into the library if that were the case." He'd called her "Sis" again. She resisted the urge to snap at him and remind him to call her Amanda. That was her name. Didn't he know it?

She softened a moment later. He was under stress too, and how could she get to know Brian if she kept putting up her defenses?

"It was very clever of him, I think." Brian said. "Because at some point that safe would have been opened."

She'd always felt part of her was missing. It was something that she couldn't explain to anyone. Twins were sometimes like that, she'd read somewhere. So why didn't she feel an affinity for him? Perhaps this would come in time. For now, her emotions for him were neutral.

Brian had stopped, beside a clump of lilac irises, to wait for her.

She hadn't realized she'd slowed down, and the gap between them had widened. Now she quickened her step until she was abreast of him. "I'm thinking something was in that letter from Scott that was vitally important to someone."

He glanced at her as they continued. "Don't know. As I said before, we haven't kept in touch."

Did Brian know more than he let on? "I hope you don't mind me asking, but I would like to know why?"

"My parents, well the ones that raised me, died in a car crash five years ago. I went bush a while before that, fruit picking or anything that kept me in a bit of money. Their deaths meant that Scott and I had no reason to see each other anymore. We were so different, and could never see eye to eye. We were both adopted. He was into...I think it was Hells Angels and some other gangs. I ended up working as a stock hand on some of the stations in the Northern Territory. Occasionally I'd send him a Christmas card. Now that I think about it, maybe this was why Scott wrote to Jean. She'd probably wanted my address, and I'd moved around so much in the last five years that she couldn't trace me."

"You sent Scott Christmas cards?"

"I know what you're thinking. That it doesn't add up after what I've just said. But, a lot of the outback stations are so large you're cut off from the rest of the world pretty much. Your only comfort is the stars at night. What I'm trying to say is that you get to feeling sentimental. He was the only family I knew about then. Not that he ever bothered contacting me." He spat his last words.

She stared at his suntanned face, at the green eyes. They seemed knowing, hardened to life, not giving much away and definitely not sentimental. "So what do you do in the Northern Territory on a station, in the middle of nowhere?"

Brian's expression softened as he continued on along the path.

"Maintenance. Round up strays. We raised prime beef cattle. It would take us about three weeks of solid riding to check all the fences and see if any needed repairing. It took us another trip lasting over a month to fix them. Then there's the calving, checking the stock to make sure they're healthy. It's okay but it gets boring sometimes."

"You said we. You didn't ride alone?"

"Not usually."

"How many others go with you?"

"Used to be Nick. He's another stock hand. A good bloke, he was. I don't know if I'll ever see him again."

"What's happened to him?"

Brian didn't speak for a while and just when she thought he hadn't heard and she'd have to ask again he answered. "He up and quit when I left for California. He said something about family needing him. I gave him a lift into Darwin the same day I caught the flight out."

"You two were close?"

"We were mates, but nah, not that close."

They stopped at the cliff face. Amanda stared at the foam-tipped waves. The wind whipped them up and crashed them against the rocky outcrops at both ends of the small beach.

The throbbing at her temples had finally gone but the tension inside remained. A few strands of hair had come loose and now they fanned over her face. She caught them and pushed them back into the short ponytail. "Any girlfriends?"

"Not at the moment. So you're a freelance photographer."

"I've been doing it for a number of years now. Taking photos started as a serious hobby when I was nearly sixteen and it grew from that." It'd saved her from totally destroying herself. While behind the lens, she could take a step back from life, from reality.

"Anything in the pipeline?"

"I just finished an assignment on the dolphins at Monkey Mia before I came over here to meet Jean."

"That's in Western Australia, isn't it?"

"Yes. Loads of tourists visit the place. The dolphins don't seem to mind them. They're such gentle creatures. They swim up to you and let you touch them." The close contact she'd had with the sea creatures, how they nuzzled her, spoke to her with those strange sounds they make, made her think about the closeness she'd dared hope to share with Jean. Closeness that now remained forever out of reach. Sadness knifed through her, stung her eyes.

"You're crying."

Amanda shook her head, and then with the back of her hand, brushed away the tears.

Brian put his arm across her shoulders and hugged her in a brotherly way. "You okay?"

Amanda took a deep breath. "Yep," she lied. She pulled out a tissue to wipe her eyes but even that seemed like too much of an effort. Her mother was dead and she was still here. "It's not fair."

Brian gazed at the sea while she wiped her eyes. They stood there for a while, not talking, just taking in the scenery. "I think I know what you're going through. This is like some horrible nightmare."

She nodded as gradually the intensity of the overwhelming emptiness of her loss receded.

Brian glanced at his watch. "We've been gone a while. Hart'll come looking for us if we don't head back."

Unable to bring herself to speak, she nodded again.

When they reached the house, Amanda went in search of Lionel. Instinct told her he knew a lot more than he'd made out.

She found him in the library making a call.

When Lionel was done, he sat back in the leather executive-chair. "Been for your walk?"

"Yes. It was good to get some fresh air. Can I talk to you?"

"Take a seat."

She sank into a club chair on the other side of the desk. "Do you know anything at all about those missing letters?"

"As I said to Hart, I have no idea of the purpose of them or their contents. And I might add, I resent the implication of this question."

"I'm sorry. I had to be sure."

He watched her. "Are you?"

She ignored his comment. "How long have you known Jean?"

Cohen's anger seemed to subside. He sighed and stared past Amanda at the formal family photos hanging on the wall. "I've been looking after Mr. Campbell's affairs for about twenty-five years."

"Then you must know everything there is to know about all of them."

His eyes narrowed. "I am their lawyer and friend, but not confidant to any member of the family. I think that's what you're getting at, isn't it?"

She nodded. "What about Dorian? The more I see you with him, I feel that you're more like an uncle, as well his legal adviser. You've seen him grow from a baby into a man."

A slight flush of pink colored the pale cheeks of a face that had probably once been striking. The jaw, as with the rest of his features, was now lost in folds of skin. A fringe of graying-black hair framed an otherwise naked head. "Yes. I watched him being shuffled from boarding school to boarding school."

"He had an unhappy childhood?"

"I did not imply that."

"No you didn't," she said.

"Look, I have a lot more calls to make."

"Please don't get defensive. I'm trying to grasp at something that I can make meaning of. I need to know so I can understand Dorian."

Lionel leaned forward, put his elbows on the desk, and formed a bridge with his hands. "His father, Murray, loved him. However, Cynthia, his mother, disliked children, even him. She died when Dorian was nine.

"He then forged a close relationship with his father. When Murray met Jean, he suddenly forgot he had a son. You have to understand, he was in love again. They were married four months later. Jean had tried hard to win Dorian's approval but...he'd resented her from the start. In his eyes, she'd come between father and son. I believe that

65

closeness he'd had with his father was never quite rekindled. Dorian always blamed her for that. But it was more that his father had moved on, as he always did."

Now she understood why Dorian's relationship with his stepmother had been strained. "I can't understand why Jean, after all these years, contacted me."

He closed his eyes and took a deep breath. "She knew her time was short. Like any of us, when we're faced with our own mortality we want to put our life in order. We want to make amends."

"What do you mean?" she asked.

"Jean was terminally ill with cancer and she had another year or so left...we were friends..." He paused. "I loved her."

Jean was going to die anyway. Amanda's mind reeled as she slumped back in the chair. She swallowed a ball of emotion that had swelled in her throat and tried to think this through. So she wanted her daughter to cheer her up in her last days and to take care of her. What about her daughter's needs? "You loved her as a friend?"

He nodded.

She remembered her mother's slow movements yesterday. Yes, the signs had been there and yet she'd missed them. She'd been too preoccupied to notice. "I'm so sorry."

Lionel let his hands drop. The raw anguish etched in his face stunned Amanda out of her melancholia.

"I might as well tell you the rest."

"Please," Amanda said.

"Murray collected beautiful things and Jean was one of them. Kept, pampered, but never truly loved. Oh sure, he thought he loved her in the beginning, but as I said, the challenge for him was winning her love, then he was on the lookout for another victory."

"What?" Amanda whispered in shock. Like herself, her mother's life was empty of love too! "No...it can't be true."

"She turned to me for comfort when he died and that made Dorian hate her all the more."

"I can't hear this." His words tore at her heart: her mothers' marriage, Dorian's hostility towards his stepmother. Had her mother found any moments of happiness?

"Was this why Jean contacted Brian and me?"

"Perhaps. What I don't understand is that from the day she buried Murray, she said that when her time came, she wanted to be laid to rest next to him."

"Oh God. Can't handle this…. I didn't expect that she'd be in a loveless marriage." She clung desperately to the knowledge that at least Lionel had been there for Jean.

Lionel didn't answer. He stared at the bookshelf, his face a map of sorrow and pain.

Amanda quietly retreated from the room.

***

"Hello," Samuel said.

"Hi. It's me, Dad. I rang to tell you that Jean's…" Amanda gritted her teeth. She had to say the word no matter how much it hurt. "Passed away." Grief tore at her heart and the pain of it gripped her chest in a vice. "Uhh," she gasped as she sank onto the bed.

"Well, you didn't really know her anyway," her father said.

She cocooned the duvet around herself and forced out the words. "There wasn't much time."

He hadn't asked for any details but she was going to tell him anyway. "The maid found her in the bathroom. We don't know any more yet."

"It's better it happened now not later when you might have become more attached." The words came across as empty and hollow. He hadn't displayed any emotion at her mother's funeral, so why would he now.

Had she expected anything more from him? She punched the duvet in anger. "That doesn't make it easier to deal with."

"I guess not."

Her thoughts went back to last month when she'd opened the

letter from Jean. And the shock when she realized she was adopted.

"Dad, why didn't you tell me years ago that I was adopted? Mother didn't even tell me before she died." She'd wanted to ask him before she left Sydney but couldn't summon up the courage. The distance between them now seemed to make it easier.

"We thought it better this way," he said.

"Better for who?" she snapped. "Certainly not for me. Why did I have to read it in a letter from a total stranger who claimed to be my birth mother?" It had shattered her but he said it was better that way.

"Now, there is no need to be like that."

"Why couldn't mum have told me?"

"She was your mother. It was the way we did things."

"She was hardly that. Why all this secrecy?" she asked.

"That's uncalled for. She was a good woman, a good mother." Amanda could hear the clink of a spoon in a cup in the background. He was making himself a coffee.

"This call must be costing you," he said.

"You're right. I'd better go." It was a relief to end the call. The gap in their relationship had just widened.

After her call to her father, she joined Brian in the family room. He sat in one of the overstuffed easy chairs watching a movie on cable.

She asked him to contact Scott about the empty envelope and he snapped out a negative reply. Was she the only one who thought this was worth following up?

CHAPTER 13

"I'll be recording this interview." Hart spoke the time and date. "I imagine that it's been a big shock for you. If you want a female present, Amanda, rather than Detective Stephan, then please tell me and I'll arrange for someone."

"This is rather formal, but I have no problem with the two of you."

"It's not usual procedure but we have to protect you and ourselves these days. Amanda Blake, would you like to tell me why you went to your mother's room this morning?" Hart asked.

It was only last night that she'd joined Jean, Brian and Dorian for dinner. Her world was shattered and it was all she could do to contain her sadness. She couldn't get comfortable in the chair no matter which way she sat. "I was putting in my earrings when I heard screaming. I went to investigate," she said.

"What did you see?"

She told him.

"Did you think she was murdered or died of natural causes?"

"How can you ask? How would I know?" She told herself to breathe but couldn't. She could see her mother lying on the tiles, her fingers trying to grasp at something. Her chest felt like it was in a vice. She gasped and reached for the puffer in her jacket.

"I must. It's my job," he said. "Are you okay? Would you like a glass of water?"

She shook her head. "G…give me a minute."

"Do you need anything?"

She shook her head again and closed her eyes.

He went over to the bookshelf, pulled a book out, and leafed through it.

What was that saying her therapist had told her to say when she was distressed? *Oh, come on, Amanda*, she said to herself. *You managed to do a fire walk with Anthony Robbins.* She'd never imagined that she could do such a thing.

"This too shall pass," she said and she took a deep breath. It worked better said aloud but it did sound odd.

"What?" He said as he put the book back.

"I was into Jane Eyre and those sorts of books at school." She pointed. "Jean has a copy there on her shelf," she said.

He had raised an eyebrow, probably thought her a bit mad. "Are you okay to continue?"

"Yes."

"I've had some preliminary information concerning everyone here. I-"

"What do you mean? Am I a suspect?" Amanda asked.

"We'll get to that if you don't interrupt me again," he said. "I believe that you defaulted on both of your credit cards and you only got them reinstated because Mrs. Campbell paid them off. You have unpaid bills to the sum of $30,000."

"How did you find out?" Amanda felt the heat rise in her cheeks with embarrassment.

"For those allowed access, your credit rating is something that can be obtained with a few clicks of the mouse. You asked Mrs. Campbell for the money."

"I didn't find out that Jean had paid up my bills until I was opening my mail the day before I flew out."

"You expect me to believe this?"

"It's the truth and I don't know how Jean found out. I did ask her but she didn't tell me. I made some bad investments and I was stupid enough to throw some more cash at that property fund thinking that it would come good. What's all that got to do with this investigation?"

"Motivation to commit a crime." Hart put the pen down and sat back.

She put her elbows on the table and pushed her fingers through her hair. "I am a suspect in my mother's..." She drew in air.

He raised an eyebrow again at her hesitation but kept silent.

"Yet, you don't know if it was from natural causes or not. Am I right?" Amanda asked.

"The lab results will take a few days. Until then we assume that everyone is a suspect."

CHAPTER 14

The phone in the San Francisco hotel suite rang for a few moments before he answered.

"Silvio?" the caller asked.

Silvio Pozzani tipped the waiter then sat down at the dining table. "What do you want?" The man was an irritation.

"It's all going as planned," the caller said nervously.

Silvio allowed the waiter to place a white linen napkin in his lap. When the door closed, he said, "It had better be. I'm not driving down the coast to meet you again. After I left you, I nearly had an accident with a dark-blue Buick. I think the man was a cop."

"Shit! How?"

"It doesn't matter how. I managed to miss him but he got a good look at the Jaguar. Even though he's probably not suspicious, I'll have to get some other wheels."

"He got a look at your face?"

"Don't worry about it." Silvio smiled as he raised the silver cover on the plate and inspected his dinner. He loved the way the Americans made salads.

"That gun you gave me, I stashed it in-"

"Not on the phone you fuckin' imbecile. I don't want to know where. Make sure the next ones look like an accident. Use the gun to finish the job only if you have to." Silvio sighed. Amateurs. The cut he and Del Condio would pocket made it all worthwhile. Del Condio would be very angry if this didn't go well. The last thing he wanted was to upset the boss.

"Accident? How?"

"I'll leave that to your imagination."

"One dead and two to go. Someone's coming." The caller broke the connection.

CHAPTER 15

A nightmare woke Amanda. Crying out, she lunged for the bedside light, nearly knocking it over. She was sweat-sticky with fright.

She'd dreamed of the moment when she found Jean's lifeless body in that blue dressing gown. Suddenly she was in another room; her hands were bloody, as in her earlier dreams. A man's shadow loomed. He tied her hands behind her. She was so scared, so desperate to escape from…something that she couldn't see. A scream had formed and died on her lips as his mouth savaged hers.

Amanda dressed quickly, grabbed her camera gear, which was her antidote to anything that was bothering her, and escaped outside as dawn broke. She hurried down nearly sixty stone steps to the beach.

This was the best part of the day for her. The first rays of light kissed the waves of the Monterey shoreline.

The tripod secured, light and shutter speed adjusted, the Kodachrome slide film in place to capture the scene, Amanda set to work. They didn't make slide film these days but she'd sourced a stash from a friend and was putting them to good use.

This had never been just a job to her. It gave her a good feeling, one that she'd missed. It made her feel real, and gave her comfort to know there was a constant among all this upheaval in her life. While behind a camera the lens became her eye, her focus on the world, all else forgotten.

Amanda took stills of crabs scurrying across the sand, of seagulls swooping, and of their mating rituals. She stopped taking photos as sadness in her grew and her thoughts returned to her mother. The word seemed strange yet it fit. A tumble of images flashed in her eyes, her mother's smile, her easy grace, the angry scene with Jean and Dorian, and finally, the discovery of Jean's body.

The sun now full in the sky, she started to pack up. Amanda unscrewed the lens. Tears started down but she ignored them, determined to finish putting away her gear, until she couldn't see to zip up her pack. She sank onto the sand, glad that she was alone and no one could see her display of weakness.

After her tears were spent, Amanda folded the tripod and started back along the coarse sand. She saw Brian at the top of the cliff face beside the leaning cypress pines.

She returned his wave. He was up early. Perhaps he hadn't slept well either.

Brian called out as Amanda neared the steps. "Coming up for breakfast?"

"Not yet," she said. Maybe later she would force something down.

"See you later then." He disappeared from view.

She was glad to spend a little longer alone. She put her equipment on a boulder, slipped on her sandals that she'd discarded earlier, dusted the sand off her white shorts, and sat on a rock.

The squawk of seagulls gliding on the breeze drew her gaze. She watched them as they landed at the water's edge looking for food. Their purpose and their needs, clear, unlike hers.

Footsteps jolted Amanda from her reverie. She looked up to see Dorian, drink in hand, as he picked his way over the rocks. Barefoot, his frayed jeans sweeping the sand, he crossed to her.

He raised his glass. "I know it's early for bourbon but what the heck. Mind if I join you?"

Alcohol at breakfast! Did he have a drinking problem? What did he want? "Pull up a chair."

A hint of a smile played on his lips, the arrogant sharp features softened by a slight dimpling of his cheeks. "You mean a rock." He moved her camera over and sat on the sea-worn granite.

"Taking photos?"

That was stating the obvious. "I have a web site where I sell some of them. Sometimes clients want to have a shot blown up on canvas and I can do that too. I can't keep up with the demand. So any chance I get, I'm doing this. When I work I get so caught up I forget about everything."

"Wish I could do that. Forget." He stared at the water as he sipped his drink.

"Then find something that you really enjoy. Doing what you love beats therapy any day." She knew that only too well.

"Words of wisdom from Amanda Blake." His demeanor seemed tense and his voice was tight. "It was goddamned awful yesterday wasn't it!"

Her chest tightened. "Yes."

He stared at his glass. "I can't get used to the idea of not having Jean around." He kicked at the sand.

"I thought the way you felt about her…well, that her death wouldn't affect you too much."

"That's the problem. It's got me spinning, and I didn't expect it. I don't know. Sometimes I think, well it doesn't matter what I think."

She hardly knew him, or any of them. They were all practically strangers, Dorian, Brian her twin, the maid, the cook, and Lionel. Whom could Amanda trust?

He glanced over. "You know, Cohen seemed shaken up by Jean's death."

"Did his reaction make you think any differently about Jean?"

He shook his head.

"You lost someone who could have meant something to you, if only you'd wanted it."

He grimaced as he stared at the ocean. It was the only indication that he'd heard her.

"Lionel cared for Jean. They were very close."

"That's what he'd have you believe," he said.

"What do you mean?" Amanda stared at Dorian. Why was he telling her this? "I'm sure he was sincere when he told me."

"Maybe he'd convinced himself of that. It was easy to see that Jean didn't want Lionel. He wasn't rich enough. My father was."

"Lionel was her friend."

"Oh sure."

"He told me so yesterday."

He shrugged. "What I do know is that she married my father for his money. We were happy 'till she came between us." He finished his drink.

Dorian had probably been against Jean from the start. "Or was it that you were jealous of anyone who took your father's affections? Jean happened to be that someone. Did you expect him to live like a hermit, just for you?"

"You don't know anything. You weren't there." Dorian stared at the rolling waves, his jaw clenched.

Was her comment a revelation to him? The silence between them lengthened. She wished he'd go.

Finally he said, "There were other women before Jean but none that lasted."

"Other women that came between you and your dad?"

"But they weren't permanent. I could cope knowing that they would eventually disappear."

"It doesn't sound like he had a lot of time for you."

"I didn't say that, did I?"

"No but-"

"But nothing! We did everything together, Dad and I."

"Are you trying to convince me or yourself?"

Dorian stared at his empty glass. "I lied."

"What? Look, let's just forget it." The man needed a therapist and she didn't plan to play the role of a shrink. "I'm going up to have some breakfast." She started to rise.

"Go on, walk away, just like everybody else. Just when I need someone to talk to." He turned from her.

She sat down, pushing her hair from her face. "Okay. Okay. What is it?" She must be losing it to stay and let someone she hardly knew carry on like this. Somehow, he'd struck a sympathetic chord.

"Dad had to go away on business a lot. It wasn't his fault."

"Was it Jean's fault that she married your father?"

He let out an ugly laugh. "You don't know how clever, how manipulating she was."

"I don't know what to think anymore." She didn't like to believe that Jean could have been like that. She'd begun to imagine that if her mother had lived they would have had a relationship built on kindness, understanding and all those things that make a mother-daughter bond special. She was torn between not wanting to know more and yet being drawn to search out all she could about her mother.

"I was just starting junior high when she became my stepmother. Even then, she couldn't fool me. That doctor who came yesterday, well he started visiting her regularly about a year ago. If she'd loved my father she'd never have looked at another man after he'd died."

"You didn't even try to give her a chance, did you?"

"She ruined what Dad and I had. She ruined it for me."

"That's what you keep saying. But how?"

Nervously, he started to jiggle his leg. "Jean never liked my friends. She was always criticizing them and the way I dressed. Turned Dad against my friends too. I could never live up to Dad's expectations, school, and sports. One time I was in a school play. I was desperate for my dad to see me on stage. But he was too busy. He turned up too late to see my part. Look, if I'm boring you."

She realized that she'd been yawning. "I yawn more from stress than tiredness or boredom. I didn't realize that's what it was until I read about it in the paper last year. God knows, I am stressed."

He seemed to accept her answer and continued. "I stopped trying. I knew I would never be the person Dad wanted me to be. Somehow, I got into college, and he was proud of me for the first time since I could remember. But that didn't last. He found out I had a boyfriend. Jean must have told him."

"How can you blame her for being the way you are? You want to blame her for everything that's gone wrong in your life."

"I'm not blaming her for that. But if she did tell him, what business is it of theirs to begin with." He kicked at the sand. "I just don't know anymore. I can't stop thinking how different it might have been if.... But you can't know how it was, growing up here. Dad. His women. He only stopped for a few years when he married

Jean. She pretended there was nothing wrong. She shouldn't have done that. The assistants. The receptionists. I hated them all. He might have stopped, if she'd only confronted him."

"I think you've convinced yourself that your father would have changed." Her half stepbrother was full of excuses for his father because he couldn't come to terms with the way he'd been treated. "You think you're the only one with an unhappy childhood? I grew up in with a mother who was a manic-depressive. You can't know what that was like. She committed suicide when I was twelve."

"Yeah, well, I didn't realize you had it hard too," he said.

He'd had an unhappy childhood and the sad thing was that he'd shut out the only person who'd tried to show him some love.

If only Samuel had been different. Life was so unfair. Again, she crucified herself when she knew it did no good. Her achievements were never enough to make Samuel bestow a word of praise. "After everything is finalized you'll be free to make a new start. Put all this behind you." Amanda rose. "I'm going up for some breakfast."

He picked up her tripod and camera. He seemed to be mulling over something. Finally, he said, "Would you have…no. I shouldn't ask."

She clambered over the rocks, and then waited at the bottom of the steps for him. "What is it?"

"If the latest will had been signed by Jean and you inherited her money, would you have kept all of it?"

She swung round to face him. He hadn't meant to pour out all his problems to her. It was all about money. She even told him some very private family things. Like a fool, she'd been taken in.

"You don't know me at all, do you! To you I'm some just some stranger that happens to be Jean's daughter."

He looked surprised by her response.

"Just for the record, I was just as shocked as you were at the idea that I was to be made the main heir. If that will had been signed, I'd have made sure everything was split evenly between the three of us."

"Would you?"

"It's still part of your father's estate and after the way you were treated by him, you deserve a decent share of it. Money wasn't the reason I came here, so the latest will remaining unsigned suits me fine. Hell, even if she left me a third, I imagine it'd be more money than I'll never be able to spend."

"The secrecy between your parents and Jean... How did you cope with that?"

"Why bring this up now? It wasn't easy. I had no idea I had another mother out there somewhere."

She wasn't going to pour out how she felt to him, especially after his comment about the will. The idea she'd dismissed last night as nonsense returned. Did Dorian have something to do with Jean's death?

"Perhaps, it was better left unsaid...you're angry."

The anger, the resentment was barely below the surface. Jesus, he was good at picking up her feelings. She'd thought she was doing a good job of masking them. "You bet I'm angry."

Amanda started up the steps, with Dorian following. Oh God, would it ever get easier to bear? She paused as her eyes misted up.

Amanda was a little out of breath as she neared the top. She slipped sideways, grabbing the wooden rail, but it came away.

Screaming, she fell, her fingers clutching at rocks and roots. The rail continued without her, bursting on the rocks below.

Somewhere...voices were shouting.

Dorian dropped her stuff and lunged out to reach her but missed. She slid. He tried again.

Amanda screamed again. Frantically, she scrabbled for anything secure until she found purchase on a gnarled cypress pine growing out of a crevice.

"Grab my hand." Dorian reached out, his foot wedged in the small gap between the steps and rock, with one arm around the upright post.

The scent of the cypress filled each gasp she took. Fighting to get a better hold, with feet pedaling at loose rocks, she tried to reach him.

"You can do it, Amanda," he said.

She had one arm wrapped around a branch, the other stretched out toward him.

A loud crack sounded, and the limb started to snap. She cried out, struggling to grab something more solid.

Dorian edged out further, his legs scissoring the post for security. "Try again."

More shouting came from somewhere. Terrified the pine might give way completely, she swung toward Dorian. Despair ebbed at her strength. "I can't."

Crack. The branch was peeling away. She let go with one hand and seized another limb with the other.

"Grab the rope," Brian shouted.

The prickly branches scratched her face but she ignored them and twisted around hand over hand, though her instincts screamed for haste. Amanda stretched out to the rope.

Missed! An overhead jutting rock held it out of reach.

Again, she missed.

She gasped for a breath and felt for the puffer in her pocket. About to spray a dose into her mouth, the trees' roots suddenly ripped free and her puffer jerked from her grasp.

"I'll try to move it over," Brian shouted.

"I lost…my puffer," she cried.

"Bring that goddamned rope across to me and I'll throw it to her. *Hurry.*" Dorian's voice was hoarse with urgency. "Amanda, turn around."

Her heart was thumping, and her lungs felt constricted. She dragged in air noisily, her hands grappling, her body twisting. Shit, she was losing her hold…breaking branches, roots snapping, needles scratching. "I'm falling."

Amanda flung herself at the trunk, tried to hug it but she kept slipping. Frantically, she spread her legs and felt for any small foothold, and found none. "I'm scared."

"I've resecured the end of the rope." Brian threw it down and loped down the steps to them, shouting encouragement as he came.

As she slid further, her foot stopped on a small ledge, a chance.

Dorian wound the rope around the rail, and coiled up the other end. "Ready? I'll throw, you grab, and don't let go," Dorian said flinging the coiled end towards her.

She caught it.

"Tie it around your waist."

"I can't. I need two hands."

"You have to try," Dorian said. "And don't look down"

Amanda attempted to do as he asked. Finally she succeeded, and wound it around her arm as well. She swung in an arc across the cliff face, bruising herself as she went but she unflinchingly clung on.

Dorian hauled on the rope and dragged her towards Brian and himself.

With a hoarse cry, Amanda caught the upright as it came within reach.

Dorian and Brian pulled her through the railing, onto the steps, and finally into a sitting position.

"Thank God you're safe." Dorian picked a twig from her hair. "Anything broken?"

"Puffer," she said.

Dorian pulled out his phone and called the house. "Estella, find another inhaler for Amanda, hurry. We're at the end of the garden."

"In my...suitcase," Amanda rasped, and Dorian relayed that.

"You had us in a panic. Are you okay?" Brian asked.

She nodded.

"Your hands look pretty bad. They must hurt," Dorian said.

At his mention, they started to throb. Her palms were crisscrossed with lacerations, and bleeding.

Brian grimaced at the sight. "I think you should see a doctor."

Estella ran over with her puffer. She inhaled and waited for it to take effect. "I've done...rock climbing a few times at one of those centers...but that was a walk in the park compared to this."

"Are you okay, Miss Amanda?" Estella asked.

"Thanks, yes." Her body ached all over. As if in a dream she stared at her once white shorts that were now torn and dirty and seconds later wondered why she'd even given her clothes a second glance.

"My camera?" It lay beside Dorian. She reached for it.

"You're worried about that?" he asked.

"I know you must think I'm crazy, but it's practically part of me. My father gave it to me after I sold my first photos." It had been a rare display of parental pride from him. She treasured it.

With Dorian's help, she took each step hesitantly. At the place where she'd fallen, she paused to glance at the surface where a shiny patch glistened in the sun. She stepped carefully over it, and gazed at the open span between the two uprights. The rail had come away from both uprights cleanly. It didn't look broken but rather like someone had sawn it.

CHAPTER 16

Garth Bartley sank back onto the threadbare couch as Dorian walked into the apartment. He pulled the thin blanket higher. "I'm feeling awful. Well, did you ask that lawyer again? Did you get the dough out of that tightwad?"

Dorian bent, and lightly kissed him, ignoring the red scabby blotches on his boyfriend's arms. "Sorry. Lionel won't release any extra money from my trust fund."

"What about your inheritance, now that your stepmother's dead?" He pushed his wavy black hair away from his face. Moments later, it fell back.

Dorian, thumbs in his jeans pockets, began pacing. "I should get a decent share. That new will she'd had drawn up would have left me worse off. The shares I wouldn't get 'till I was thirty. Anyway she didn't get to sign it, did she?"

"So when will you get your hands on all this cash? You know how much I'm suffering." Garth coughed a few times then drew a long noisy breath.

Dorian, guilt-ridden at not being able to obtain the money for Garth's medical treatment, sighed. "We have to wait for all the legal stuff to be done. The biggest problem is that these twins of Jean's are probably going to get a reasonable amount too."

Garth frowned. "You can't accept that."

Dorian shrugged. "When Amanda was climbing up the steps from the beach this morning, she slipped and fell through the railing. Brian and I rescued her. She could have been killed. It's a long way down the cliff face to the beach."

"You saved her?" His voice was laced with disbelief.

"I was closer to her than Brian. Couldn't stand there and do nothing, could I? The doctor's bandaged her hands. They were pretty bad."

The roar of a Greyhound bus leaving from the terminal nearby came through the open window.

"Can't you put me up in something better? I can't stand this dump."

"I didn't think you wanted me to find you something else. Last time I offered, you refused."

"I didn't know you as well then."

"I'll start looking first thing Monday." He picked up Garth's discarded shoes, took them to the bedroom, and then returned. "I'll get us some coffee. Do you want anything else?"

Garth's smile was strained. "Warm me up that leftover pizza in the fridge too. My appetite's returned. It's late and I haven't eaten lunch yet."

CHAPTER 17

Amanda woke to the sound of someone turning off a water faucet. Afternoon had turned to night.

As she rolled over to turn on the bedside lamp, pain shot up her arm, reminding her of her earlier accident.

The doctor had come and gone this morning. He'd sutured the small wound on her upper arm and cleaned up the cuts and lacerations on her face and body. Then he'd wound gauze around her hands. He'd prescribed sleeping pills for her when she'd let slip that she'd had some restless nights lately. She'd been very lucky to escape serious injury, the doctor had said.

At first, she tried to put the accident from her mind but the fact that she might not be alive now had shaken her too much. Finally, she'd slept.

Estella walked in from the adjoining bathroom. "I will run bath for you. It will make you much better. Jes?"

"Thanks. I feel useless like this."

Estella sat beside her and carefully unbound her hands. "Looks very bad."

Amanda studied her swollen palms. They were crisscrossed with cuts and gashes. Something nagged at the edges of her consciousness. "Look."

"What's wrong?" the maid asked.

"It's my nightmare. I've been having it for weeks. I dreamt that I found someone in a blue dressing gown. That was Jean. Then I look at my hands: they're all…bloody." The mention of her mother's name wasn't getting any easier. It was as if a huge wound had opened inside. It pained and tore at her. Tears cascaded down her cheeks.

She had to create some defenses, otherwise she was going to be a blubbering mess most of the time and that wasn't acceptable.

Estella paled. "You make me frightened, Miss Amanda." Then in a firmer tone, the maid added. "No more bad dreams for you."

Amanda nodded as she brushed away the tears, hoping Estella was right.

"You upset. Poor Miss Amanda," the maid said.

She blew her nose. "I'm okay." She hoped she was.

Estella slipped disposable gloves on Amanda's hands and secured them at the wrist with tape. "No water will get in. I wait outside."

Amanda slipped off her chemise. Why did she feel so vulnerable? Her nakedness had never bothered her before, never made her so edgy. She shivered as if a cold wind had suddenly blown in through the closed window. Goose bumps covered her body. She glanced around. There was no one there. No one seemed to be lurking in the shadows cast by the bedside lamp.

"Estella? Are you still outside?"

No answer. Amanda tensed, about to call out again, when she heard the maid reply.

"You want help?"

"It's okay thanks." She forced away her uneasiness and padded into the bathroom.

The lavender-scented oil Estella had poured into the water filled the air. Her blue dress and clean underwear were on the vanity. She stepped into the warm water.

Amanda lay back and felt herself relax. She couldn't wash herself properly but a good soak would be great.

When the water began to cool, she stepped out, toweled herself dry and called Estella to help her dress.

With her hands freshly bandaged, Amanda shuffled to the stairs. At the landing, she gazed down hesitantly as she remembered her fall this morning. She stepped back and took a deep breath. This was stupid. She wasn't going to fall. Slowly, one step at a time she descended. When she had finally reached the bottom, she sighed with relief.

The click clack of her sandals on the tiles echoed in the hallway as she looked for Brian. She hadn't seen him since this morning.

He was pouring a whisky for himself at the wet bar in the family room. Glass shelves stacked with liqueurs and spirits lined the wall behind him. Two overstuffed caramel-brown sofas and some easy chairs faced the TV and entertainment system.

He looked up. "I thought you'd be resting."

She smiled as she crossed the room. "I'm not sick and I've stayed in bed too much already."

"Do you think you'll feel up to going for that drive we talked about on Monday?" he asked.

"Monday. Oh, I just remembered." She looked at her watch. "Maybe it's too late to call him now," she said.

"Who? What?"

"It's someone I met on the plane. We had agreed to take in some sights on Monday."

"A stranger?" Brian asked.

"It's not what you think. Guy and I just chatted like old friends on the flight. It's not a date or anything like that." Did she detect a little concern for her?

"All I know is that we both need a break from this place."

"Since you put it like that, I guess I can't refuse," she said.

"That's the shot, Sis." He added some ice, and then tasted his drink. "Not bad. You want some?"

He'd called her that name again. She gritted her teeth. "*Sis.*" She'd have to learn to like it. Or, at the very least tolerate it. After all, she owed him. "The house is so quiet. Where is everyone?"

"Rosa and Estella have gone to bed and Dorian took off after dinner. He didn't say where. Still sore?"

She nodded. "A little. I haven't really thanked you for saving my life."

"Forget it."

"Without your help I don't know if I'd be in one piece," she said.

He glanced away. Was she imagining it or did he seem embarrassed? Nah…he surely wasn't the sensitive type.

"What can I offer you?"

"No alcohol for me thanks. I can't with the tablets I've been prescribed." She didn't drink much at the best of times anyway. "I have a call to make," she said.

"Don't let me stop you."

"I have to let Guy know that I can't make it Monday."

"Bring him along."

"Are you sure?"

"Hey, I wouldn't say that otherwise." He pushed the phone to her. 'Unless you want to use your mobile? It'll cost."

"I got a phone card at the airport." She had her mobile in her pocket but didn't feel comfortable with Brian listening in.

He smiled. "See you later."

In the hallway, Amanda could hear muted voices coming from the veranda. Dorian was out; Rosa was in her room as was Estella. The gardener and chauffeur had both gone home. No one was supposed to be out there.

Not wanting to make a sound, Amanda slipped off her sandals. When she reached the back door, which was slightly ajar, she peeped out. Although the light was off, she could make out two figures near the outdoor setting.

The male was smoking a cigarette and the female had her back to Amanda. All she could hear was the low rise and fall of their hushed voices.

The breeze sent two words across to her. "Not yet?" Estella's voice and accent were unmistakable. The man threw down the cigarette and ground it out with his shoe. Then he leaned over and kissed Estella on the cheek. As he walked towards the back entrance to the garage, past the lamppost, the light momentarily caught his worried expression. Ricardo.

Amanda pulled back. Why were they meeting like this, and in secret?

A door slammed somewhere, jolting her. She did not want to be found tiptoeing in the hallway. Before she knew it, she was in the library, shutting the door behind her.

She felt foolish but she had this feeling that there was something wrong. Ricardo and Estella may have been discussing their chores and nothing more. Then why were they out there in the dark?

She stared at her sandals dangling from her bandaged fingers as if they might offer an answer to the questions haunting her. Had Jean been murdered? If she had, who was the killer?

Amanda stepped into her shoes, and leaned back against the door. Footsteps echoed along the hall. As they came closer, she peeped through the keyhole and saw Dorian pass by. He hadn't mentioned where he was going, or with whom he was meeting. When she glanced at her watch, she realized a few hours had passed since he'd left. It was after ten. Her mind was working overtime; she was getting suspicious of everyone.

Just then, the computer made a pinging sound. She opened the email that had just arrived. Surprised, she stared at the message.

To: jeancampbell@campbellbearepharm.com.
Hi Jean
I've found out something that changes everything. That you were partly right is no consolation for the news I have for you. Please contact me tomorrow at the number I gave you and I will explain further.
Regards,
Scott McMahon.

It sounded so secretive. What was going on? Her palms were suddenly sweaty. Anyone could access Jean's emails if they wanted to. She closed the email, created a new sub folder, and dragged the email into it. No one would think of looking there for it.

Then she clicked reply and sat thinking. What should she write? Finally, after retyping the message a few times she settled for a simple one to Scott.
Hi Scott,
Please call me on the number below.

I need to speak with you urgently.
Kindest regards,
Amanda Blake.

CHAPTER 18

"I don't want to ring Scott. It'll be a waste of time. I've told you we don't get on." Brian glanced at his watch. "I don't know the time difference between here and Sydney anyway. Can't we discuss this later?"

Amanda glanced at Jean's library of books. I'm doing this for you, she said silently to her mother. "I'd rather call now. The staff is busy, and Dorian's upstairs studying. No one's likely to walk in on us. I'll just check the time zone on my phone." She tapped on the application. "It's two p.m. here and seven a.m. in Sydney."

"What's got into you? Why all this sudden interest in Scott?"

"I thought we'd both agreed that you should speak to him."

"I was just...well you were upset and all. You know that detective will probably contact him about that empty envelope."

Should she tell him about the email? She couldn't decide. "Well I...er...have a feeling Hart won't bother." Perhaps, she'd tell him later. "Anyway, I can't stand a mystery. I want to know why he wrote to Jean."

"Can't call him. I don't have his number with me."

"I found his home number on the internet."

"Okay. Okay. You win." Brian picked up the receiver and dialed. "Hi, Scott."

Amanda hovered.

"Yeah, I guess it must be a surprise." Brian expelled a breath. "Look-"

"I just wondered-" Brian pushed his fingers through his dark blonde hair. "Look it's about the letter-" He gripped the receiver.

"Can I talk to him?" Amanda asked.

He shook his head. "Can't you put our differences aside this time?"

"Bastard." Brian hung up, and expelled a long breath. "Sorry about the language."

"I was hoping he would be more co-operative. Let me try?"

Brian's laugh seemed strained. "He's always been the same. That bikie gang he hangs out with would sooner bash you than say g'day. Ring him back now if you like to be insulted, sworn at, but I'm sure you won't get any further than I did."

"You're probably right. Thanks anyway. I think I'll have a little rest. See you later." As she walked upstairs, she wondered why would Scott ask Jean to call him? What information did he have? Nothing added up.

Amanda closed the door to her room and tried the number she'd asked Brian to call. She hoped that Scott wouldn't be as hostile with her. The phone rang repeatedly but no one answered.

Afterwards, Amanda called her best friend, Anna.

"Hi. I hope you're not asleep this time."

"Nope. As it turns out work is flying me to a client in Melbourne and the taxi's coming any minute to take me to the airport. What's happening, Funny Face? I tried calling you but no answer. I didn't bother leaving a message. Figured I'd get you sooner or later," Anna said.

"I'm a mess." Amanda told her about her fall.

"No broken bones I hope. I'm giving you a hug. Here it comes."

"Thanks. I need it. Can you do me a favor?" Amanda asked.

"Anything," her friend said.

"I found this weird email from Brian's step-brother, Scott. I came across it in Jean's inbox." She told her its contents.

"I can't imagine you being a super sleuth but that email sounds like it's worth following up. Did you try emailing him back?"

"Yep. And, I keep sneaking into Jean's office and checking her emails for a reply as often as I can. So far nothing."

"You replied to him only yesterday, didn't you? There's not much more you can do then," her friend said.

"I was hoping you could try contacting him for me." She gave her the landline number.

"What am I going to say to him?"

Amanda told her. "Ask about the email, and give him my mobile number, please."

"How can you be sure that he'll talk to me about the email?"

"I can't but it's worth a try. It's all I've got."

"How are you holding up?"

"Not so good," she said.

"Hey. It must be tough and I wish I could be there for you," Anna said. "I won't be able to call him until I get home tonight. I'll let you know what gives when we've spoken. I'll have to go; I think the cab's outside now. You take care, hear."

"You too," Amanda said.

CHAPTER 19

Shadows from large white clouds filtered the sun's rays over San Francisco. From the top of Twin Peaks, Amanda saw the flat roofs of houses, apartment blocks, and straddling the hilly city, roads and highways teeming with vehicles. Out on the ocean, cargo ships and other vessels looked like children's toys bobbing on the horizon.

Guy Robertson, in chinos and jacket, slotted some coins into the telescope. "Over here, Amanda." He adjusted the scope and peered into it.

She edged, through a group of tourists, to him. Originally, she'd expected to be doing this touristy thing with just Brian and her mother. However, it was better to be out and about than moping around that house.

"There's Alcatraz. Look." Guy lowered the scope to accommodate her height.

Amanda pushed back the hair fanning across her face. Then she stared into the lens, saw the old prison, and watched a tug tow a liner into the bay. She swung the scope to focus on the city, watched the constant movement of people, trucks, cars, and someone walking their dog. "Thanks."

She glanced up at Guy, who had been standing patiently beside her. Before she had any idea what he planned to do, he kissed her.

Her cheeks burned as she pulled away. Amused faces watched them. "Guy, please don't."

"Sorry. I didn't know you were so shy." Guy's lips creased into a boyish grin, his eyes glittered mischievously.

"Well…" She fiddled with a button on her white blouse with the few fingers that were free of the bandages. She was not usually embarrassed this easily.

"It seemed to me that you enjoyed it?"

"Not in public. Let's remain just friends." His insistent pressure against her mouth hadn't stirred her. She hadn't thought about any man in a sexual way since she'd broken up with her ex-fiancée, Charles, early last year. Since then, she'd avoided getting involved. She didn't need any complications in her life ever again. She almost hadn't responded when Guy struck up a conversation with her on the plane, but she'd been charmed that such a good-looking man was pursuing her.

"Then I'll just make sure we're completely alone the next time."

Not if I can help it, she said silently. He didn't acknowledge that she'd wanted to be friends only with him.

"Where's Brian?" Then she saw him. A German looking couple, wearing socks with sandals, had handed their camera to him to take their photo. With an experienced eye, she watched him as he turned the settings backwards, then forwards.

"He's got no idea. I'd better go help." Amanda hurried across the expanse of patchy grass. "Not like that. Don't turn it to sunny." She leant over him. "It's a dull day. The shutter won't open long enough, and the pictures will be dark."

Brian smiled a tolerant smile. "Okay, I'll leave it to the professional." He went to give the camera to her.

"I can't hold it properly. The bandages don't come off for at least another day. "You hold while I adjust." She peered through the viewfinder.

"So why'd you bother to bring your camera?" Brian sighed as she worked the settings.

"It's much smaller and easier to hold."

"Sorry. We ask too much. I take the camera," the man said stepping forward.

"It's okay." Amanda said. "Would you please join your wife. No, that's too far back. Come forward away from that tree. That's better."

"Are you sure everything's right now, Amanda?" Brian asked.

He sounded angry with her. She was only trying to help. "Take the shot."

"Thank you. We cause you too much trouble." The tourist took his camera.

"I can't believe anyone still takes shots with an actual film anymore."

"I still do, though not as a regular thing. There are lots of buffs who still do the old fashioned thing." Her brother was so rude.

He turned to the couple. "Sorry about my meddling sister."

Amanda bristled and waited until they were out of earshot. "You just can't take it when someone gives you advice no matter how well intentioned."

"Who the hell do you think you are dishing out advice anyway!"

She was about to hit back with a retort of her own when Guy joined them.

"Where to now?" he asked.

"I don't know. Ask her," Brian said.

Guy winked at Amanda. "What about a cruise around the bay later?"

He'd obviously mistaken her friendliness to mean something more. She'd have to set him straight when she got the chance. "Sure."

"Okay, okay," Brian said. "I know what you're going to say, Sis. That I'm a grouch." He started towards Guy's Mercedes parked down the road.

"*Sis!*" Jesus, the more he used that name the more it irritated her.

Guy gave Amanda a questioning…what's happening look? "I'll tell you later," she said as she went after her twin.

"I didn't say that, Brian. But I sure was thinking along those lines," Amanda said.

He slowed down. "You're so bossy. You know that?"

"You've got a short fuse."

He swung around to face her. "Who wouldn't with you fussing like that?"

"I don't know what all this is about, but how about we move on. What's next, the cruise or Chinatown?" Guy said.

"Anything that will make her happy." Brian opened the back door and climbed in.

Before Amanda could get to the passenger door, Guy opened it for her and smiled.

***

Three green-pagoda roofs— the highest one in the middle — spanned the street. Circular plaques of Chinese characters set into the sidewalk welcomed visitors to Chinatown.

Clumsily, with her bandaged hands, she tried to adjust the settings on the camera while Brian and Guy brought some ice creams from a stall. The fat-bellied laughing Buddha with a small child staring up at it would make a great shot.

"Yours was chocolate chip and chocolate, right?" Brian asked.

"Mmm, thanks. Hold it for a second while I take another shot from a different angle." She knelt down on one knee, gingerly holding her camera. Every time she tried to capture the scene, someone would walk past.

"Can you stop trying to take everything you see," Brian said. "You can hardly even use the thing."

"I can manage," she said.

"Eat your ice cream. I'll help you after that."

"But the sun's at the perfect angle now. It won't take long."

"Oh, for crying out loud Amanda. The damn thing's melting."

"Fine." She turned around and took a shot of Brian and Guy eating.

"You know I hate having my picture taken. Are you going to bloody well eat this thing, or do I bin it?" Brian glared at her.

"You don't have to be like that." This brother irritated her more and more. "Guy, will you hold my camera?"

"Sure." Guy finished of his last of his ice cream and took it.

They passed a Chinese herbalist. Amanda paused to watch the man weighing dried roots on an old-fashioned scale for customers while she tried to calm down. She had to get a grip.

Her mobile beeped. It was a text from Anna.

'No luck with Scott McM. Will try again when get time. lul Anna xx.'

'Ta.' Amanda texted back and then slipped the phone back into her handbag.

"I've always wondered, if what these herbalists do actually works. Have either of you tried?" she asked.

Brian said. "It's all nonsense. How can a few dried things replace drugs?"

"I'm with him," Guy said.

"So many people believe in it. I'd give it a go if someone recommended a good one," she said.

"I can't stop loving yoooo," a drunk sang a medley out of tune as he passed them. "Yoooo got my heart on a string. I need lovin. Some hot lovin." Then the drunk stumbled into a waste bin and fell. She remembered her uncle being just like this man. He was always in between homes. Her mother despised any weakness in character, never mind that she'd committed suicide.

Two Chinese men were playing Mah Jongg at a sidewalk table.

"Hey, this will make a perfect shot. What do you think, Guy?"

"I want you standing near those men playing. It'll be something that you could pass off as being in Hong Kong," she said.

"You, not me." Guy took the camera from her as Amanda stood next to Brian.

"Come on, Brian. You and me together?"

He shook his head.

"Spoil sport." She took up a goofy pose and waited. "What are you doing, Guy?" She started forward. "It's on auto."

"Looking at the photos you've taken today. Get ready." He took the shot.

"I've never been to Asia. The smell..." Brian wrinkled up his nose as he watched the players.

Amanda licked the melting ice cream. "I have. I was supposed to be on holiday in Hong Kong, but I bumped into an editor I knew over there and well, he was desperate for someone to do some publicity shots. The bloke who had the contract had been in an accident."

"Come on Brian. It's one game you probably don't know how to play." Guy kept step with Amanda.

Brian said. "The one on the right was winning."

"You told them to go find someone else. After all you were on holiday," Guy said.

"The poor man was in a fix with a deadline." She took a last bite and binned the paper napkin.

"You're a workaholic," Brian said as he trudged up the hill.

"Well. I guess I am. Probably get bored too easily or something."

A Vietnamese man shouted at his two little girls when they began to run ahead of him. She remembered her father taking her to the circus one time and when she'd run ahead, he'd been so angry that he'd taken her back home without seeing the show.

"And you're Mr. Perfect. You must have a failing."

Guy glanced at him with what seemed like reproach. "Come on, Brian. Tell all."

"Well…" Brian cleared his throat nervously as he paused to stare at a man who was hanging a red flute above the doorway of his grocery shop.

She'd keep needling him. He'd given her heaps today. "Come on. It must be one of the big ones. I know you don't smoke. Maybe it's wine, women and gambling?"

He looked away, but not before she'd noticed his cheeks redden.

"It's gambling and women and beer."

"But there weren't any females on the station you worked at, were there?"

"That's another thing I hated about the place. Except for the homestead where the owner and his family lived, which was out of bounds to us workers, there were no other women. I'll never go back to that."

"I thought you liked it?" This was incomprehensible for her. Up until recently she'd believed most people liked their jobs. She'd never considered that she was one of the lucky few.

"I guess I needed to get away from the city and clear my head for a while."

They were at the edge of Chinatown. A cable car clattered to a stop down the street from them, expelling and absorbing passengers.

"So what are you going to do now, job wise?" she asked.

"Look, Sis! I don't know why you've decided to pick on me, but..."

"How about that trip to Fisherman's Wharf then that boat ride?" Guy said.

She gritted her teeth. Her twin had called her *"Sis"* again.

"Suits me," Brian said. "I've seen enough of this place."

Amanda could have ambled around for hours. Her brother was so different from her. "Let's go."

After Amanda stepped into the cable car, Brian hopped in, with Guy last on. He gripped the rail with one hand, and in the other, he held her camera. Someone pushed past him and the camera hit the floor, and tumbled out onto the road just before the door closed.

"Shit," she said. "Tell the driver to stop." Then she heard a crunch.

"Hell," Guy said.

"It's wrecked now." Amanda, despondent, sat down next to a woman as the cable car sped down the steep hill.

"I'm sorry." Guy put his hand on her shoulder, and left it there for a moment.

"It wasn't your fault." She tensed. His touch had lasted a few seconds longer than necessary. She didn't want to encourage him.

"I'll buy you another one when we get off," he said.

"Thanks, you don't have to."

Luckily, she'd put a new card in this morning: so the only pictures she'd lost were of the views from Twin Peaks, Chinatown, and a few of Brian and Guy eating their ice creams. She dialed Scott's home number and hoped that he would pick up. There was no answer. She couldn't even leave a message. Was the man ever at home?

***

It was late afternoon when Guy, Brian, and Amanda arrived at the security gates of the Campbell mansion.

A Monterey mist—with its tendrils floating like swathes of chiffon across the landscape—had begun seeping in from the sea.

Brian stepped out of the Mercedes Benz and punched in the code on the security panel set in the wall bordering the property, then the gates opened and he climbed back in.

Guy drove slowly as the mist was thicker here and they only caught glimpses of the neat hedges and borders of flowers.

Brian leaned forward. "Thanks."

"No problem." Guy glanced at Amanda in the seat beside him. "I hope today wasn't too much?"

"When I rang you last night I wasn't sure I would be in the mood to go today but I enjoyed it; even that cable car ride."

"You needed a break from this," Guy said.

"How about coming in for a drink before you drive all that way back to San Francisco?" Brian asked.

"Can't stay long." Guy pulled up outside the Campbell mansion.

A Buick stood on the driveway. Hart stepped from his car and plodded over to them.

What did he want? More questions. Or, did he have some answers? Hart's expression seemed serious. Whatever had brought him here was not good. Amanda's stomach tightened at the thought. She flung open the door of the Benz and stood. "Detective Hart."

"Good afternoon, Ms. Blake." He waited for Brian to get out. "Mr. McMahon."

"You know how to spoil a day. What brings you here?" Brian asked.

She thought that Brian had done a good job of that himself.

"The usual." Hart stared at Guy still sitting in the car.

Guy buzzed down the window and introduced himself. "I'll pass on that drink, Amanda." He shot her a look that seemed to say: sorry,

I can't help it.

"But I thought...."

"The mist is getting even heavier and I don't want to be late for my meeting. I'll catch you later."

Damn. She would have liked his support as well as Brian's. Guy was running out on her.

"Call you. Promise." He drove off.

Amanda trudged up the steps wishing that she were somewhere far away. The weight of the past days' events was building to a crescendo in her thoughts. She rubbed her temples, trying to ease the pressure.

The three of them entered the living room and Amanda immediately went to the glass doors and pulled aside the drapes, remembering Jean doing just that the other day. She closed her eyes to contain the deep sadness welling inside her. It hit her just when she'd thought it under control. She stood for long moments until she felt calmer. The grief was still there but eased a little. She fronted the detective. "Why have you come?"

Hart was silent.

Why wouldn't he answer her? What was so horrible that he couldn't bring himself to tell them? Her stomach tightened and she was sick with worry.

Brian jerked forward from the sofa. "Damn you. Stop playing this out."

"Murder is a serious matter." Hart searched his pockets. Found a packet of gum and offered some to them. With no takers, he popped a stick.

"So it was murder," Amanda said. To suspect that it may have been that was different from actually knowing.

Brian, rigid, gaped at Hart.

"It's not fair." The ache inside her grew. "Damn you!" She sank onto the sofa. "Do you have any idea who?"

"Our investigations are continuing," Hart said.

Tears cursed down her cheeks. God, would they ever stop. She was a mess. She brushed them away and blew her nose. *Pull yourself together, you're useless like this*, she said to herself.

She forced her head up and said, "You must have some suspects?"

"We are still establishing motives and movements for those few days before your mother's death. Mind if I sit?"

"If you want," Brian said.

"Have you narrowed it down to anyone in particular?" Amanda asked.

"I'm not at liberty to say."

Amanda wanted to grab him by his crumpled lapels and shake him, make him tell her. "You talk in riddles."

"How was she killed?" Brian asked.

"The Medical Examiner's finding was that she'd ingested a fatal dose of potassium cyanide."

"Cyanide?" Brian asked.

"Correct."

Brian leaned forward. "How? When? The security here is excellent."

Hart nodded. "Very high tech. Hard for anyone to break in."

There had to be a killer in their midst, Amanda thought. Someone who could have come and gone as they pleased: that someone knew her mother.

"Have you found how she was poisoned?" Brian asked.

"We haven't found traces of cyanide in any of the items we collected." He flipped open his note pad. "We searched for traces in the…pills, toothbrush, toothpaste, lipstick, and compact, and found none."

Ricardo and Estella's rendezvous Saturday night suddenly took on a more sinister meaning. Dorian, why did he go out right after they discovered Jean's body? And what about their conversation on the beach about the inheritance, and that unsigned will? None of it pointed conclusively to any one person. Amanda would have to keep alert for any small thing that might give the murderer away. This detective knew more than he let on; perhaps he already knew the killer's identity.

"What happened to your hands?" Hart asked.

"I was planning to tell you," she said.

Brian looked at her in an intense way and she couldn't fathom whether he wanted to say something but couldn't because Hart was here or whether it was something else that bothered him.

"I think it was an accident," she paused, and then added, "but one that could have killed me. But if you want to know…." Then she told him about her fall and about Dorian and Brian rescuing her. "It happened yesterday."

Hart stood, his eyes widening as she told the story. "Why didn't you tell me this before?"

"I admit I was worrying about it. But I thought you might think I'm being a hysterical female. I kept convincing myself of that, and that I was making more of it because of…of Jean."

"Something was spilled on the steps, you say?"

"I'm sure of it." She shivered as the implication of what he did not say sunk in. This had been an attempt on her life.

"I'm going out there now to have a look."

"Even if we turn on all the outside lights, it'll be dark on the steps," Brian said.

"Then get me a flashlight," Hart said, trudging towards the door.

Brian buzzed Estella and asked her to meet them with one on the veranda.

Amanda was edgy as she followed Brian and Hart outside. This was like some B-grade movie. None of it made sense.

A few minutes later Estella joined them, light in hand. The two men went to investigate while Amanda waited on the veranda with Estella.

"What are they looking for?" the maid asked.

"Hart didn't say," she lied. There was something different about Estella. Then Amanda noticed the maid's hand tremble. She seemed to be afraid of something or someone.

Brian and Hart returned moments later and Estella went inside.

"The mist is so heavy that I can't see a thing," Hart said. "Has anyone used the steps since your accident?"

"Everyone has been told not to use the steps until the handrail is repaired," Brian said.

"Where is the handrail now?"

"It's still at the bottom of the cliff. I think Dorian rang a carpenter to build a new one and take the old one away," he said.

"I'll be back first thing tomorrow and have another look at those steps and the handrail. Brian, find a barricade and put it at the top. I want both of you to stay in tonight, and be very, very careful from now on."

"Goodnight." Brian went to the garage in search of something he could use to barricade the steps.

Amanda took Hart through the house and out the front to his car. She kept her voice low. "I want to tell you that I found an email from Scott McMahon on my mother's computer. That's Brian's step-brother. He asked her to get in touch with him. He had some information for her. It sounded important."

"When?"

"Last night."

"Why didn't you tell me this sooner?"

"M...my mother's...murder, puts a different slant on things."

The detective was silent for a moment. "What information could he have for Mrs. Campbell?"

"I don't know."

"Do you think Brian might know?"

"Brian's had very little contact with his brother in the last few years. Anyway, I haven't shown the message to him yet. Aren't you in the least bit suspicious?"

"But I don't like jumping to conclusions. I'll get in touch with McMahon."

When, she thought, next Christmas?

"Have you told anyone else?"

She shook her head.

"Then keep it that way. Please forward it on to me."

He gave her his card with his email address and they said their goodbyes. He climbed into his vehicle and she raced inside. She'd never been afraid of the dark, not even as a child locked up in the broom cupboard for hours when she was naughty, until she came here.

CHAPTER 20

Amanda had spent all day waiting for the opportunity to search her mother's room. Finally, no one was about. As she put her hand to the doorknob, the image of Jean lying on the bathroom floor assaulted her. She doubled over and told herself to breathe.

A puff from her inhaler helped her lungs but not her emotions. She had to make herself do this. As she bolstered her courage, Estella appeared at the top of the stairs. Amanda smiled at her and pretended to be going back to her own room. The maid disappeared into one of the other bedrooms with a vacuum cleaner and she hurried back to Jean's room. She took a deep breath and opened the door. The scent of wildflowers drifted to her and she remembered her mother's warm embrace. Sadness washed over Amanda and tears slipped down her cheeks.

About to step inside, Amanda heard someone hurrying up the staircase. She retreated, closing the door. The idea of searching her mother's room abandoned for now.

"What have you been doing?" Brian asked as he stepped into the hallway. He was dressed casually in jeans and t-shirt.

Had he seen her coming from Jean's room? "Nothing much. I'm going down for dinner."

"I've already eaten. I could get used to all this."

But she couldn't get used to the idea that her mother was gone. "You didn't wait for me?"

"Didn't know where you were. I'm getting changed and going to the casino." Brian took a few steps to his room and turned to her. "Do you want to come?"

Maybe he hadn't wanted to be in her company after yesterday. Now he was feeling guilty and invited her out. But how could he think about enjoying himself now? "No thanks."

Amanda went downstairs and passed the library on her way to the dining room when the phone rang. She went to the desk and answered it.

"Amanda Blake?" Hart asked.

"Yes?"

"I have the lab report on that substance you slipped on the other day. Suntan oil. Did you take some with you to the beach?"

"No. Nor did Dorian. Anyone could have spilled some."

"Did you notice it on the way down to the beach?"

"Come to think of it, no. Do you think this was deliberate?" she asked.

"I can't say that just yet."

The man was so guarded. However, what he said sounded very much like a yes. "Someone wanted me to fall," she blurted out. "That can't be possible. Maybe Dorian or Brian saw something?"

"Do not discuss this with anyone," Hart said. "As I said before, we don't know for certain if it was deliberate, but don't go down those steps to the beach 'till all this is cleared up."

"That's why you were interviewing Dorian again yesterday, wasn't it?"

"We had to know his version of why you went first up the steps."

"It was just the way it happened. Dorian took the tripod and I carried the camera. He followed me up. No, wait. Dorian carried the camera and tripod."

"We know that he followed."

"Do you think I staged it? Is that what you think?"

"Not at this point."

"Jesus, small comfort that is! Do you seriously think I'd want to hurt myself?"

"Do you?" the detective asked.

"I don't know what you think of me but I would never do that."

"Maybe you have an enemy," he said.

"How would I know? I'm living with people who are practically strangers. Have you called Scott McMahon?"

"In due course."

That would never do, she thought.

"Is there anyone you can think of, even friends who might hold a grudge?"

"No one. By the way, after I clean my teeth, I always rinse them with mouthwash. I was doing that last night when I remembered something."

"What are you talking about?"

"In that list of items found in Jean's bathroom, you omitted to mention the mouthwash."

"Hold on a minute. Let me read my notes."

Amanda stared at the family photos of the Campbell family. They were stiff and formal. Dorian, always standing apart from Jean, and a man that Amanda guessed was Murray. There didn't seem to be that much family resemblance between father and son.

Hart recited the items they had found. "No bottle of mouthwash was collected. Are you certain you saw it on the vanity?"

"Positive."

"Okay. When does the garbage go out?"

"Tonight, I think. Do you want me to check?"

"No. I'll get someone to pick it up right away. Don't say a word to anyone."

Their call over, Amanda hung up. Her hand was stiff and clammy. She'd been gripping the receiver harder than she realized.

CHAPTER 21

A flock of arctic terns flew overhead, their calls cutting through the subdued voices of mourners grouped around the burial site. Amanda gazed at the rows of black and white granite slabs shimmering in the heat.

She stood stiffly between Brian and Dorian in her new black dress. Her pumps were sinking into the soft earth that was still moist from an overnight shower. Faces glanced at her, at Brian, then away. Their expressions were ones of surprise. From the responses she'd received when she'd arrived at the church for the service, she'd realized that no one had known Jean had had children.

Estella, wearing an ill-fitting polyester suit, chatted to Rosa and Ricardo.

The priest waved away a fly that buzzed lazily around his head and began his sermon.

Amanda glanced at Dorian and saw he was looking gray, obviously upset about today. She held her tears in check as she fingered the long strand of South Sea pearls that Jean had given her less than a week ago.

Her thoughts drifted back seventeen years. Back to when she'd been twelve, and in class doing math. She hadn't liked mathematics much then. She'd been summoned to the principal's office. Her dad had been inside waiting for her. As she'd walked down the corridor, guilty thoughts had raced through her mind. Was it because she'd pulled that stupid girl's hair? No, it had to be something worse than that. Parents only came when you'd done something terrible or when they had unhappy news.

The two sad faces, the principal's and her father's, had said it all. It was serious. "Why are you here?" Amanda demanded, her loud voice masking the quaking she felt.

"I've just come from the hospital. I'm sorry. It's mum. You know she was having trouble…her medication for her nerves…she kept forgetting to take it. Sometimes she'd take extra to make up. They couldn't do anything for her. It was too late."

"How too late?"

"Well...she's gone to heaven."

"She's not gone. I want to see her. Please let me see mummy." Amanda usually called her mum. Only when she was frightened, she called her mummy, and she was very frightened now. "I want to see her. She wouldn't leave me."

"No. I explained to you that mum has gone to heaven, Amanda." Samuel had put his hand on her shoulder. "And there's nothing else to say on the matter."

"It's not fair. Why did she die?" She'd shrugged off the only attempt her father had made to comfort her.

"Your mother wouldn't have wanted you to show any weakness." Samuel lowered his voice. "So, stop your sniveling."

She hadn't cried at Elaine's funeral and she wouldn't cry now, no matter what.

The priest's voice broke into her thoughts. Jean's gravesite loomed at her with a sadness that etched deep into her soul.

"Ashes to ashes, dust to dust."

Her scream was silent. She glanced up expecting everyone to have noticed her inner struggle. No one had. They were staring down at the polished wooden coffin, all still listening to the steady drone of the priest's voice.

The emotional pain when Elaine had died, which had remained locked away, surfaced again, but this time, it was for Jean: the woman who had reached out across the ocean to her. Amanda couldn't kid herself that she hadn't been hurt, that she hadn't felt anger against Jean and against her adoptive parents. At least Jean had attempted to make amends.

Why is it that the funeral directors think it gentler to lower the coffin so slowly? As if anything could make the event easier to bear. It seemed to take forever. Amanda squeezed her eyes shut. Tears of anger welled in her eyes against that unknown someone who had taken her mother's life. The anger grew in intensity and she grabbed hold of it, closed herself around it—befriended it and found purpose in it. That would be her driving force, to seek answers and justice.

A tall man with caterpillar eyebrows went to shake her hand. She pulled back. Even though the bandages had been removed, her palm was still tender. She offered only her fingers.

"I'm Ira Bowen, manager at the company's branch in Denver, Colorado. A touching service, Ms. Blake." Ira adjusted his tie.

She hadn't been aware Campbell-Beare Pharmaceuticals had a branch there, not that she knew very much about the company anyway.

"Yes it was," she said lamely, not knowing what else she should say as Ira moved on to Dorian.

Another mourner swanned over in black stilettos and a figure hugging dress. "You're Jean's daughter, Amanda?"

She nodded.

"Felicity Beare," she stared haughtily from under her wide-brimmed hat.

Before Amanda could respond, the woman added. "That's the Beare, in Campbell-Beare."

"Thank you for coming," Amanda said.

"It must be such a comfort to know that Jean is resting beside Murray," Felicity said.

"Lionel said this was what she'd wanted," Amanda said.

"Did he?" Felicity had an open mouth smile, which didn't reach the corners of her lips. Botox had done its job too well, thought Amanda.

"You must come visit me while you're in town." She air-kissed Amanda. "Promise?" Not waiting for a reply, she waltzed off to someone else.

Amanda felt like a puppet in a play, reacting and responding the way that was expected of her as people approached and offered their condolences.

"I had no idea our mother was so well known." Brian watched

another couple move away as he loosened his tie. "It's a hot one today."

Like herself, Amanda had expected her twin to be upset by her mother's death. If he was, he'd been very good at hiding his emotions so far.

A stocky powerhouse of a man joined them. "Hi, you must be Amanda. You look just like Jean." He gripped her hand briefly. "Horace Beare. And you're Brian." He did the same with her twin. "Jean was always batting a thousand."

"Everything's baseball with Horace," Dorian added.

"She was a great lady, but she'd reached the end of her game. As we all will one day," Horace said.

"Thank you." Amanda was sure the man was offering his sympathies.

After Beare moved on, Dorian made his way through the crowd, pausing now and then to speak with mourners until he reached a tall student type with blotchy skin wearing dark sunglasses. They seemed to share a close bond as they talked, their heads bent, their shoulders almost touching. The friend kept running his hand through his untidy black hair.

A straggle of people began to leave. Hart stood apart from everyone. His gaze darted from person to person, taking everything in.

"Let's go under that tree," Brian said.

Amanda retreated past other gravesites to the dappled shade of a jacaranda coming into bloom.

Ricardo and Estella waved goodbye to both of them. As they went to their car, Ricardo spoke to his sister. She nudged his side when a couple walked by them, silencing him. Amanda wondered what had he started to say.

That feeling of unease she'd had when she'd seen them whispering in the courtyard the other night returned. They couldn't be trusted. What were they plotting?

Brian touched her arm. "Is something worrying you?"

Could he guess at what she'd been thinking? "Where's Dorian?''

He scanned the crowd. "He's over by that white headstone with that weird mate of his. I'm glad that's over. I hate funerals.''

"It was your mother's," she said.

He looked at her with a contrite expression. "I hardly knew her. I know that's no excuse but, look, I'm glad that I met her…I'm making a complete mess of this."

"Yes you are," she said. Dorian and his friend were busy talking, or were they? Perhaps they were arguing. The man was pointing at Jean's gravesite, a burst of words poured from his lips. Dorian's strained features said it all. This person was pushing him into an emotional corner.

"I want to have a quick word with Lionel before we leave. I'll be back," her brother said.

"Okay." It seemed that Jean had been the source of friction between Dorian and his friend, and whatever the problem, it was not solved yet.

Her stepbrother noticed her gaze and his lips turned up at the corners: his smile seemed strained. Then he mouthed a word. "Home?"

She nodded.

After a few parting words his friend left, and Dorian came towards her.

Hart intercepted. Her stepbrother frowned as the detective spoke. What had the detective said to make Dorian fold his arms defensively?

Amanda walked across the uneven ground toward them. Her gaze took in Dorian's stance, his wiry frame, and the hands that had pulled her to safety. Was he capable of murder? Would he have saved her if Brian hadn't been there? His friendship took on a new uneasy meaning.

"Good morning, Ms. Blake. Let me offer my condolences to you," Hart said.

"Thank you."

"I'll see you both later," the detective said.

Brian shouldered his way between Dorian and Amanda.

"Is your friend coming to the wake?" Brian's voice implied that he did not want to hear a yes.

Dorian stared back. "He's gone home. He's been sick for the past few weeks."

"What? Oh, sick of you." Brian said.

"No!" Dorian started for the funeral car. "Coming, Amanda?"

"Give me a moment." Her gaze moved over the wreaths and bouquets that lay over the green carpet covering the open gravesite. She had said her silent goodbyes in the church. There, Cohen had addressed the congregation. Who better knew Jean? His eulogy had moved some to tears. Even Dorian had shifted uncomfortably in his seat. It was Lionel rather than Dorian who invited the congregation to the wake.

Lionel waited for them at the car. His balding head damp with perspiration. His face was a white mask. "I dislike these events intensely."

Dorian said "Then why did you bother to come?"

"I cared about Jean. This has been a sad closure for me," Cohen said.

"Bullshit," Dorian said.

The chauffeur opened the doors.

"I don't deserve this from you. I was there for you so many times. I tried to be like a father for you," Lionel said.

"You were never that."

"Dorian, please," Amanda said as she slid into her seat.

"For you, Amanda. Not for him." He pressed his lips together. There, he did it again, controlled his temper for her. It didn't make sense.

Lionel turned and strode away.

CHAPTER 22

Caterers had served a light, buffet-style lunch and refreshments on the veranda for the eighty or so people who had come back to the house.

After the last of the mourners left, Lionel Cohen summoned the family, the staff, and Hart inside for the reading of the will.

Amanda entered the living room with Dorian, who was nursing a drink.

Brian, comfortable in one of the wing-backed chairs, was talking to Lionel. "So you enjoy a good game of poker. Then we'll have to set up a game soon."

"Needs more ice," announced Dorian, as he stared into his glass.

"I'm rather busy at the moment," Cohen watched Dorian leave. "Do you play often?"

"I haven't had a game in ages. Does sometime next week suit you?" Brian asked.

"I'll let you know."

Weary from the day's events, Amanda sank into the chair beside her twin.

Dorian came back in. "Glad that's over. I hate small talk with people who are practically strangers to me." He took a gulp of his drink, and sat.

Amanda tapped her fingers nervously on the armrest while she waited for the others to arrive. Just knowing that Jean had loved her was more than enough. She didn't want or expect Jean to have bequeathed her anything. Sure, there were plenty of people out there who would greedily grab whatever they could. One such man, working for the family company, had flirted with her, gave her his phone number, and said with honeyed insincerity—you're the most beautiful and sexy woman I've ever met. Please go out with me. I won't be able to stand it if you don't. The line was so well-worn that she'd nearly burst out laughing there and then. His motives were so transparent. Chat up the maybe heiress to the family fortune, and if she got the cake, he would latch on to her and have his slice too. She should have told him that he was wasting his time, and that she was not so gullible and she'd no idea if she was to receive anything at all, but his constant chatter prevented her from doing so. Still amused by the sound of his prattle going through her head, she smiled for the first time today.

"What's so funny?" Brian asked.

"I'll tell you later," she whispered.

Cohen glanced up from the bundle of papers he was leafing through. "You find me funny?"

Amanda met his gaze. "No. I was thinking about something that happened to me earlier."

"Oh. The funeral!"

Cohen's barb caught her by surprise. She squashed her initial vicious retort—*you bastard, you are deliberately trying to upset me.* "That's not what I meant at all. I don't want to go into it now."

"Why, Lionel?" Dorian jiggled his foot.

He was standing up for her and she couldn't understand why.

Lionel jerked over another page. "You really want to know?" It fluttered to the floor. He reached for it.

"Not really." Amanda tried to ease the tension. Jesus, it was bad enough sitting here and waiting for the reading, let alone having to deal with Cohen's sarcasm. She did not want or need a full-scale argument happening now.

Dorian stilled his foot and sat rigid. "Lionel, Amanda deserves-"

"She...reminds me too much of Jean." His face was devoid of emotion, but his hands betrayed him: they trembled as he closed the folder.

Stunned, she sat back, willing herself to keep calm. Her resemblance to Jean was no revelation to her. His admission that this was the reason for his behavior was. A private hell of his own making, and she was part of it.

Hart trudged in. Rosa, Estella and Ricardo followed.

Cohen glanced up, all signs of his rancor seemingly gone. "Please make yourselves comfortable. Now that everyone is present, we can start." He put on his reading glasses.

"I, Jean Marcie Campbell, being of sound mind..."

Dorian tapped his foot again on the carpet: the muffled sound propelled Amanda to another level of tense.

"The estate is to be divided equally among Dorian Murray Campbell, Amanda Marcie Blake, and Brian William McMahon." Cohen paused. "In plain English, that means each of you will receive about sixty million in shares and bonds to be held in a family trust. The details will be fully explained later. Jean made provision for Mr. Beare and the Campbell-Beare Pharmaceuticals board to continue to run the company. The shares presently produce a dividend of approximately seven and a half million per year. There are three main beneficiaries. This home is bequeathed to Dorian as well as the apartment and office block in New York, including the art works contained therein to be held in the family trust. Two homes in Paris, one in New York, one in Milan and one in London are bequeathed to Amanda, including the art works contained therein to be held in the family trust, plus all of Mrs. Campbell's jewelry, which she may use as she sees fit. The three dairy farms in New York State and the two beef ranches in West Virginia are bequeathed to Brian to be held in the family trust."

Amanda sat motionless, trying to absorb the news. "I had no idea the estate was so large."

"Neither did I," Brian said.

The more she thought about it the more it worried her. One thing was clear in her mind, she would spend every cent if she had to find Jean's murderer.

She glanced at Brian. He was gripping the sides of the wing-backed chair so hard that his knuckles were white.

"Estella Periuz...." Cohen said in his usual measured voice.

The maid sat stiffly next to her brother.

He continued, "...will receive $400,000 for her loyal service."

Amanda heard a swift intake of breath from Ricardo. The noise seemed to echo in her head until Lionel spoke.

"Rosa Estivariz, for her loyal service will receive $150,000."

The cook thanked Lionel.

"Ricardo Periuz, for his loyal service will receive $100,000."

Ricardo gawped in amazement. "Mucho?"

Estella drew her tissue out and blew her nose. "So generous. She was good employer."

Ricardo gripped Estella's hand and whispered. "It will help our mama."

That expression of need from Estella and Ricardo had surprised Amanda. They were benefiting from Jean's death, much more than staff usually did.

Lionel continued. "The money will go into the family trust initially and if any of the beneficiaries, or should I say trust members, Dorian, Amanda and Brian, die, their share will be divided between the surviving members. This trust takes precedence over any provisions they may have made."

What had made Jean do that? She remembered Cohen saying that it had been drawn up immediately after Murray had died.

"Family trust? What does that entail?" Brian asked.

Amanda knew she should listen but the way Cohen tried to explain how the trust worked was too confusing.

She wondered about Scott and the email he'd sent. Why did he want Jean to contact him? Where was he? And what information did Scott's missing letter contain? Five times, she'd attempted to contact him this week. It must have been sheer luck that Brian was able to speak with Scott that one time. Not that Brian had thought it luck at the time.

"I should also mention something that Detective Hart already knows."

Amanda sat upright, her attention captured.

"The will that Jean did not sign had a clause that I have withheld until now. It stated that in the event of Amanda's death, a quarter of the estate would go to charity and the rest would be held in the bloodline trust for Dorian and Brian, for a period of fifteen years before they could access this money. Estella and Ricardo would only receive $100,000 and $50,000 respectively."

Had Jean lived, Dorian and Brian would have been much worse off as would Estella and Ricardo. Greed was a very strong motive for any killer.

This waiting for Hart to continue his investigations was driving her mad. She had to do something. The killer was out there enjoying his freedom, and her mother was in the ground.

Ricardo glanced at his sister and pressed his full lips together. It was a silent message that Amanda didn't understand but it worried her nonetheless. What were they plotting, she thought?

"Thank you, Mr. Cohen. We very grateful for the money Mrs. Campbell left us. When can we have it?" Ricardo rose.

Cohen blinked. The directness of the question must have surprised him. "The usual procedures must be adhered to. In any event, it will be after probate. I can't estimate exactly how long that will be."

"It won't be soon enough for me," Dorian was still swinging his foot.

Cohen smiled but didn't speak.

Amanda stared at Estella's worried face. The maid should have been pleased to inherit such a large sum. So, what was wrong?

"Thank you." Ricardo, with his hand in the small of his sister's back, propelled her out.

Brian loosened his tie. "What do you plan to do with your money?"

Amanda shrugged. "I haven't had time to think about it yet. And you?"

"Maybe a yacht and a new Lamborghini. But first, I have a few debts to clear up once I figure out how this trust works."

"Oh." *Me too*, she said to herself. Later, she would ask Cohen to explain the trust to her again.

"Do you want to go for a walk, Brian?" Amanda asked.

His gold-flecked green eyes had a faraway look. He seemed lost in thought. "Yep. I need some fresh air."

His tone was flat. Was he worried about her or something else entirely?

Hart struggled out of his chair. "Amanda, can I speak with you alone for a moment?"

"Let's go into the library. Catch you later, Brian." What now, she thought? Her stomach tightened as she went in.

"What's this all about?" she asked.

"I'll explain shortly," Hart said.

Amanda followed the detective into the library. Hart shut the door behind them.

"I think you should consider hiring a bodyguard." He searched his jacket pockets. "A friend of mine, an ex-cop, works as one."

"Thank you for the offer, but I'm fine. It's not necessary." She would not be here long enough. She wouldn't tell Hart that. He would not agree to her plan of action.

"But I think it is." He pulled a business card from his inside pocket. "You must realize that this is serious, especially because of your fall the other day. I don't believe that the handrail was sawn; it was just joined at that point. Today the gardener gave me the missing bolt from the hand rail."

"Where was it found?" Amanda asked.

"In a garden bed that was quite a distance from the steps. If it were found near the steps or just below where the handrail should have been then I would have thought it was normal wear and tear."

Someone wanted her dead. No. She tried to reject the thought, but a trickle of fear was building and she couldn't squash it no matter how hard she tried.

"Any fingerprints?" She toyed with the card.

"I expect to find a perfect set from the gardener. Other than that, we'll have to wait and see."

That heavy shower last night, thought Amanda, would probably have washed any others away.

She had to play it right. She put the card into her pocket. "I'll contact this man tomorrow."

"The sooner the better," the detective said.

"Was there anything else?"

"We found the mouthwash in the garbage."

"You've tested it?"

He nodded. "It was empty, and someone had gone to the trouble of washing it out and removing any prints, but the lab still found traces of cyanide."

"Oh God."

"It's easy to swallow small amounts when you're gargling and Mrs. Campbell could have been using it for days before it…well…it did the job."

"Well, you'd better catch that murdering bastard." Amanda reined in her emotions. "I'm sorry. I…I didn't mean to say that." She rubbed her forehead, trying to ease the tension inside her. "That email from Scott is worrying me."

She went over to the bookshelf and picked up a copy of Jane Eyre, flipped to the first page and saw her mother's name written there. She turned to him. "This book was my mother's from her childhood. I think I'll keep it."

"You haven't tried to follow up on this yourself, have you?"

"I haven't made contact with Scott, if that's what you mean." There was a name for this: twisting the truth. Not something she normally excelled at but today, she did. "Have you spoken to Scott?

"We will."

"Was there anything else you wanted to know?"

He shook his head. "Please contact that bodyguard tomorrow."

"Mmm. I'll see you later." She hurried to her bedroom, and texted Anna. 'Any luck w Scott?'

Her friend replied. 'Nope.'

'Damn. Speak soon. lul, Amanda xx.'

She went into the hallway and stopped to listen for any sign that someone might be coming. All was quiet.

She stole along the hallway to Jean's room. With everyone occupied downstairs or outside she would take the opportunity to search her mother's room without interruption. She hoped to find something that would explain why Scott had contacted Jean. Or even the contents of that envelope.

At least four times this week, she'd attempted to go to her mother's bedroom.

As she turned the door handle, the image of Jean's lifeless body flooded her senses again. Amanda wanted to scream. Her legs felt like they were buckling. Her knuckles were white as she clenched the knob.

"Oh God." She put her hand over her mouth to stop a scream surfacing. The urge to turn and run almost overwhelmed her. It took all of her willpower that she hadn't known existed to stay. She shut her eyes and took a few long shaky breaths.

Finally, she opened the door.

Estella spun round, the waste paper bin in her hands. "Susto?"

"What are you doing here?" Amanda stared. She thought Estella had gone out with her brother.

"I did not empty the bin. I did not come in here since…since, but after, but all the money, Mrs. Campbell left me…I was ashamed. I want to clean up."

Amanda walked over to the bureau. "Give it to me."

The maid shrank back. "It is only Mrs. Campbell's trash. The policemen already look at everything."

"You've been watching them!"

Estella shook her head. "Please. I was only passing when I see them look through Mrs. Campbell's things."

Amanda was in two minds. She should tell Hart about this immediately. But if she did, there'd be men swarming all over the place again. She couldn't afford that now. This woman was sneaking around too much for her liking.

She would have to tell Hart eventually. "I'll have that waste basket."

"Yes, Miss Campbell...sorry, Miss Amanda." Estella's hands trembled.

"I don't like you tiptoeing about like this. You're not to enter this room again." She noticed the key pinned to the maid's pocket. "And I'll have the key too."

"Please. I am sorry. I should have asked. I did not think it would matter. I am not a thief."

Amanda took the key. "I don't know what you are. What I do know is that you're not to be trusted. I intend to tell the detective about this."

"You think bad of me. I tell you I am not a thief."

"So you say."

"You do not believe me. I work for your mother for many years. If she was here, she would...upset."

"How dare you involve my mother in this, today of all days."

"I will not work here anymore. Finish now." Estella turned to go, then swung back. "But I musto warn you-"

"What are you two doing?" Brian stood in the doorway.

"Well I...." She'd wanted to search Jean's room for clues, "I caught Estella snooping around."

"Doing what?" he asked. "Why are you holding the bin Amanda? And what's in it."

"Don't know, but I took it from the maid."

"Only trash," Estella said.

"Estella has resigned," Amanda said.

Brian raised his eyebrows. "Why?"

"You must be very careful, Miss Amanda." The maid strode out.

"Why's she acting like this?"

"Wait. Come back a minute. What did you mean? Are you threatening me? Come back," she shouted.

'What's going on here?" Brian asked again.

'I'll explain later," Amanda went into the hallway.

Estella was already at the foot of the stairs.

"Come back and explain yourself," Amanda shouted.

Estella ran towards the kitchen.

She started down the stairs until she heard the back door slam. She trudged back to her mother's room where Brian was waiting.

"Why did she quit?"

Amanda told him. "And she tried to tell me she was only tidying up. Tidying up in here when Jean's been gone almost week. Well it just didn't wash. She was acting too suspiciously."

"We should tell Hart about this."

Amanda sat the basket on the desk and pulled out some of the crumpled paper. "You can tell him later, when I've left."

"I'd rather ring him before Estella clears out. What did you say? When…why…you're leaving?"

"I'm going to visit Scott, see if I can get to the bottom of the letter he sent to Jean. I've booked a red-eye flight to Sydney. I'm convinced that someone didn't want that letter around. And I want to find out what was in it."

"Scott wouldn't know anything. I told you before that Jean had probably contacted him to get my address."

She straightened a page: a reminder to ring Mr. Beare. "The day I arrived, Estella mentioned that she'd been to Wollongong. She has a cousin there."

Brian raised an eyebrow. "So how does that connect with Scott?"

"Perhaps he's found something out about Estella or her brother. Anyway, I just want to find out what was in it. I should have told you before. I don't know why I didn't. Scott sent an email to Jean."

Brian, silent, stared hard at her.

"I forwarded it on to Hart." She told him what it contained as she pulled out another crumpled page. It seemed to be a spam letter.

"What was it about again?"

"Nothing that I could make head nor tail of. I tried to contact Scott a few times. Even replied to the email but I got a fat zero back."

"You shouldn't have bothered. You were there when I rang him.

Just because of a silly email and that supposed letter. All right, there was an envelope. So what. You're going on a wild goose chase."

She glanced at him. "Don't you think it's strange that you're brother's never home? Something's wrong and I'm going to find out what."

"He could be on holidays or something."

"Then I'll track him down." How could she explain that she was convinced that message was more sinister than he thought?

"Don't be so bloody…. Oh never mind. You shouldn't go."

Every time she read the email, it had left her feeling uneasy, and positively desperate to find out what it all meant. "I've made up my mind."

"You can't go on your own. I'll come too."

"Thanks for the offer but I don't think it would be a good idea. The two of you would only argue. I won't find out a thing."

"Someone's got to protect you."

"I can look after myself. And if we both go, Hart will probably contact the Australian authorities and I don't want them hanging around. If you're here, you can fob him off with excuses and he need not know where I've gone straight away." There seemed nothing of importance among these papers. About to throw them back, she spotted a newspaper clipping under a bill. She glanced at it. The man looked somehow familiar. The name underneath, Eddie Delensky, which didn't mean a thing and yet she felt she should know him, had seen him somewhere. Perhaps he had one of those familiar faces.

He shook his head. "I don't like it. What have you found?"

Amanda scrunched the papers in her hand. "Nothing really."

"What are you going to say to Dorian? Or are you just planning to disappear for a while?"

"I want to speak to him about Estella before I go. I'll tell him about my trip then." She threw the rest of the rubbish back, and put the basket on the floor, while she pocketed the newspaper clipping with her free hand.

"I still don't like you going alone. I've already told you my brother's bad news. Tell Hart to send one of his men."

"He'll only contact the Australian authorities and wait to hear from them. It could take ages. I'm going. It's the quickest way to get to the bottom of all this."

"Scott's mixed up in the drug scene and God knows what else. You're being foolish."

"I've made up my mind."

"You're a stubborn woman, Amanda Blake." He hugged her. "Take care, Sis."

CHAPTER 23

Guy Robertson breezed into his San Francisco hotel suite, with a décor of cream leather this and that. It would be at least another week before his work was finished and he could head off home. He loosened his tie, slipped it off along with his jacket, walked over to the built-in closet and hung them neatly inside. Mamma had trained him well, so well that he was always tidying up, and he hated walking in on a mess.

Amanda Blake, what an exciting woman. He closed the closet door. She had the qualities he liked in a female—easy on the eye, strong-willed, yet there was an underlying softness about her. He would coax her along a little: she would be his soon enough.

The funeral had been on today and afterwards Amanda had found out how much she would be worth. The thought thrilled him. He picked up his mobile and tapped in her number.

"Hello."

She sounded worn out.

"Well, how did it go?"

She told him about the day's events.

"Do you want me to come over tonight?" Guy picked up the pen by the phone and started twirling it.

"Can't. I'm leaving for home later."

Guy dropped the pen. "*Australia?*"

"Yes. I'm going to see Scott McMahon."

"Why? Who's he?"

There was a long pause on the other end of the line. "I'll tell you more when I get back."

Hell. His plans were out the window. Perhaps he could delay her. "Whatever it is it can't be that urgent. Why don't you wait a couple of days and see how you feel. You're not thinking straight. Upset about your mother and all."

"Sorry. The flight's booked. I don't plan to stay long."

This would just about ruin everything. She was slipping away from him. "Amanda." He'd have to think fast and make the best of it somehow. Have all bases covered.

"Yes."

"Ring me when you're on your way back. I'll be your welcoming committee, and I'll pick you up from the airport."

CHAPTER 24

SANTA CRUIZ

Lionel Cohen rummaged through the stack of folders on his desk. Where was the file on the Zackerman case? It had to be here somewhere. As he looked deeper, the top ones slid one after the other to the floor before he had a chance to save them. He leant over, and picked them up. "Fuck it." The clients would be here soon. He finished picking up the folders and put them in order, all the while looking out for the missing one. He buzzed through to his assistant. That stupid goddamned woman must have mislaid that file. "The Zackerman folder is missing. Find it now. Make sure you bring it in the minute you do."

"But Mr. Cohen, you took it home last night. Don't you remember? It should still be in your briefcase."

She was right. How could he have forgotten? "Yes. But I thought you'd taken it out." No sooner had he switched off the intercom than she was buzzing him.

"Mr. Cohen, Mrs. Beare is on line one. Shall I put her through?"

"Yes." He pulled off his glasses as he switched lines. "Hello, Felicity."

"You were supposed to meet me for breakfast. I waited for over an hour for you. What happened?"

"I'm really sorry. I wanted to call but…" he had to lie, she'd never believe he had forgotten, "I've been so pushed with work I didn't have time."

"Time." She spluttered down the line. "Horace will be back in three days. Is there someone else?"

"There *is* only you. Will you come to dinner at my place tonight? My meeting will finish around four, and then I'm heading home. I'll order some of that Five Star Fine Dining take out that we like."

"I've already made arrangements to dine with one of Horace's cousins visiting from out of town. Just thought of a way. Half way through the meal, I'm going to develop a headache. I should be there by eight."

He looked forward to making love to her again. This time he hoped big john, as she'd so fondly called it, although not lately, would work.

Felicity had a high sex drive, and she was not afraid to experiment. That, plus her striking looks, had attracted him initially. However, she was not the most understanding of women. She had been patient and he knew that would not last for much longer. The last time they'd met, she had told him to see a doctor about his problem or else. Then she'd added that her trainer had all the right equipment, and she just might try him out. He hoped she wasn't serious.

His doctor had told him it was a temporary problem that almost every man experienced at least once in his lifetime. The doctor suggested he should try subdued lighting, soft music, and to empty his head of all his worries and let things happen naturally. If only it were that easy. One more time, and then he'd resort to those pills that everybody was taking nowadays. Maybe he should get a prescription and take them anyway. Damn, he didn't have time today to visit the doctor.

He would make sure all his thoughts were positive. His member would stand like a soldier for her. He would take her in all the ways she liked. It would be a night to remember.

CHAPTER 25

CARMEL VALLEY

Ricardo Periuz yawned, and stared at the plastic clock on the wall. "Hell. I've barely got time for breakfast; I'm expected at the Campbells' at nine." He pulled out the carton of milk from the fridge and shook it. "Nearly empty."

Estella looked up from her bowl of milky cereal. She was dressed in a chain store suit. When she had collected the paper this morning, she had noticed an advertisement for a maid; called, and arranged an interview in two hours' time. She apologized. "Lo siento."

How could she have been so thoughtless? If Ricardo had not taken her in after she had left the Campbells', she would have had nowhere to go; she could not go back to live in Ensenada. Their poor mama could hardly look after herself as it was. In addition, Estella did not want to go back to Mexico; her future lay here. With a new job and the money from Jean's estate, she had more than enough for a substantial down payment on a place of her own. Also, she would be able to afford a nice nursing home here in California for their mama.

Ricardo grumbled as he buttoned up his shirt and said in their native tongue, "I haven't got time for shopping. I guess I'll just have to go hungry." He sat on a threadbare armchair, and pulled on his socks.

The small two-bedroom bungalow in Carmel Valley was twenty-five minutes or so away from the Campbell's house.

Estella finished her last mouthful. "It's my fault; I should have left you some. Finish dressing while I get some more."

The neighborhood strip mall, which had a small market, two restaurants, a misplaced souvenir shop and a gas station, was a block away.

She collected her purse from her room, and then slammed the front door behind her as she left. She ran down the steps, and

132

stopped suddenly at the bottom when she saw him.

What was he doing here? Visiting someone? But the purposeful way he walked toward her left her with no doubt that he had been waiting for her.

He approached. "Hello, Estella."

"What do you want?" She had never liked him. He reminded her of those polar bears she had read about in magazines. Beautiful to look at, yet so deadly, one could tear a man apart in seconds.

"I want you to come with me. Now." One hand remained in his pocket.

"Why?" She stood rigid, defiant. "What wrong?" She'd bluff her way through this.

"Just move."

"My brother, Ricardo is inside. I'll-"

"You don't understand." His tone was menacing.

Her stomach tightened as she tried to think of something else to say.

He lowered his voice. "I have a gun. If you call out and Ricardo hears, I'll have to shoot him."

A gun. Her legs were suddenly wobbly from fear. She glanced back hoping to see Ricardo staring out of the window, but the blinds were shut.

"Get moving."

She hoped her brother would come outside. Or at least see her situation and call the police. "Why you do this?"

He did not answer.

Estella guessed this man was trying to scare her because he realized how much she'd seen and how much she knew.

A couple holding hands were strolling along, enjoying the sunshine. She stared at them, hoping they would see her distress. They went by, too preoccupied to notice. Her heart sank.

What choice did she have but to do his bidding? He opened the door to his sleek new sports car. "Just don't try anything. Don't make me hurt you."

A few more people passed. One glanced admiringly at the car but hardly noticed her.

"Tell me what you want?" She was shaking as she did up her seat belt.

"Shut up! Put your hands in your lap." He pulled out a length of zip-tie.

She obeyed, too numbed with fright to do otherwise.

He looped the tie around her wrists and pulled it tight.

She stared at her bindings, distressed. How could she escape now? *Ricardo, help me*, she cried silently. The front door remained shut.

A few more pedestrians hurried along. Again, she hoped that one of them would notice her. None did.

He started the car.

Their neighbor, a retired man, came out of the once-white clapboard house next door. She wanted him to look her way. Please. Desperately, she sought his gaze. Her body sagged in bitter disappointment as she watched the man turn and shuffle away in the opposite direction.

Her kidnapper accelerated away from the curb, driving past a pizza joint and other shops, past small bungalows and the local elementary school. Squeals and laughter from children going into class rose in a crescendo, and died away as they drove on. The children were carefree. She wished that for a split second, she could be one of them.

Ricardo would go to work mad with her for not arriving with the milk in time. What was she thinking? What was wrong with her, what did all that matter? He would be more concerned that she was missing than about the milk. Her stomach knotted. Please God, she prayed silently, let him find me, wherever I'm taken.

Along the coast, they passed a blur of large bungalows perched on hilltops overlooking the ocean.

The tie hurt her wrists, but she said nothing. She stared out, trying to memorize the route. Fear her companion.

He took her south along State Highway One.

Sometime later, they passed a sign that read Los Padres National Forest. The air was pine-scented from a horizon of tall dense redwoods, but Estella hardly noticed. She wanted to break the silence. Move him somehow to change his mind. "Please, will you stop here? We talk. Then you take me home."

He did not answer.

He must be taking her to some hideaway log cabin. How long would he keep her there? What would happen to her? She stared at him; he had not looked at her once.

Then he turned off the main road onto one of the many dirt tracks into the park.

Estella shivered, as the redwoods seemed to close around them and slivers of sunlight streamed through the foliage. She studied their passage with increasing desperation as he drove further and further along the meandering rutted track.

He turned off the main track onto a more overgrown one, and followed it along until they had reached a small clearing. When he had shut off the engine, he turned to her.

Where was the log cabin, she wanted to ask.

What she saw in his eyes set her trembling again. She was scared; she had never been this scared. "No...please. I do not know anything. We talk now. You take me home. Please. You...take me...home."

"You've been snooping around. And you know too much already."

"I know...nothing." She had guessed this man was Jean's killer. She had seen the glint of greed in his eyes, seen him pour the sun tan oil on the steps leading down to the beach. He had failed to kill Amanda that time. "I will not tell anyone that you bring me here." Estella rubbed her wrists as best she could. They were aching.

"That's right."

Fool.... Fool. She should have gone to the police and told them all she knew. She had wanted to go and see that Detective Hart right away when they first suspected him but Ricardo had said they did not have any proof, and they were illegal: wetbacks. Even so, she had made an appointment to see Hart this afternoon. Too late, it was much too late!

She glanced at the door.

Escape?

As he got out, she leaped from the car, made to run, and then she heard the unmistakable click of a gun.

"Go on. Make it easy for me."

Estella glanced back and found she was staring into the barrel of a gun.

Her heart pounded at her ribs like a trapped bird.

"Over there." He jerked with his revolver, at a fallen redwood. "And hurry up."

"Please. I not know what you want? No. Do not do this." She looked for a sign of him weakening. She willed him to feel something for her, some spark of compassion.

There was none. "Walk."

She stumbled forward.

A perspiration of fear trickled down her face and under her arms. She stopped beside the fallen tree. "Please...please, Signor let me go. I know nothing. And of this, that you have brought me here today, I will not tell anyone. Not Amanda. Not Mr. Hart. Not anyone."

"Shut up!"

She nodded wildly, willing, for now, to do anything that would save her. Her hands shook as she brushed away her tears. She should have tried harder to persuade him earlier. However, she had convinced herself he was going to keep her somewhere for a while.

His eyes were the color of a calm tropical ocean, his smile benign, but beneath this cool exterior beat the heart of Jean's murderer.

And now, he wanted to do the same to her.

Oh, God help me. Her stomach turned to liquid.

He stood still, seemingly contemplating, for a moment.

"No, please." She implored, still hoping to reach him.

He fired, and she felt the bullet slam into her. The impact jerked her back then she slumped forward, surprised.

She had expected pain, but there was none. She stared at the wound in her chest as blood began to seep out. She tried to stem the flow but it pumped ever faster through her fingers.

Estella gasped as pain suddenly tore through her. It burned and stung. She had no defenses against it. She sank to the pine needle covered ground.

A spreading pool of crimson colored the dirt beside her. Her breath became labored and noisy.

Estella stared up.

He was watching her. Did she see a flicker of regret in those cold eyes? No, she must have imagined it.

He backed off toward his car.

She was so scared, she was not ready to die, did not want to die. She should have been smarter and gone to the police when she saw what he had done. Estella hoped Ricardo would.

The pain grew: it throbbed through her entire being. Ricardo, she screamed silently, where are you? She wanted her brother to find her now. "Ricardo, I need you," she sobbed.

Darkness was closing in and she was so cold, and so desperately alone.

CHAPTER 26

AUSTRALIA.

So far, the morning had been uneventful.

Amanda had picked up a hire car at Kingsford Smith airport in Sydney, and had started down the Princes Highway to Wollongong, past rows of tile-roofed houses.

The usual mix of cars, trucks, and the occasional semi-trailer on the highway south were moving again. The bumper-to-bumper morning peak hour was nearly over. She opened the window and breathed in the familiar cocktail of smog.

She knew if she'd taken her Honda, first she'd have had to catch a cab to her duplex at Roseville, and then if she bumped into her neighbor who'd been friends with her father since their school days, he would be sure to tell Samuel she'd been home. She didn't want to see her dad just yet.

Her mobile rang and she turned on the speakerphone and answered the call.

"Hi. It's Justin from Now Bank. Just a friendly call to remind you that you are behind on your mortgage payments."

"My mother just passed away in California. I've just returned from the funeral."

"I'm sorry to hear that. Have you received our letters?"

"I haven't been home," she said.

"Well, you've missed three months payments. If you miss one more month, we will have to take action. "

"Is that all?"

"Well-"

She cut him off, angry at his lack of compassion. If she hadn't sunk her money in that property trust she'd been talked into, she wouldn't be having these money worries. She'd have to ask Cohen when she would be receiving any money from the estate.

Even though she felt tired as she'd only cat napped on the plane, the bitterly cold autumn day kept her wide awake. She turned on the radio. Rod Stewart was singing one of his hits. Elaine used to listen to him. She switched channels.

Past Heathcote there were fewer houses as acres of Royal National Park edged them out. Bottlebrushes, wattles and other natives grew by the roadside; gum trees waved in the wind, their spent leaves sent spinning into the air.

Amanda turned up the heating as her leggings and a long top weren't enough to keep her warm. Dark clouds crowded the sky, promising heavy rain. She spread her cold fingers across the stream of warm air. She hoped Scott would be home and wouldn't turn her away. Her mobile rang. "Hi Zac."

"What's cooking, Amanda? You ready to join us?"

"My mother passed away and I'm going to have to ask you to hold for another week or so, please."

"I'm sorry to hear that. But you know what these editors are like. I'll try to do some background stuff 'till then. I can't hold them off forever. Call me as soon as you're free. Speak soon."

They said their goodbyes and she switched off her speaker. He was a great guy. She had to make a decision to join him or hand the job over to someone else in the next two weeks.

It had taken a little over an hour of steady climbing to reach Mt. Ousley. She continued on, noticing warning signs asking trucks and buses to use low gear; the road ahead fell away steeply. Shredded truck tires by the wayside, a reminder of yet another careless driver.

Scattered down the escarpment were houses and trees, and out to sea, tankers and ships waiting their turn to unload. Large raindrops splashed against the windscreen. Moments later they had formed rivulets on the glass. Amanda turned on her wipers. She didn't like driving down a mountainside in this sort of weather, it made her edgy and she was already that just thinking about Scott—in all probability unsociable, or even unwilling to see or talk to her. She switched radio stations and the sounds of Mozart filled the car as she tried to relax.

A semi-trailer's air horn blast made her jump. She glanced in the rear-view mirror. Where had he come from? She hadn't noticed him behind her 'till now. He edged up closer, blasting again. Her mouth went dry as his chrome bumper almost nudged the Mazda trying to make her go faster.

Hell. He was so aggressive. Nervously she gripped the wheel, accelerated, and then changed to the innermost lane. A window-height cement divider on her right side made her feel boxed. When she lost sight of him, she breathed a sigh of relief.

The roar of the semi as he accelerated from further back ramped up her tension again. Shit, the madman was overtaking vehicles and coming toward her. He swung across her path. She jammed on the brake. Her Mazda skidded towards the concrete divider. She eased her foot off, steering to bring the car under control, her knuckles white as she gripped the wheel.

"Stupid idiot," she cried as he swerved back into the middle lane.

She slowed to give him space and allow him to get ahead.

As the road curved and the descent increased, he dropped back. About time he had some sense, she thought.

Now he was beside her. Was he trying to rattle her? Well, he'd succeeded.

Then that metal monster swerved towards her. She braked. They were going to crash. "No," she cried.

Seconds seemed to stretch into eternity.

Tires from the cars behind her shrieked as their brakes gripped. He slammed her into the concrete, the side window shattered. Glass showered her as the impact whipped her sideways, then forwards. Her head hit the airbag. Metal, like a giant orange skin, peeled away from the side of the Mazda, with a high-pitched tearing sound. The door was gone. The car was still moving. He rammed her into the divider again. Amanda heard grinding metal. Showers of sparks seemed to go on forever as more of the car ripped away.

Darkness enveloped her.

***

Someone screamed. It was so loud that it disturbed her slumber. Amanda wished they'd stop. Wished they would leave her alone.

People in flowing gowns walked towards her, beckoning. She looked back and saw emptiness. Nothing seemed to matter. She turned to these people, welcoming their smiling gentle faces. Behind them, a rainbow of light shone, giving them a golden glow. They were so beautiful. They stretched their arms out to her. She longed to be cocooned in their embrace. She floated towards them. But when she reached out to touch them, something pulled her backwards, no matter how hard she fought it she couldn't get any closer. Then suddenly, the gowned people dissolved and were gone.

"She's a mess. At least she's stopped screaming. Let's get her out." The male voice said.

Her throat felt sore and someone pushed something stiff around her neck. Then two people lifted her onto something flat.

Amanda opened her eyes to see a man in an ambulance uniform attending to her on a stretcher.

He checked her pulse.

Something was wrong. Her head ached. Her body hurt. A sticky substance trickled down her cheek, and she brushed it away. Her unsteady hands were bloody. "I'm...I'm...bleeding."

"Don't worry. We're here to look after you."

What had happened? Where was she? Then she saw the strange sculpture of twisted metal that had been the hire car. Amanda realized she'd been in a car accident. "Am...I all right?" She started shaking.

"Don't worry." He pulled a blanket over her.

"It...it was that damn semi that changed lanes and pushed me into the divider."

"Just relax." The paramedic strapped the stretcher into the back of the vehicle.

"Where's that semi driver?" She propped herself up on her elbow.

"Lie back." The paramedic eased her down. "Driver took off. The police should track him down."

The throbbing in her head increased, making it hard for her to think. "My handbag. My puffer."

"Ventolin?"

"Yes."

"Just keep still. You could have concussion."

The paramedic told his assistant to find her inhaler and the rest of her things.

"Just relax now while we take you to hospital. I'm going to put an oxygen mask on your face. Okay?"

"I haven't got time for that. I've got to see Scott."

Then she was falling…falling into blackness again.

CHAPTER 27

"Accident victim, possible concussion," the doctor in Casualty said to the nurse as he studied Amanda's chart.

He drew the curtain around the bed. "No broken bones. You're very lucky, Ms. Blake. How's the neck feel?"

"It's stiff." Since Amanda had woken, she had been dressed in a hospital gown, taken to x-ray, then wheeled to the overflowing Casualty area.

He felt around the base of Amanda's neck. "How does it feel?"

"Sore."

He began to press her ribs and she winced. "That hurts,"

"Mmm." He continued feeling around her stomach.

"That hurts there," she said.

"Nurse. Can you chase up that x-ray? Ms. Blake, can you sit up please?"

"I feel a bit light headed."

"Understandable." He flicked a penlight, from one eye to the other.

"What?" she asked.

"Hang your legs over the edge of the bed please." He tapped her knees. "Okay. From what I can see, you may have concussion." Then he examined her forehead. "We'll have to see to the cut above your eyebrow. I'll give you a local first. Lie back."

"Okay." She tried to remember what exactly had happened and couldn't.

He cleaned up the cut then swabbed the skin in preparation for the injection. He turned to the nurse still hovering in the background. "We're admitting Ms. Blake. And while she's under observation she is to have no analgesics even if she has any pain." The doctor made notes on her chart, and began to stitch her cut.

The chubby-faced nurse helped Amanda into a wheelchair, and pushed her down the long corridor and into a patient room.

Light flooded in through two tall windows. The nurse pulled back the blankets. "I'll help you up."

The nurse opened one of the two narrow metal lockers and pushed Amanda's things into the bottom.

Amanda wiggled to get comfortable; the pillow was too flat.

"I'll get you another pillow. Then I'll clean you up." The nurse drew the curtain before she left. The bed opposite was unoccupied.

Amanda slumped back, tired. Her body ached. Against all her efforts to keep them open, her eyes closed.

She must have drifted off, because the next thing she knew someone was sponging her face. Amanda stared up at the slim blonde bending over her. Cindy Castles was the name on the nurse's badge.

The bottle blonde was chewing gum. "Been in an accident eh!" She continued to sponge her.

"What happened to the other nurse?"

"She's busy. Don't ya worry. Just lie back and I'll fix ya up." The nurse pulled down Amanda's hospital gown then washed her blood-caked upper torso.

A few of the cuts stung and Amanda winced. Cindy continued without noticing, her touch rough over even the most bruised flesh. It was just a job to some people.

"So how did it happen?"

She told the nurse. "And talking it over with you makes me wonder if the semi was more than just careless."

"Ya think he was trying to run ya off the road?" the nurse asked.

"Yes."

Cindy shook her head. "Ya kidding me, right. Just relax and get ya-self better."

Someone had been trying to kill her. But, Cindy didn't think so. Perhaps she was overwrought.

The nurse pulled up Amanda's gown. "There ya are."

A male doctor stood in the doorway. "Nurse, I need your assistance with a patient."

"But I'm-"

"It will have to wait. I need you now." He marched away.

"I'll be back with your injection."

"What's it for?"

"To help take away the pain."

"I…I don't want it. The stitches aren't sore."

Cindy smiled. "Doctor's orders."

Amanda was sure the doctor had said not to give her anything for her pain. Perhaps he'd changed his mind.

"Nurse," the doctor called.

"I'll be back with your injection, Miss Blake."

She watched the woman stride out in bright pink sneakers. Since when did nurses wear those? Didn't they wear those black lace ups? The hairs on the back of her neck prickled. Something was wrong and Amanda was not going to hang around to find out what.

She had to get out of here now.

Her imagination was not running wild, of that she was certain. She wasn't overreacting about that man in the semi. Nor the menacing way he'd edged up behind her. Nor the way he'd changed lanes twice. The most damning thing was he hadn't stayed around to see if she'd been okay. Was it because he hadn't expected her to live?

Her skin went clammy with fear at the thought.

Someone wanted her share of the inheritance. They had sent a hit man to kill her. There was no reason why they wouldn't try again. Was Cindy Castles her next would-be assassin?

Amanda winced as she ripped the drip out of her arm. She stood and immediately felt woozy. She sat until the feeling settled, then opened the nearby locker. She rummaged through her cabin bag and pulled out a pair of jeans, t-shirt, a cashmere cardigan, her puffer, some fresh underwear, shoes and her Nikon but then put the camera back. She'd have to return for it when she could. Dressed in her street clothes she tiptoed to the door. There was no sign of Cindy.

Down the corridor, a man with a menacing sucked-in boxer's face had an open newspaper in his hands but his bulging eyes never looked at the printed sheet, they scanned the corridor constantly. With his large paw, he jerked over a page.

She pulled back.

He wasn't her bodyguard so there was only one other reason for such a man to be there...to make certain she didn't leave here alive. She closed her eyes and took a deep breath, even though it hurt her ribs. Get a grip she told herself. This wasn't CSI or Miss Marple. However, her stomach was a tight ball and she had an awful tingle of tension at the back of her neck.

Further along, a doctor and a nurse were discussing something at the nurse's station.

Three chatting women walked by her door. She joined them.

Amanda kept pace with the women, her heartbeat drummed in her ears as she passed the man. A few moments later, she heard heavy footsteps behind her.

Startled, she glanced back and saw the boxer as he loped towards her.

She hurried down the corridor, her shoes clicking noisily on the tiled floor. As she reached the doctor, she cried out. "Call the police. He's...."

The doctor looked up from his notes. "Pardon?"

She snapped her gaze back to see her pursuer reach inside his jacket. Did he have a gun? "Oh God." She bolted.

"Just a minute. What's wrong?" the doctor called after her.

She turned left. Ahead were some opaque plastic doors with a sign that said Authorized Entry Only. Amanda crashed through them and nearly into a surprised patient in a wheelchair with a nurse behind him. She careered into another corridor. Her pursuer's footsteps echoed closer.

She glanced wildly into rooms as she passed. A ramp led down to a storeroom. She ran in.

Shelves of bandages, cotton wadding, and more lined the walls and cabinets. The smell of iodine pervaded the air. Large supply boxes stacked one on top of the other in the corner became her cover as she crouched behind them. She pulled one stack of boxes towards her to close up the gap. The woozy feeling returned but she fought to keep it from overwhelming her as she drew in the spray from her inhaler.

The door swung open.

Amanda shrank lower. He was breathing hard. If she could hear him then he must be able to hear her. She tried to minimize her gasps for air until she felt she would suffocate.

He searched, and then cursed. His heavy tread came closer.

She tensed. He kicked at the cartons in front of her. Her first instinct was to jump at the sudden noise but she willed herself to be still, her body damp with fear. Then she heard him move to the far end of the room. The door slammed shut.

Amanda expelled a pent up breath. He was gone. Thankfully, so was her dizziness.

She rose and saw the boxer waiting.

"Stupid bitch," he said, his bulging eyes blinking.

As he made a grab for her, she pushed the stack of boxes at him.

"Fuckin' bitch." He knocked them out of his way and lunged at her.

"Let me go." She punched his stomach but it was as if she was hitting a wall. As he pulled out a gun, she kneed his groin.

The boxer groaned his unshaven face suddenly white, his grip loosened.

She tore the weapon from him. "Get back."

"You wouldn't use it," he said, complying.

"Just try me." She aimed the gun at his groin with shaking hands. "This close, I can't miss. Now take your pants off."

"Don't be stupid."

"Don't test me." Her hands had stopped shaking. She knew she would need her puffer soon, but tried not to think about that. "Do it now or you'll be pissing like a girl."

He unzipped his black trousers and let them fall.

"Throw them to me. And don't move or I'll shoot," she rasped as the need for her puffer escalated.

As she backed up, she kicked his trousers toward the door. "I'll shoot you if you try and follow me."

Amanda slammed the door shut behind her and propped an invalid chair against the handle. That would give her a little time.

She grabbed the trousers, stuffed the gun into the back of her jeans, where it couldn't be seen under her cardigan, and scooted back the way she'd come as she tried to give herself a dose from her inhaler. Up the ramp she went and through a blur of corridors until she reached some plastic doors with a bin nearby. She stuffed his pants and the gun into it. At least he had to find something else to wear before he could come after her again. Then she pushed through the doors to another wing. Finally, she saw the glass entrance doors.

There he was outside dressed in disposable scrubs, hunting for her.

Amanda retreated.

Where to go? Her gaze took in the endless carpeted corridor and more closed doors.

Amanda saw her pursuer in the doorway at the same time he saw her. She turned, and pushed past people into another wing; saw a blur of people in the patients sitting room, crying relatives and an empty nurses' station.

Where to now?

Her room was ahead. She should grab her things. There'd be no coming back later.

She halted at the threshold.

Cindy, back to the door, hunched over, was searching Amanda's cabin bag. She punched the woman in the back. The blonde fell in a tangle of arms and legs.

Amanda grabbed for the bag.

Cindy twisted and clawed at air as Amanda sidestepped her. On all fours now, Cindy lunged at Amanda. She swung the bag and knocked the nurse backwards.

Breathing hard, Amanda retreated from the room into a young

doctor. She shouldered him aside.

"What's going on?" the doctor said.

She pumped past the nurses station, and up another corridor where there were crying babies and pregnant women.

A lift pinged somewhere. She turned the corner and hurried towards the bank of elevators. The doors opened as she approached.

Two doctors, deep in conversation, stepped out.

Amanda burst past the surprised doctors into the lift. She jammed the door close button as hard as she could, over and over.

Seconds ticked by, a number of hurried footsteps echoed on the tiled floor. Hurry up, she screamed silently. Cindy and that boxer reached the lift as the doors closed.

Exhausted, she slumped into the corner, bag beside her, her heart pounded. She tried to ignore how much her body ached.

The lift slowed to a halt. She dashed past incoming people, and down a silent corridor searching for a hiding place. She pushed open the ladies room door. A teenager was washing her hands. The nurses' lunchroom had someone there too. Then she saw a linen tub on wheels. The tub was half-full of sheets. She flung her bag in, and clambered in after it and pulled some sheets over her head.

Someone approached. She tensed and tried to quieten her breathing; each intake of air drew in the smells of unwashed sheets.

A breathless female shouted. "Seen anything unusual, or a blonde running around?"

"All quiet here," the orderly said as she began to wheel the tub.

"Just patients," another voice said.

"Cheeky," the first orderly said.

The sound of people further away gave her a temporary reprieve.

She prayed no one would notice the pile of sheets were higher now. The orderly stopped pushing and walked away.

It would be only a matter of time before… Then Amanda heard the familiar heavy tread she'd come to dread…the boxer.

Perspiration wrought from fear wet her face. She was aware of each intake of breath, which sounded like bellows to her.

He stopped close to her hiding place.

Was he going to look inside? She closed her eyes and prayed silently that he would not.

Never before had she felt like each nerve ending in her body was standing to attention. His musky scent barely cloaked the underlying odor of his adrenaline-soaked body sweat.

Amanda felt someone dumping something on top of her. More dirty linen. Smothered by the extra layer, Amanda pushed a small space in the sheets and opened her mouth so she could take in deeper gulps of air.

Finally, the boxer moved away. She heard the lift doors open, then close. He'd gone. Safe for the moment…the thought circled inside her head.

Amanda tensed when she heard voices nearby until she recognized them. They were the familiar tones of the orderlies who'd been collecting the linen.

The trolley was moving.

"It's hard to push this thing today. The wheels must be stuck," a female said.

"Here let me," the second orderly said.

She felt a jerk and then the trolley moved again.

"You're right, it is stiff. I'll have to report this," the second orderly said.

"Another two hours before I knock off. Then it's home to make dinner."

"Your other half doesn't?"

"Cook? Are you kidding? He can't even make toast."

When the lift bell sounded she knew they were taking the trolley to another floor. Then they were moving again.

Many footsteps passed by them, and Amanda kept still until the trolley had stopped. Finally, all was quiet.

Amanda pushed aside the sheets. The laundry room had bags stacked all over the concrete floor. A truck was reversing outside. Someone was coming to collect the linen. She dumped her bag on the floor. Then she tried to clamber out of the trolley, but her aching and bruised arms had no strength left in them. Finally, she leveraged the top half of her body over and fell. She lay still gathering, from somewhere inside, the strength to get up.

Her shoes were still in the trolley. Barefoot, she wouldn't be able to run that well. She slumped against the trolley and breathed. *Come on, Amanda*, she told herself....*get those shoes*. She listened for any indication that someone had heard. Then, she climbed in and retrieved them. When she tried to get out, she fell again, tearing a hole in her jeans and bruising her knees.

The corridor was empty. The door to the back entrance was open. Two males, backs to her, were smoking beside the laundry truck. She knew by their build neither of them was her pursuer. She raced down the ramp. The men turned to glance at her. Amanda froze. Were they after her too? But when they resumed their conversation she realized they weren't. They were just passing time. She limped along the service road towards the front entrance, but her energy had long gone and only the will to stay alive powered her on.

Amanda flagged a cab that had just expelled two passengers.

She jumped in.

"Where to?" the greasy-haired driver asked.

As she shut the taxi door, she saw the boxer and Cindy coming out of the entrance doors.

"Take me anywhere, away from here. And hurry." She slumped out of view, hoping they hadn't seen her.

CHAPTER 28

SANTA CRUZ, CALIFORNIA.

"Lionel, what's wrong?" Felicity asked.

Moments ago, he had hungered for her like an animal and he knew it had frightened her as much as it had excited her.

Felicity pressed her body against Lionel, but it didn't arouse him. His lust had evaporated.

"The way you jerked me against you as soon as the front door was closed I thought you'd be unstoppable," she said.

How could he tell her the high he had been on when she first walked in had plummeted to a bottomless low? The release from his torment had been temporary as he slipped further and further into a well of hopelessness.

"What have I done wrong?" She sat up and turned on the bedside lamp bathing his bedroom in soft light, the black satin sheets sliding from her almost naked body. "Was it because I slipped off my dress first? Did I spoil our little game for you? I'm sorry, but you seemed so impatient."

He rolled over and glanced at her bruised mouth. He didn't understand what had come over him. He'd savagely kissed her until he could taste the blood from her lips.

"Don't you want me?"

"It's not that." He could not put into words how low he felt.

"Did you bother to go see a doctor?"

"I'm okay. He said the usual things."

"What then?" She got up and stared at herself in the mirrored closet doors. "Is it because I'm not appealing to you anymore?" She turned to face him with her hands cupping her breasts. "I know my boobs are beginning to sag. I know the massages aren't working anymore. If it's that don't worry, I've booked in for a procedure next month."

"You're still as lovely as the day I first made love to you." Forty and she was more attractive than any woman who was ten years younger, even though her waistline had thickened a little and her succulent full breasts were ready for the surgeon's youth-making knife.

She turned to him, a half smile playing on her mouth. He watched her breasts rise as she tidied her hair that was the color of dark honey. It usually excited him when she did that and he knew that's what she was trying to do. However, it was not working. He felt useless, sucked of energy as melancholia drew him further down.

Her lace panties, which barely covered that triangle of dark hair, were firmly in place, another reminder of what hadn't happened. He sat up; his shoulders slumped. "It's my fault."

"I'm standing practically naked in front of you. Waiting to be ravished."

"My mind's on other things."

"Other things? Or other women? Aren't I enough for you?" She stared at him.

He looked down at his feet as he slipped into his robe, unwilling to meet her gaze, his mouth dry. "Believe me. There is no one else, only you."

"Liar. You son-of-a-bitch." She fastened her bra.

He watched her lean forward and adjust each breast into it; his hands should have been doing that. Instead, he stood as he knotted the sash around his waist. "It's me. I can't seem to...."

"The goddamned thing used to always work before. After all I've gone through for you. Twice a week for the past five years I've sneaked out behind Horace's back to come here. I was happy to do it for you, for us. What we had between us was special." She slipped on her Dior dress and zipped it up.

"It still is." Why was she attacking him like this?

"Are you kidding? It hasn't been like that for weeks and weeks. Until now, I didn't want to face the truth. I didn't want to see what was there. And now it's Jean's death, isn't it?"

Why did she have to mention it now? She was trying to inflict pain on him. He shook his head as he spoke. "Problems at the office."

"Do you think I'm going to swallow that? Why don't you just say that Jean meant a lot to you?"

"I love you, not Jean."

"Love *me*? Jean still means more to you than I do. She always has. I was a fool to think that now she was gone our relationship would get better."

"You're wrong. It's you I love. She was a close friend and someone who employed me. That's all." He watched her smooth down her dress. He didn't know what to say. What to do? She didn't want to listen.

"Do you know that I was even considering asking for a divorce? I know you like to gamble, and even with a good settlement, I'd have had to go without my little luxuries. Like Horace's jet to take me shopping to Paris. No holidays on his island."

He was stunned that she'd been considering this. He'd never dared ask her to leave Horace, even though he'd said as much to Dorian. "You mean it? You were going to do that for me?"

"Not now." Fuming, she grabbed her purse. "I don't know what I ever saw in you. You're getting old and fat anyway. There are plenty of younger men out there."

"You are the one I love. It's only you I want. Let's go into the living room and have a drink." He needed one, badly.

"Fuck your drink, and fuck you. I am not going to swallow your lies anymore. I'll give you one last chance to come clean." Breathing hard with anger, she stepped into her stilettos.

"I'm sorry, I can't. Please, I still love you."

"If you loved me, then you'd keep no secrets from me. I am not going to come second to anything or anyone. It's enough that I've always come second with Horace. Do you know how that feels? Obviously not, because you're doing it to me." She opened her purse and flung some coins at him. "That's the last you'll see of that. You son-of-a-bitch."

He cringed. "Don't do this. We had something good."

Her eyes glittered with rage. "Had is right. I can't even feel like a woman with you anymore."

"Just give me some time to sort myself out. That's all I ask."

"That bitch is coming between us even from her grave. I hate her. Don't bother to call me or try to see me." She strode from the room.

"You've got it all wrong. Please, Felicity, let's not finish like this. Not like this. I need you."

With Lionel at her heels, she stormed through the tiled hallway to the front entrance.

"Please." He had to convince her. He grabbed her arm.

She shook herself free. "I'll ask you one last time. What's going on?"

"It's not what you think. I'm sorry."

"How could I have even contemplated leaving Horace for you? I must have been crazy." She left, slamming the door behind her.

CHAPTER 29

WOLLONGONG, AUSTRALIA.
Amanda still felt a little shaky when the taxi driver stopped outside Scott McMahon's home. Was it sheer madness for her to continue this search for the truth? After her escape from death on Mt. Ousley, then her harrowing chase at the hospital, perhaps it was. Something inside her wouldn't let her give up no matter what the outcome.

Perhaps she should have spoken to the police first before being so impulsive as to come here. Would they have believed her story? Even to her all of this seemed like something out of a movie. They too might think she was nuts. She pulled out her mobile and texted Anna. '@ Wollongong. Going 2 c Scott.' lul. Amanda xx

Her friend replied. 'Crazy? Where r u?'

'Outside Scott's place.'

'Good luck. Let me no what gives. lul, Anna xx'

"Is this the address?" the driver asked

"Yes." She scanned the neighborhood. A man was mowing his lawn two doors down. A Subaru 4WD wagon was parked in the driveway on the other side of the tree-lined street. There didn't seem to be any suspicious cars with people in them waiting to get her. All seemed well.

The driver stared at her expectantly.

She handed him the fare, and picked up her cabin bag. Her body ached all over as she stumbled out into the afternoon autumn sunshine. "Can you wait five minutes until I'm sure someone's home?"

He nodded.

The sixties dark-red triple fronted brick house she stood in front of was similar to the one in which she'd grown up.

Bricks and mortar only meant that your neighbors didn't know what happened inside. Amanda pushed away those unhappy memories as she went through the gate. The Scott she'd imagined didn't fit in this place. After the picture Brian had drawn, she'd imagined Scott existing in a broken-down fibro cottage, the screen door hanging off its hinges.

Shading the house were two large camellia trees, their tight buds covered with droplets of water from this morning's rain.

She set her bag down, rang the doorbell, and yawned while she waited. She was jet-lagged and jumpy...not a good mix. Perhaps Scott didn't live here anymore.

About to retreat, she stopped when she heard footsteps inside. Would he be hostile, or welcoming? She took a deep breath and prepared mentally, as much as she could, for the confrontation.

Someone turned the key in the lock. There was no backing out of this now. She'd been through too much and come too far.

The door opened. Afternoon sunlight revealed a man in dirty navy overalls. He looked like a mechanic. His grease-smudged, tanned face creased in a frown as he ran his hand through his wavy auburn hair. "I'm not buying encyclopedias or religious books."

She blinked, startled at the image. "Sorry. I'm-"

"Well I'll bet you've got something to sell in that bag." He began to close the door.

"Wait. I must see Scott McMahon."

"Yeah, yeah that's what they all say."

"Does he still live here?"

"Well, all his mail still comes here. Who wants to see him?"

"It's about Jean Campbell. I've come to-"

"What did you say?" He swung the door open wider.

"I'm Amanda Blake and I want to speak with Scott. Do you know where he is?"

He stared down at her. It seemed he was uncertain of what to say or do.

The mechanic had seemed so sure of himself at first that she guessed this was probably a rare occasion. "Look, if you know where he, is please tell me. I've come all the way from California to see him."

Finally, he wiped his hands on his overalls, looked hard at her, and then gripped her cold hand in his warm one and shook it. "You've taken me by surprise. I'm Scott and I'm pleased to finally meet you."

"Oh," she blurted. Why had she expected him to look like Brian? After all, just like herself, Brian had been adopted. Scott didn't seem as threatening as her twin had described, but she was not about to relax.

"You haven't come all this way for nothing so you'd better come in."

She'd rather have chosen the safety of standing on the doorstep in full view of passers-by. She turned and waved to the taxi driver and he drove away.

Hesitantly, she tailed him through a living room furnished with a wide screen TV, a black leather sofa, and the top half of a cabinet that was filled with books, CD's and DVD's.

"You read these?" She indicated to the books.

"Yep." He kept walking.

A direct question hadn't gotten him talking. For some reason, that made her more nervous.

He led her into the small kitchen with granite bench tops and light wood cabinetry.

"Take a seat while I wash off the grease." He indicated to a table with four chairs around it.

Amanda looked out the kitchen window at the backyard. A clump of irises was the only plant in an otherwise naked garden bed at the end of a neat sloping lawn. The leaves on a maple tree were turning red. A study of the room—back door to the left and the bedrooms to the right, where Scott went—gave her a rough idea of the layout if she needed to make a hasty exit. She sat on the edge of the seat, ready to bolt if she needed to. The sound of running water reassured her that he was actually cleaning himself up.

She drummed her fingers on the table. Should she be direct or take her time to find out the information she needed?

He returned. "I was working on my Harley when you rang the

bell." He moved to the sink. "Can I offer you a drink? Tea, coffee, water or maybe a beer? You look like you've had a rough day."

"Coffee please." She wanted to get this over with, but she was thirsty. Since she'd arrived in Sydney this morning, she'd had nothing to eat or drink. She watched him move about the kitchen, fill the jug, and slice cake.

"Chocolate cake is all I have. Is that okay?"

"It's my favorite." Why was he playing nice guy in the kitchen? After what Brian had said about him, she couldn't reconcile his behavior today and surroundings.

He sliced the cake, and poured out the coffees. "So what can I do for you?" He said as he put the drinks and cake on the table.

One step at a time, she said to herself. "It's about the letter you wrote to Jean." He straddled the chair.

His direct stare was unnerving, which made it doubly hard to say what she wanted to say. She wished he'd respond instead of staying silent. "I would like to know what was in it. I mean could you tell me what it contained?"

A dog started to bark which made her jump and spill a little of her coffee. "Sorry."

Scott reached into a nearby cupboard, and pulled out a roll of paper toweling. "Use this."

Amanda mopped up the spill.

"You're nervous as hell, aren't you?" he said.

Shit, she could feel her cheeks flush. "I...I...tried to call you from California last week but you weren't answering." She bit into the slice of cake

"What's happened to you? I didn't want to ask before, but it looks pretty bad."

When she tried to swallow, the crumbs stuck to roof of her mouth. Amanda took a sip of coffee to help wash it down. She touched one of the taped up wounds on her forehead. "Car accident.

Scott said, "You must have been calling my land line not my mobile. I came back from Darwin last night."

What was he doing there?

"When did this accident happen? The bruising on your neck looks like seatbelt burn," he said.

Her hand went to the spot. Her touch was light but it hurt. "Ouch."

The doorbell rang. She jumped in fright, and lunged for the knife Scott had left on the bench.

In one movement, he pushed back the chair and rose, his mouth open. "What's got into you?"

The bell went again, and again.

"Hang on, I'm coming. Are you all right? You look dangerous with that thing in your hand."

She stared at the knife. Incredible. Her instincts for survival had made her reach for it, yet she'd always been against any form of violence. What was happening to her? "I…I'm fine." What a lie. She put the knife on the table.

He had started toward the living room.

Amanda lunged at Scott, and grabbed his arm. "Wait."

"What the hell?"

"Someone's after me." She let go. *Wants to murder me*…was what she'd wanted to say, but…she didn't know Scott, didn't trust him.

"Why?" Scott asked as he moved more cautiously now through the living room, and to the front door.

"The car accident was deliberate," she said.

Two men: she heard their exchange. Something clicked. It was a sound she would never forget.

Scott's suntanned face paled. "Get down." He dived pulling her with him.

An ear-shattering hail of bullets from a semi-automatic splintered the wooden door and the plaster walls around them.

"Come on." Scott grabbed her arm and, on all-fours, dragged her with him as he retreated to the kitchen.

A second volley of bullets came moments after the first. The sound echoed in her ears. Amanda froze.

Scott squeezed her arm hard. She winced with pain.

He shook her. "Come on. You want to die?"

Those words were enough to make her come to her senses.

Thump. These men were kicking in the door.

He grabbed her cabin bag. Together, they raced from the kitchen to the laundry. Scott frantically pushed the washing machine across the door as a barricade.

"Let's go." He flung open the internal door to the garage.

Pieces of Scott's motorbike lay on the floor. He locked the door behind them.

She could hear the killers running through the house.

"Get in. Always keep a spare magnetized to the frame." He grabbed the key from underneath the Range Rover.

Hurry, Amanda wanted to urge him. However, she stayed silent, and willed him to get the car started. *Now*. Precious seconds went by, and when the engine kicked over, she shouted. "Hurry up."

He revved up the car, and then activated the automatic garage door.

The back screen door slammed. Someone had been there *waiting* for them.

She heard the laundry door splinter and fall.

They were coming.

Slowly, the garage door started up. Her heart pounded as she willed Scott to exit.

As the internal door opened, he threw the car into gear and tramped hard on the accelerator.

The growl of the motor did not mask the roar of the semi-automatics spewing out lead.

CHAPTER 30

Scott sped away from the killers.

Bullets shattered the back window and thudded as they pierced the roof of the cabin. Amanda screamed.

Shattered glass cascaded over the rear seats. The wind rushed in.

"We're still here, so get it together," Scott shouted.

Police sirens wailed in the distance.

She covered her mouth to stop herself moaning with fright.

"Shut up or I'll have to slap you." He changed gears.

"What?" She rallied. "Don't you dare!"

"That's better."

"Oh Jesus," she said as she looked back.

The Subaru wagon Amanda had noticed in his neighbor's driveway was tailing them. She'd thought it to be a neighbor's car when she'd seen it earlier.

He turned left.

The momentum flung Amanda against the door.

"Seatbelt now," he shouted, and cornered again, flashing by a streetscape of boxy houses, driveways and local shops. The Subaru was closing with each heartbeat.

Scott swerved to miss an oncoming car. The vehicle braked, skidded into the gutter as Scott barreled on. "Who the hell's after you?"

"I don't know."

"Why are they after you?" He careered into another street.

"I'm not sure. I think-"

"Not sure! Don't know! Well, I'm sure as hell being shot at. What in the bloody hell have you done?"

"It's the inheritance." In a cold sweat, she grabbed hold of the seat belt for extra security as he narrowly missed another car.

"What?"

"Careful," she screamed.

"I'm trying to keep us alive."

"Sorry. That was a stupid thing to say." What had she been thinking of? She wanted him to lose those assassins no matter what it took, she though as she pulled out her inhaler.

Red lights ignored, brakes screeched, horns blared, as Scott hurtled through the next intersection, down the hill to the beach, and down the boat ramp. Then he changed to four-wheel drive as the car hit the sand. "Hope we shake them now."

The Range Rover ploughed across the soft yellow grains. They headed towards the hard wet surface near the water's edge. "Tell me, what inheritance?"

"Jean's millions." As Amanda looked back, the wind whipped her hair across her face. The wheels flung salt water high into the air in a continuous fountain. "We're losing them."

The Subaru followed. As soon as the rear tires hit the soft sand, the vehicle slowed. It struggled along the ruts from Scott's car until it reached the water's edge.

Bullets whistled past them.

"Down." He pushed her as he steered one handed.

A flock of seagulls scattered in surprise, their frightened squawks filled the air.

Seconds passed before she looked out.

The Subaru had dropped further behind.

Scott sped past a couple open-mouthed in shock. He and Amanda ducked together as another bullet smashed into the roof.

Droplets of salt spray gathered on the windscreen. He switched on the wipers. "I must have been mad to open my door to you."

"Let me out now then and you'll be rid of me," she said with false bravado, though she desperately hoped he would not.

"Don't be stupid. You think I could live with that on my conscience?"

He glanced at the slight rise on the left. "I know there's a road here somewhere."

Even though she could hear the tension in his voice and knew he must be scared too, he seemed cool and in control.

The gap between the Subaru and them had widened.

"There," Amanda shouted.

He jerked the steering wheel when the sand met a grassy area. The Range Rover skidded as the tires flung up sand. He gripped the wheel so hard his knuckles were white.

"Shit!" Amanda clung to the seat. They had to get away.

He tramped on the accelerator.

The wheels on the passenger side spun free and it seemed the car might overturn, but moments later, they thudded to the ground again. He corrected the skid, and drove the car over the grass towards the road ahead.

"Where did you learn to drive like that?"

He changed gears. "I race Midgets."

They burned rubber through quiet seaside streets. "Brace yourself," he shouted.

She clung on as Scott cornered.

"Midgets. That explains-" She was jolted as they thudded over a roundabout, then past a blur of factories.

"Went racing in the U.S.A a month ago. I'm taking us to my workshop. My men would've gone home by now." Scott careered into a concrete drive that ran along half a dozen light-industrial units. He screeched to a halt outside Scott's Motor Repairs. The area was deserted. He grabbed a set of keys from the glove box.

"Be ready to take the wheel." He jumped out, and unlocked the corrugated roller door.

Amanda scrambled over the gearshift to the driver's seat as the metal door rose. She accelerated in past a jumble of cars as the door slammed shut behind her. The noise made her jerk her foot off the clutch and the car stalled.

She jumped out with her things, ducked under a car on a hoist, and hurried across the concrete to Scott.

He pulled a dusty curtain aside and peered through the only window. Beside him, the wall held shelves of tools, and on the floor— stands of batteries and spare parts.

"Thank you. You saved us," she said.

He shot her a steely look, his face still pale. "I don't recall having much choice. I was scared shitless. I still can't take it in. Gunmen were firing at us. Us! I felt like I was back in the Army. They were mostly mock battles I fought in then; this was for real."

"Army?" she asked.

"I'll explain later." He took a deep breath. "When we left the beach, I lost sight of them. I hope we shook the tail."

"We're in trouble if we haven't." As she dropped her bag, she heard a clink. "Damn."

He jerked his head round. "What was that?"

"It's my camera."

"I've been jumping out of my skin since those guys turned up and that's all you're worried about?" He resumed his watch.

"Hell no! I'm terrified that they might find us. It's just that this Nikon means so much to me. My dad gave it to me after I sold my first professional photos."

"So!"

"Look, I wouldn't exchange my life for it."

He released the curtain. "All's quiet out there."

She slumped against the wall, relieved. "Thank God."

Scott rounded on her. "What the hell are you involved in? I could've been killed. Did you think of that?"

"I'm sorry to drag you into this."

"Sorry doesn't explain anything."

"How was I to know they'd be waiting opposite your house."

"Who are they?"

"I don't know."

"Try again because I want some answers right now. You must have some idea."

"I don't."

Scott started unbuttoning his navy overalls.

"What are you doing?" She shrank back.

"For goodness sake, I'm not going to touch you."

"You're right. I don't know what I'm doing anymore. It's all been too much."

"I'm going to change before we plan our next move." He stepped out of his overalls. Underneath, he wore casual shorts and a white t-shirt, which strained across his muscular chest. "I'm waiting to hear your explanation."

She had to trust him. He'd just saved her life. She owed him. Besides, who else could she trust? Hart's name came to mind but he'd seemed completely uninterested in this lead. And to top it off, he was on another continent. "Someone's trying to kill me, and I think it's because of Jean's will. Someone is trying to get my share of Jean's millions."

"She's dead? What happened to her?"

"My mother died a week ago. Someone poisoned her."

"Are you kidding me!" he said in disbelief.

Amanda's still raw grief for her biological mother came flooding back. She wanted badly to cry.

His eyes darkened with sadness. "I'm really sorry."

"M…my…mother was buried yesterday."

"Jeez. It must be tough for you."

"Yes." She crossed her arms in an effort to contain her sadness. She wished she'd been more like a daughter in the short space of time they'd known each other. If only she could rewind time, and try again.

"Have the police found her killer yet?"

She gingerly touched her forehead. The area felt swollen and sore. "If they had we wouldn't be in this predicament."

"That happened in the car accident, right?"

"A semi-trailer rammed my car." She told him about the accident, and about the chase at the hospital.

He stared at her in disbelief. "Holy Moses! You've had all that happen to you before you came to see me! Now we have some gunmen chasing us. We can't deal with this alone."

"No," she said.

"You're not against calling the cops, are you? Or is there something else you haven't told me?"

"I meant, no we can't handle this alone. And I've already told you why those killers are after me."

"Okay, okay." With Amanda at his heels, he marched into the office then dialed 000.

"This is an emergency. Someone's trying to kill us. Been shooting at us. My name is Scott McMahon and I'm at-"

An explosion sent a whoosh of blast-air vibrating through the building.

He stared at the receiver. "How? The junction box." He threw the receiver down. "It's dead. And I haven't got my mobile phone on me. Have you got yours?"

She dug through her bag. "It's got to be here, but I can't find it."

"Forget it. We've got to get out of here."

"Oh God," she said.

He grabbed a pair of jeans and a sweater draped over a chair. "Let's go."

She started for the Range Rover.

"Not that one." He sprinted across to a white Honda and threw the clothes in the back.

"The keys are in the ignition. You'll have to drive out while I handle the door."

She jumped into the driver's seat.

The aluminum door was half-way up when gunfire echoed through the building. Scott flattened himself against the wall, one hand still on the chain.

Amanda ducked below the windshield.

Every breath, every sound, seemed like claps of thunder to her.

Bullets studded the concrete walls and everything else in their path with lead.

Every muscle in her body screamed for the noise to stop.

When it did, she glanced up cautiously. The man with the sucked-in boxer's face, her pursuer from the hospital, edged his bulk under the door. When he caught sight of her, he grinned.

Like thickening old honey spilling out of a jar, time slowed. Split seconds seemed like hours. Her heartbeat hesitated to a single thud.

The killer straightened. His semi-automatic aimed at Amanda.

Scott? What was he doing? The force of her desperation made her come out of her mind paralysis. Peripherally, she was aware of him. He seemed frozen, immobile. Suddenly, he let go of the chain holding the door.

It hurtled down.

The killer looked up, his face contorted…fear… The door…slammed into his skull. His fingers uncurled. The weapon slid from his grasp…clattered to the floor. A loud gurgling sound was his last struggle for life. Then he was still.

Amanda stared…mesmerized.

Then she started to tremble; a scream ballooned in the back of her throat. She swallowed that down with the bile that had risen. Amanda felt sure he would lift the door and get up, but he didn't move. Death had come quickly.

Scott grabbed the man's gun.

"Get over here and work the door." He inspected the firearm.

She climbed out of the car on rubbery legs. "N…no. I can't," she whispered.

"You might have a death wish but I don't. Move. Move!" He aimed the weapon at the door. "There's got to be more of them waiting outside."

Amanda ran across to the entrance, and pulled on the chain.

"Faster." Scott stood beside her.

She obeyed, at the same time flattening herself against the wall.

As soon as there was a gap, he fired, took cover from a similar answer outside and fired again.

Someone groaned. One or more of Scott's bullets had found their mark.

Scott fired a volley of bullets again. When he stopped, a car engine started.

Outside, the Subaru screeched down the long drive, and away.

"Let's get moving before whoever's left comes back with reinforcements." He dragged the dead man outside, clear of their exit.

Then he returned. He secured the chain to a mechanism. "Hold that lever. Don't let go 'till I drive out, or the door will start down."

Scott raced over to the Honda and started it. As he drove through, he flung open the car door and she scrambled in.

Another body lay sprawled face down, further along the drive. In a depression in the concrete, the man's blood formed a macabre design.

It drew her gaze, this pool of red. She wanted to shut her eyes, but couldn't, not until they had driven past. Then she did but the sight had formed an indelible picture in her mind.

She wasn't aware of her surroundings, only that she was alive, breathing and numb with fear.

They had been driving for about ten minutes before it occurred to her that she didn't know their destination. "Where are we going?"

"Sydney. A friend of mine has an apartment there he hardly uses. Brad's overseas at the moment. We should be safe there."

Safe? Would she ever feel safe again? She slumped back in the seat, drained. She was so tired, she wanted to go to sleep, but for now, her body was too alert. The adrenaline was still pumping.

CHAPTER 31

SYDNEY.

Amanda woke with a start. "What? Where are we?"

Broken lines of fluorescents bathed the underground parking lot in light. Scott was in the driver's seat beside her.

"Elizabeth Bay." He continued backing into a parking spot. "I'm glad you woke. I was beginning to think I'd have to carry you upstairs."

"I must have dozed off when we were on the expressway."

Scott switched off the engine then expelled a long tense breath. A lock of his auburn hair had fallen onto his forehead. With a tired movement, he pushed it back.

He turned to her, his intense blue eyes holding her gaze.

She'd expected more recriminations from him. However, as the silence between them lengthened she tried to guess what he was thinking, but couldn't. In addition, the sudden rush of, of whatever it was she was feeling... caught her by surprise. Attraction? It couldn't be that. It must be gratitude for saving her life.

She stifled a yawn then shivered from a growing inner coldness that had nothing to do with the chill of the night air. It was from knowing how precarious life, her life, really was.

"Are you alright?"

"I'm still here and I'm grateful for that. Elizabeth Bay you said?"

"Great views of Sydney Harbor." Then he added. "And safe."

Safe trumped everything else right now. "At the moment I don't give a damn about the views."

"My friend always said that they're a five minute wonder and I'm inclined to agree."

"What do you mean?"

"How much time does anyone spend looking at the view? He estimated about five minutes. Brad's a smart cookie. He only bought this because of the capital gain." He grabbed their things from the back seat and they walked to the lift.

"How are we going to get in?

He held up the key ring. "They're on here. My mate left his car with me for servicing."

His half smile that everything was fine wasn't convincing. She watched him pull his jumper over his t-shirt. "What's the security like?"

"All I know is that it's got all the latest devices. You were asleep when I punched in the code to get us in."

"Then I'll stop worrying." However, she couldn't. How could Scott be so sure no one had followed them?

They stepped into the lift. She glanced at the parked cars as the doors closed just in case someone was lurking there. Had he noticed? If he did, he didn't say anything. Perhaps he'd been looking for people lurking in the shadows as well. His brow was knotted with what she assumed was worry. They got out at the top floor.

"Here we are." He unlocked the door and turned on the lights.

The wide foyer opened up into a spacious apartment. Two long fawn-colored sofas, some low tables, and other ultra-modern furniture decorated the space.

"You didn't mention if anyone might be home?" She couldn't face making small talk with a stranger right now.

"I did tell you earlier that Brad's overseas…actually he's in Europe for three months."

"Sorry. After what's happened, my memory's like a sieve."

"Make yourself comfortable while I go and change." He disappeared down the hallway to a room that she supposed was a bedroom.

A quick inspection of the place gave her an idea of the layout. This apartment had larger living areas than her townhouse. She pulled open the drapes to reveal a glass sliding door with a balcony that overlooked the bay.

Amanda pulled out a few essentials from her bag and wandered down the hall in search of a bathroom. She washed her hands and as she turned off the taps, her reflection in the mirror stilled her. She looked a mess of taped stitches and purple bruises. Still, alive is better than dead, she thought as she did her best to forget those bodies lying on the driveway.

She peeled back the tape above her eyebrow and inspected the sutures. An egg sized bruise had developed there too. Gingerly, she touched the area. The pain brought tears to her eyes and the dull throb at her temples intensified.

Her hair was a tangled mess. She picked up her hairbrush, and pulled it through her hair in an effort to dispel those sights, sounds, and smells of death.

She winced repeatedly as the bristles caught; but she continued to tug regardless. The action, as the knots disappeared, was mundane enough to lull her temporarily.

Scott knocked. "Are you okay?"

She put down the brush. "I'll join you in a minute." She found a face cloth in one of the drawers and did her best to wash her face.

When Amanda entered the living room, Scott, in jeans now, was gazing at the starry night sky. He swung round, and watched her walk towards him. "I think we both need a stiff drink. Scotch okay?"

"Thanks."

He went over to a small bar in the corner of the room.

The view was something that at another time she would have appreciated. Rows of well-lit yachts moored at a jetty. Here and there, their lights dispersed the cloak of watery darkness.

Her reflection in the glass mirrored a younger version of Jean and her thoughts took her back to Monterey to dwell on her first impressions of her mother. The welcoming smile, the accepting hug—one that she hadn't returned, which she now sadly regretted. When her mother had kissed her, the scent of sandalwood and wildflowers had lingered when she withdrew. A week ago, that scent had lingered in Jean's bathroom. Amanda closed her eyes as her sadness deepened.

Scott was so different from the way Brian had described him.

How could Brian have been so wrong? Perhaps their differences, their constant friction, colored his view of Scott.

She wanted to spend more time with her twin and catch up those lost years if it were possible. It was true, you didn't know what you had until you lost it. She hoped that Brian would stay in her life for a long time to come.

Was a killer stalking Brian too? Her stomach knotted. The thought that her twin might be in danger was too horrible to contemplate.

Who had the most to gain? Dorian? If not him, then it had to be Estella and Ricardo?

Scott brought her drink over. "How about we check the kitchen for some food?"

"I have to find my phone." All she could think about was her twin, and how she had to contact him.

"That can wait. We need to eat. Neither of us has eaten since we shared that cake."

"That was the first thing I'd had all day." Amanda followed him in.

The pantry had plenty of bare shelves and a couple of cans of baked beans and spaghetti. Scott held up a tin of each. "You pick."

"Wait." She opened the freezer. "Well there's plenty of ice cubes, and...a tray of something. It's lasagna. That'll do me."

"Me too."

Amanda popped it into the microwave.

"You want a refill? I sure as hell need one."

"I haven't even tasted mine yet." Amanda slumped onto the stool opposite him. She took a sip. It warmed her throat as it traveled down. "Nice."

He poured himself another measure of Chivas Regal. "I killed two men today." He stared at the glass as he turned it. "I don't know what I should feel but I don't regret saving our lives."

"You had no choice."

He leaned across the bar, towards her. "You think I bloody don't know that! Otherwise we'd be the ones...dead."

She tensed. "I know."

"We should contact the police."

"Brian could be in danger. I have to warn him," She watched the color drain from his face.

"The cops first," he said.

Did he hate his brother that much? "Fine," she said, though it wasn't really.

What was upsetting him aside from the obvious? "Just don't tell the cops where we are. Not yet at least, or they'll be swarming around us in no time. I'm scared they could attract these assassins to us."

"Hell, I've just remembered, there's no landline here. Brad's away so much he hasn't bothered."

She went over and got her cabin bag. "I make no excuses for all the stuff I keep in here. Let me find my mobile." She tipped everything out and started searching.

He smiled. It was the first time that he had and it lit up his face.

"So much for alerting the cops, huh."

"I hope I haven't lost it," she said.

She breathed a sigh of relief when she found it. "Want me to call them?"

"Up to you. It's your phone," he said.

"On second thoughts, you can. I can't face having to explain to them," she said.

He dialed the emergency number, and told the operator about the two bodies at his workshop and gave them a worker's number to call for access to the workshop and then hung up. "What's wrong? You look more on edge than you were a moment ago."

"I'm being paranoid. I thought that you were going to tell the operator where we were."

He sounded strained and tired. "Can't blame you. Today has been one day of hell. Mind if I call my head mechanic?"

"Go ahead," she said.

He told him briefly about the shoot-out, and that the police would be contacting him and to notify the two other mechanics about what had happened.

"I'll let my friend know that I'm okay." She texted Anna. 'Hi Anna. @ Elizabeth Bay. Been in shoot out. Am ok. Speak soon. lul Amanda xx'

Her phone rang. "What the hell's been happening to you, Funny Face? Dropping a bombshell and telling me not to worry. Jesus, Amanda. Explain."

She did as briefly as she could.

"Got time to connect tonight?"

"Sorry. No."

"Take…strike that, keep safe. No more shoot outs. Crap, my heart's jumping just thinking about it. My boss is calling me. Got to go. Speak soon."

"Thanks. Bye." She called off. She was about to text Brian but decided to wait until after dinner and call him instead.

The silence between Amanda and Scott lengthened, and when she glanced at her drink, she was surprised to see she'd finished it.

Scott refilled her glass. "Nine years I've had that car repair workshop. Do you know how hard it is to build up a successful business from scratch?"

"I'm a freelance photographer. So, yes I do. But, I hope this doesn't harm your business."

"I've put all my savings into it. If my customers find out what happened today it could ruin me." Scott slammed down his glass. "We've been shot at, chased, and you, you just sit there as if nothing has happened."

"This is a bloody nightmare. We both know that. I'm having trouble coping, myself. I don't suppose you've even considered that."

"Point taken."

"I'll apologize again but it won't reverse today. I wish it had never happened. What more can I say?"

"It's just that this past week has been the worst one in my whole life. And today…."

"Don't say it." She shut her eyes. The stench of death was with her again.

"What the hell made you come all the way from California to see me?"

She rocked backwards and forwards, her teeth clenched, as she hugged herself. She had to pull herself together. Push away those images of guns and blood.

"You okay? You've gone white."

Amanda gulped her whisky. It washed down the bile that had risen in her throat.

"I'll have another please," she said. "On the rocks."

"Are you sure? I don't want to get you drunk."

"Let me decide." She threw it down as soon as he'd made it. The chaos in her mind gradually receded. She'd traveled to see Scott for a reason and it was time to find out what only he could tell her.

When she looked up, she found him staring. "I need to know the contents of that letter you sent to Jean Campbell?"

He seemed startled by the question. "That again. We didn't get to talk about that earlier. It was Jean that first phoned me. Brian had arrived at her home and she wanted me to send an up-to-date picture of him and tell her something about Brian that only the two of us could know. I wrote about the time he and I went fishing. It was years ago. I didn't get a bite but he caught six eels. Had a hell of a time bringing them in, too. When we brought them home, mum screwed up her nose and said that she wasn't touching those awful slippery things. So Brian struggled for ages, skinning them and wouldn't let dad help either." He paused. "He loved fishing and he always came home with a catch." His voice trembled with emotion.

She knew so little about her twin. "I don't understand why she would ask you that? Brian must have some pictures he could've given her of himself?"

"At first, I couldn't work it out but then I got to thinking. He said he'd come over before he left for California and he didn't."

"Brian? But weren't the two of you enemies."

"Where did you get that idea? We were very close."

"Brian said-" She jumped when the buzzer on the microwave went off. Every noise was sending her bananas.

"Dinner's ready." He went to the kitchen and came back to the bar with their meal.

Although she hadn't felt too hungry before, with the aroma of hot tomato mixed with melted cheese and beef, her appetite returned.

Scott put a plateful in front of her, then skirted the bar and sat opposite. He finished a mouthful then continued. "Our parents were killed in a car crash about ten years ago. We were all that was left of our family." He paused. "That pulled us together."

"Wasn't it five years ago that your parents died?" That's what Brian had told her.

"I should know when my father and mother died."

"I guess you should." He was lying and she wondered why.

"Anyway, Brian took their deaths very hard. He dropped out of university and went bush. I was worried about him. He was nearly twenty then. But every week he'd call no matter where he was. He used to do all sorts of odd jobs. I still remember the day, three years ago; when he rang to say he got a job as a stock hand."

His features softened into a sad half smile as he spoke. "I was at the workshop and had my hands full with some difficult customer, didn't really have time to spare, and he rambled on. It was in some outback station in the Northern Territory."

She finished a mouthful. "But Brian said the two of you didn't get on."

"That's crazy. He was always telling me that we had to stick together."

"Are you sure? That's not what Brian said. I can ask him again. He's in California right now." The conflicting information between the brothers had her head spinning. Who was lying?

He shook his head. "God in heaven, how I wish he was." He closed his eyes and took a long breath.

"I don't understand. When he rang you last week, you wouldn't let him talk. You hung up. I know because I was there beside him."

Something was upsetting Scott. Maybe it was because she could easily refute his relationship with Brian. Then, why would he make up this story? It didn't make sense.

Scott pushed away his half-eaten meal. "For the last week and a half, I was in Darwin."

"Liar. He spoke to you." She'd produce the copy of the email next. See how he wiggled out of that one. Perhaps her brother was right about him after all.

He slammed down his fork. "Liar am I? Let me explain why I was there before you decide that." His nostrils flared as he took deep breaths.

"I'm listening." What the hell was he was up to? Her appetite disappeared.

He leaned forward, tense and angry. "I'll tell you one more time. The arrangement was that he'd visit me on his way through to California. When he didn't show I got worried. It wasn't like him. He would always call if he was late. So, I contacted the station where he'd been working. Someone there told me that Brian left with Nick Delensky, the odd jobs man there. They had left for Darwin three days before, and then both of them were flying on to Sydney. I half expected Brian would bring Nick over. Last Christmas, when Brian came down to visit me, Nick Delensky tagged along too."

"Brian mentioned something about some workmate that went out fixing fences with him. That must have been Nick." However, the last name Delensky: it rang bells in her head. Where had she heard or seen it before? She couldn't remember.

"I know if Brian had been in Sydney he would have called in. I couldn't shake off this feeling of unease I had. So, I contacted the police up there and told them my brother was missing and Nick might be too. Went through the usual stuff with them. Anyway, they called back and said Brian had caught his flight but Nick Delensky never had and he hadn't been in contact with any of his mates since he left the station. They said they'd ring me if anything that I should know about came up. Then there was Jean calling me out of the blue with questions about my brother. My guess is the police must have contacted her about Nick. Why, I have no clue."

"Are you trying to tell me that Brian made Nick Delensky disappear? I find that hard to believe. And what for?"

"At that stage, I didn't know anything. But, I had this gut feeling that something was very wrong." He closed his eyes and was silent for a moment.

"I contacted the police again and got the same standard answer." His eyes glistened with emotion. "Then they rang and told me they'd found a body. Would I be able to come up and see if I could help them identify the man's personal effects because the body was badly decomposed." He took a long breath. "A body in that heat would be unrecognizable, even after a week. It could look like it had been there for ..." He closed his eyes and seemed to be clenching his jaw in an effort to hold in his emotions.

"What are you saying?" The horror was not over. "I find it hard to believe Brian would...would...I don't know."

"Stop it. Will you bloody well give me a chance?"

Amanda sat back staring at him, her heart thudding in her ears.

"Yes the Brian I knew wasn't capable of anything like that. He was too gentle."

"Then what are you trying to tell me?" She had a feeling that she didn't want to hear his answer.

He gripped the edge of the bar, his knuckles turning white, his voice a whisper. "That person they found was Brian. He's dead!" Tears glistened in his eyes.

She jumped from the stool. "Who the hell do you think you are? My brother's very much alive. You're some cruel bastard."

He stared at the counter as he expelled a slow breath. "The sergeant showed me dad's cigarette lighter which was found with the body... Brian never went anywhere without it." His voice, strained with sorrow. "He was found at the bottom of a ravine...a bullet...in his head."

She backed off. "I'm sorry but you've made a mistake. It's got to be a mistake. It can't be Brian. It can't. I just left him. He's back in California." Tears threatened to surface and she blinked them away.

"Like hell he is. Do you think I would have spent the whole of last week trying to retrace Brian's steps if I wasn't convinced that my brother was…gone." He paused and took another shaky breath. "We were so close… It hurts." He clenched his jaw again as if the pain of the memory was more than he could bear.

Amanda turned away unable to look at the raw anguish in his eyes.

He was so sure but he had to be wrong. Otherwise…she couldn't think about the otherwise.

'The dental report came through yesterday," he said. Then he thumped his fist into the counter. "It's not fair."

Amanda jerked backwards in fright.

"Sorry," he said.

She put her hand to her lips, fighting to contain her apprehension, that what he was telling her was true.

Where had she seen that name Delensky? Then it occurred to her. "I've got a newspaper clipping I want to show you." She ran to get it from her bag in the bedroom. Ever since she'd found it in Jean's waste paper bin, something about it had nagged at the edges of her thoughts.

It had to be here. Her hand trembled as she frantically searched all the zippered pockets until she found the clipping. She pulled out the copy of the email, as well as the camera with photos she'd taken of Brian at the dinner table. This was her proof that her brother was alive and well. She stopped to compare the photo in the clipping to the one she'd taken of Brian. Did this bearded stranger look like her brother? She was shocked to see that they did look alike. She sat back on her heels.

"I just don't know. Read this."

Scott was hunched over on the bar, his cheeks wet with tears. "Just leave me for a minute."

"Please, I just need you to read it."

Scott lifted his head: his eyes were red-rimmed.

When he finished he said, "Yep. That man in the picture is Nick Delensky but his name in this news report is Eddie Delensky. How many names does this man have?" He shook his head in disbelief. "Wanted by Interpol…some formula he's stolen from Campbell-Beare Pharmaceuticals. Isn't that Jean's company?"

Amanda pulled out her puffer.

"I saw you use that in the car chase. Asthmatic?"

She nodded.

He glanced at the clipping again. "The men who set up the grab are after him. It doesn't say why. Bloody hell, they're involved in illegal gambling. And all sorts of bad stuff." He threw the clipping down. "Those few days Delensky stayed with me, made me feel like I should watch my back when he was around. That bastard was too smooth, too slippery. I told Brian how I felt but he didn't listen. He trusted everyone."

"I just don't know what to think anymore. This Nick or Eddie Delensky could have been killed by some gangster." Brian had saved her hadn't he, when she fell from the steps down to the beach. He was there for her at the funeral.

Scott spoke softly. "It was Brian they found. Brian had broken a collarbone at football when he was fourteen. While I was there they sent for x-rays from his doctor, and they matched." He stared into his empty glass. "There was no doubt."

"No! How can this be true?" If…no…impossible. She was so scared. "Then who is this?" Her hand shook as she showed him the photos on the camera.

"That's not Brian."

The evidence was piling up. "P…please, don't say that. I…can't deal with this." She wanted to crawl into a dark cupboard, of the sort Elaine used to lock her in when she'd been naughty girl.

"When I met Nick…Eddie…whatever his name is…last Christmas, I was surprised how much he looked like Brian. It would have been easy for the bastard to take my brother's place." He held up the clipping. "Take a look. If Delensky's hair was cut and his beard shaved and his hair lightened. That man you think is Brian has got to be Nick…Eddie Delensky." He sat forward and put his head in his hands.

As she stared, she crushed the copy of the email into a tight ball, as tight as her emotions. A well of anger was building inside her. "Why didn't I notice how similar Brian and this Eddie were before today? I'm a photographer, I should have noticed."

"Sometimes the truth is too hard to deal with."

"Th…then it could have been him that poisoned J…Jean…I…I can't breathe." She gasped. "Got to get out."

She dashed to the glass sliding door. Tore it back and stumbled onto the balcony. A moan that turned to a scream surfaced from somewhere deep inside her.

Then Scott was there pulling her inside. "The neighbors will call the cops."

She heard him but she couldn't stop. It went on…and…on.

Amanda dragged in a breath, her throat, raw. She doubled over then slid to the carpet. "Not Brian. Oh Brian," she sobbed, for the brother she'd never known. "I've never heard the sound of his voice or seen him smile." She didn't want it to be true: she wished it were some trick some horrible lie. She ached for those shared times that would never be. She fought the pain, but it grew until there was no room for anything else, nothing but agony and despair.

Deep in anguish over this terrible loss, her thoughts slowly turned to Jean, who'd been murdered by Delensky masquerading as her son. Jean must have suspected that evil bastard; otherwise, she wouldn't have attempted to change her will. Her hatred for him grew with each passing second.

Gradually, she became aware that Scott had drawn her into his arms, and of his support. She clung to him in an effort to block out the world and to allow the warmth of his body to try to thaw her growing desolation.

CHAPTER 32

Scott helped her up. "Let's get you to bed."

Amanda, too numb to care, allowed him to lead her through the apartment, and to the main bedroom. He threw back the comforter on the queen size bed. "I'll sleep next door. Is this room okay?"

Amanda didn't answer. Right now she didn't want to make decisions, no matter how trivial.

He touched her arm. "Are you all right?"

"It's not fair. I just wanted to know Brian," Amanda whispered as she turned to bury her head at his shoulder. "Delensky...we should let the cops know."

"That shit of a bastard murdered...my brother," his voice, tight with anger. "Where's your phone?"

"I don't know. It must be somewhere in the living room. Tell them to contact Detective Hart at the Monterey City Police Department. He's the one investigating Jean's death."

"I'll tell them where they can find Eddie or Nick, whatever his name is. Do you have a phone number for that detective?"

"I don't know where I put his card."

"Never mind. They should be able to contact him. There can't be too many detectives named Hart in Monterey." He wrapped the comforter around her. "That should help warm you up."

Holding on to the comforter, she shuffled after him. Scott found her phone in the kitchen and made the call. He turned to her. "The cop wanted to interview both of us. I told him we'd be in tomorrow."

"I heard that bit. Anything else."

"Not really. I'm bushed. And you look terrible. It's bed for both of us, I think."

They went back to the bedroom. He put his hands on her shoulders and gazed at her intently. "I'll see you in the morning."

Her pain was mirrored in his eyes. She couldn't stand it; she turned from him as a lump of sadness caught in her throat.

"Goodnight, Scott."

He shut the door behind him as he left.

***

"Don't touch me. Please don't hurt me," Amanda cried as someone shook her.

"Wake up. It's me, Scott."

He'd turned on the bedside lamp. Still trembling with fear, she sat up. "What's going on?"

Scott was in pajama trousers. "You've been calling out."

She finger combed her hair back from her face.

He sat on the edge of the bed. "Are you okay?"

"I've had this nightmare before. But this time it was worse. My hands were all bloody. I was tied to an old iron bed. I tried to free myself but something held me there. A faceless man came in. I saw the knife in his hand, and that's when I screamed. He was going to kill me. I know it. I know it," she sobbed.

"It's only a crazy dream." Scott shifted his weight on the mattress.

Was he leaving? "Stay. Please. I don't want to be on my own. Not now."

"Are you sure?"

She nodded. "Please."

"Well, I wasn't sleeping much anyway." He switched off the lamp, and climbed in beside her.

CHAPTER 33

Weak morning sunlight filtered through the bedroom drapes. Amanda stretched to try to ease her tight muscles and then turned to glance at Scott, fast asleep on the pillow beside her.

His wavy auburn hair had fallen across his forehead. At some other time, something might have sparked between them, but they had both been too overwrought to allow it. She'd taken comfort in the warmth of another caring human. Like her, he hadn't slept much.

Amanda eased out of bed, not wanting to wake him. From her cabin bag, she pulled out some fresh clothes and then tiptoed across the room to the ensuite bathroom.

She closed the door, slipped off the borrowed pajamas, stepped into the white tiled cubicle and let the hot stinging water cascade on her skin. Still shell-shocked from Scott's information last night, she went through the motions of soaping up and rinsing off like an automaton. She flicked off the shower when the skin on her toes started to look wrinkled. A hand towel was all she could find to dry herself.

There was a knock but before she could sing out, the door opened. Scott stopped short. "Sorry." He yawned.

Surprised, Amanda held the towel against her. "You barged in."

"I didn't mean..." Scott withdrew and closed the door.

Amanda expelled a pent-up breath. She threw on her mauve blouse and jeans with more haste than necessary and made her way to the kitchen.

The microwave was on. Scott was on the phone to someone telling this person where Delensky could be found.

"I just rang the Darwin police. I didn't think to last night. Sorry about before. I should have waited for you to...but I was half asleep."

She tried to appear cool and casual about it. "Don't give it another thought."

"I hope leftovers are okay. There's nothing else. Coffee?" he asked.

"Sure."

"There's only long life milk," he said.

"I said sure. Didn't you hear?" She tried to quell her temper. Space, that's what she needed. He was making her edgy.

"Sorry, I should have asked before I used your phone again," he said.

"It's cool. I'm on a good plan."

"We've made this morning's news on the radio," Scott said.

"So soon," she said.

"They announced that the police found two bodies outside my workshop. They were asking for witnesses."

His casual glance made her conscious that the two top buttons on her blouse were undone. She did them up.

"Amanda, I'm really sorry about before."

"It's already forgotten." Damn, the man knew what she was thinking. All she needed now was to blush.

He picked up the phone again. "I've got to make a call to my head mechanic again. Explain more of this to him."

She went back to the living room where she'd left her purse. She pulled out her address book, and flipped to the page where she'd written Jean Campbell's name. On the next page, she'd written Dorian and Brian's names.

Amanda sank onto the sofa and stared at Brian's name. No. She grabbed a pen, wrote Delensky over it. Then she crossed it out over and over until the page was torn.

Angry tears blurred her vision as she tore the bits of paper out. This bastard was not her brother. She wished she could obliterate him as easily.

How she hated that she'd been so completely taken in by him, his slimy casual charm, and his supposed concern for her. Murderer. Murderer.

That fall she'd had at her mother's house made sense now that she knew who Brian really was. Brian...Delensky had waved to her before he'd gone in for breakfast that morning. He must have poured something on the steps after Dorian had joined her because she was pretty sure the surface was fine when she went down to the beach. Had that fall been set up for her, or for Dorian? Perhaps it hadn't mattered which of them had slipped?

She knew now Delensky had thrown down the rope to her because he'd had no choice; her screams had alerted the Campbell staff. Her stepbrother was the one who'd really saved her. She'd been blind. If Delensky had sent killers after her here in Australia what was to stop him from sending more after Dorian?

When he was finished, she asked. "Do you think the police here would have contacted Hart yet?"

"I don't know."

She tried calling the Campbell home, and prayed that Hart had Delensky behind bars by now.

Scott carried in a tray with two cups of coffee and the left over lasagna.

While she was waiting for someone to answer, he put the lasagna on the low table beside her. "Thanks," she whispered. She took a sip of coffee.

"It's an odd breakfast, I know." He sat at the other end of the sofa, but to her it was still too close. She was aware of the quickening of her pulse.

"Good evening, Campbell residence," Rosa said.

Thank God. She'd been ready to hang up if it had been Delensky. "Hello, Rosa, it's Amanda. Can I speak to Dorian?"

"Poor Mr. Dorian. He in hospital."

"What?" Amanda jerked forward, spilling coffee onto her jeans. She put down her cup as Scott gave her a napkin.

"Had terrible bad accident. He uncon..."

"Unconscious."

"Yes. A car hit him when he cross the road at campus. A careless driver...not stop."

"Delensky." Thank goodness, he hadn't succeeded and Dorian was still alive.

"What you say?" Rosa asked.

"I'm stunned." Delensky would stop at nothing to get his hands on the entire estate.

"Please I sorry. You very upset. And I not tell you very well."

"Is he going to be okay?"

"He, very sick, Miss Blake. The eyes, they closed. But sometimes they open, just a bit. Is then he calling for you. I not know why. He calling for you."

Amanda's stomach knotted. "Where is he?"

"St. Euphemia's Hospital. He need you. You must go see him Miss Blake. You come back soon?"

"I can't. I have to…. Yes, I'll come. Can you give me Detective Hart's number?" She waited until Rosa found it and told her. Then she rang off and slumped back, stunned, the napkin still in her hand, unused.

Scott looked at her. "What's happened?"

Amanda told him about Dorian.

She forced down a forkful of lasagna, hardly tasting. "I have to go back to the States."

He put down his fork. "You're kidding? You're not taking off now?"

"Dorian's been asking for me. He probably saw who ran him over. There's also the inquest coming up. I have to be there for that." She drank some coffee.

"Let's go and see the police first."

She shook her head. "You go. I have to see if Dorian's going to be okay. He saved my life and I never thanked him." She told him about her fall.

"Fuck me. Delensky's been trying to kill you from the start. You can't go back. It's too dangerous."

"It's risky no matter where I am until I'm sure they've put Delensky behind bars. I mean, he had a truck driver try to run me off the road here in Australia." She wished he'd stop staring at her so intently.

"I still don't like it. Why would Dorian be calling for you? You hardly know each other?"

"I wish I knew. But, I feel I should go. It's got to be important."

She googled the hospital number, and placed a call. A receptionist gave her the standard response about Dorian. Then she tried Hart and got a busy signal. She left a brief message for him to call her, as the low battery noise started. She put the phone on the charger.

"I'll drive you to the airport and see you safely onto the plane. That's the least I can do."

He got the cups and followed her to the kitchen.

Amanda stacked the dishwasher as she listened to the news report on the radio, and heard another mention of the two bodies outside Scott's workshop. She slammed the dishwasher door shut.

"It was only a matter of time before we made the news," he said.

"So far we haven't been named. I should let dad know that I'm okay but I've been holding off because he'll ask a million questions and I'm not up to talking about what's happened too much."

"So when will you be ready? You have to call him."

"I know." Her phone was still charging and she went to the living room and dialed but her dad didn't pick up. She left a message telling him that she'd been involved in an accident and a shoot-out but she was okay. That should stop him worrying too much, she hoped. She had to prepare herself for when he did call. There'd be a ton of instructions on what she should do.

Scott was leaning over the rail on the balcony, looking at the wind-capped waves.

She sensed sadness in him; it was the way he was just staring, as if he wasn't seeing anything at all.

Amanda slid the door open. "Does your friend own one of those yachts?"

He didn't answer.

"I guess I'd better book that flight."

He continued to ignore her.

"Is it something I've said?"

"No." His voice was flat. "I can't stop thinking about Brian…the way he was killed. Bullet to the head. God, he didn't stand a chance."

"Don't." She shrank away. "Not him." She swung round blindly reaching for the door. Tears stung her eyes.

He came after her as she ran inside.

"I don't want to hear about that. I…I can't talk about him yet." She pressed her hands over her ears.

"It's hard for me too."

He was holding her, just in a comfortable way. She buried her face in the security of his shoulder. Gradually he drew her closer. The spicy scent of him filled her senses. She didn't think about what was happening. She just let it happen. It felt good to be within his warmth, and by just being there, he eased her hurting.

Scott's breathing deepened.

He cupped her face in his hands. His gaze seemed a feather-like touch on her skin, her mouth.

Her pulse quickened.

Hesitation hung between them for seconds.

Then his lips brushed hers, slowly, sensually, igniting fires within. He pushed his fingers through her hair, deepening their kiss, playing his tongue against hers. Her heart pounded, her body throbbed: wanting to feel all of him.

Then she knew: she needed this.

An eddy of sensations buffeted her along. Her ache for him increased, pushed away her sadness, her grief, and her fear. Nothing else mattered.

Scott groaned, and then released her as if he'd just realized what he was doing. "Sorry. I shouldn't have."

"Don't apologize." She drank in his blue eyes darkened with passion. No thoughts, just, he was here and he was the man she wanted, she reached out. Then she did not know whether she'd started to kiss him this time or it was the other way around. They were in each other's arms.

"Amanda," he whispered, "You're making me crazy."

"And you, me!"

He started unbuttoning her blouse and trailing his mouth along her milky skin.

"I'm drowning," he whispered into her ear, and sensually nibbled it.

Desire fired her blood. She touched his chest, his muscular shoulders. His hips rode against her.

"You sure you want this?" Scott asked.

"You know I do." This was the first time she'd been so open with any man. The wanting was unbearable.

He broke away. "Sorry."

"Is it because I look so bad with all these cuts and bruises?"

"Where did you get that idea? I just didn't want you to think I was taking advantage."

"You're not. I'm still sore so be gentle with me."

"You won't even know that I'm touching you."

"That's not what I mean."

Then he was caressing her neck, her shoulders as he pushed her blouse away.

She pulled at his t-shirt wanting to feel his skin against her.

He kissed her again as he removed more of her clothes.

Then he picked her up and carried her to the bedroom.

Amanda lay watching.

He kicked off his shoes, unzipped his jeans and joined her. "You're so beautiful,"

She locked her hands around his neck and pulled him down with her.

"I was hooked from the moment I saw you standing on my doorstep."

Amanda laughed. "You didn't want to buy my encyclopedias. You were going to send me away."

His mouth covered hers in reply, and then moved to her neck, kissing her there. His lips burned her skin wherever they touched her.

He removed the last of her clothing, and kissed her breasts as she moaned in delight.

"Take me now." Amanda arched her back.

And gently, he did just that.

Locked in a passionate embrace, they moved in unison in a slowly increasing rhythm.

A kaleidoscope of sensations sent her spirit soaring.

"Mandy." He whispered out as she clung to him.

She cried out as he drew them to a climax.

Then it was over and she felt bereft when he withdrew.

The sound of their breathing gradually returning to normal filled the room.

Scott drew a lazy finger across her lips. "Wow."

"Likewise. Mandy?" Amanda asked.

"It's my nickname for you. I'm totally smitten. Can't you tell?"

She smiled happily; he'd lifted temporarily the darkness that had been swamping her. But she didn't answer. She just wanted to coast along, not make decisions right now.

Nothing like this had happened to her before. The few couplings she'd experienced before were awkward non-events. It was the closeness of another human she'd been seeking then. This time it was different.

She used to think that the intensity of emotion other people shared was not something that she would ever experience.

As if sensing her inner turmoil he said, "No regrets Mandy?

"I…no."

He nuzzled her neck and she began to cry. "I'm sorry. I can't help it. I'm a mess."

"Just relax against me." He put his arm around her.

CHAPTER 34

Scott, in jeans and t-shirt, reached over to stroke Amanda's cheek, as she stood by the sofa. "You bring out the cave man in me." He smiled.

"Flatterer."

Scott undid the top button on her blouse.

"What are you doing? I have to book the flight."

"I like to see you like this." He undid another button, and pushed back her mauve blouse, then kissed her neck.

"Knock it off. I-"

"You talk too much." He rubbed his mouth against hers.

His arms encircling her felt so good. It would be all the harder for her to leave. "You taste nice."

"Keep talking. I like what you're saying," he said.

She looked into his blue eyes. "I need to make that call."

"Mandy, I don't want you to go."

"We've already discussed why I'm going." She reached for her mobile on the low table and then sat on the sofa.

"I know. But, I can't help being worried. And after yesterday I've good reason to be."

Amanda saw that she'd missed a call from Detective Hart. She tried his number but had to leave a message again. She told him that she was returning to San Francisco and would text him her flight and time of arrival. "No luck with Hart. We keep missing each other. I'm going to ask Guy to call Hart and for both of them to meet me at the other end." Then she booked her flight.

"Who is Guy?"

"Just a friend who's in the States on business. He's someone I met on the flight over to see Jean."

"What sort of a friend?"

"You're getting paranoid. He's a nice bloke."

"So far your judgment hasn't been the best."

He was criticizing her. "How could anyone have known that Delensky was an impostor?"

"Jean guessed."

"Okay. Okay." She didn't like to be wrong.

He sat beside her. "Look, I'm sorry. You didn't deserve that."

"Well, I'll bet it didn't occur to you that after what happened yesterday Delensky's probably got a contract out on you as well."

"I can look after myself."

"Don't I know it."

Scott turned on the TV and switched the channel to a morning chat show.

She picked up the receiver and made the call to Guy.

He yawned and then said, "Amanda. How are you?"

"I'm fine. Sorry to wake you."

"I was up anyway. What's wrong?"

"Does that offer still stand about picking me up?"

"Of course it does. What time and when?" Guy said.

She told him and asked him to contact Hart.

Scott got up and went down the hallway.

"Can't wait to see you," Guy said.

She wished he hadn't said that. They could only be friends, nothing more. "Oh, one more thing…is it okay if we go straight to St. Euphemia's Hospital. Dorian's been in a car accident." She glanced at the screen hardly noticing the antics of the host and the guests on the show.

"That's terrible about Dorian. I'll see you tomorrow then."

Amanda texted Anna. 'Still @ Elizabeth Bay. Flying 2 SF 2day.'

'What t hell's going on this time? U sure u should go?'

'Got 2 c Dorian in hospital. He's been in accident.

'Don't think u should go.'

'Got 2 c Dorian. Speak soon.' lul. Amanda xx'

'Then watch yr back. F u got some explaining 2 do.' lul. Anna xx.

As Scott walked in, a news flash came up on the screen. Help was needed to identify the body of a woman found floating in Sydney

Harbor. Her throat had been cut. A sketch of the woman's face appeared on the screen. Oh God, the blonde nurse from the hospital. Cindy Castles. Amanda dropped her phone and stared blankly at the screen.

CHAPTER 35

MONTEREY.

Eddie pulled out of the Campbell drive in his on-approval sports car. It was only a matter of time before the money would be all his. He would sure live it up.

This mooching around here drove him crazy. Casinos and bars were his scene. He was here to get his hands on the Campbell money and nothing or nobody was going to stand in his way: especially not Amanda Blake.

That bitch was proving more difficult to kill than her brother was, and Silvio Pozzani had lost no time in calling a meeting about that.

The phone call early this morning from Pozzani was short and blunt. "Giuseppe isn't happy. Meet me down at the wharf at dusk. You know where."

Giuseppe Del Condio. The thought of the boss reaching for him made Eddie shiver with fear. He'd tried to escape his tentacles once before. Del Condio's man Pozzani, the devil's angel, was here to watch over him.

A truck horn blasted. Eddie snapped out of his reverie, and glanced in the rear vision mirror. The idiot was right up his bum. He accelerated. Then he turned onto Highway 101 San Francisco bound.

He snaked in and out of the traffic, trying to escape, all the way from Australia, the hot breath of old man Del Condio. It was making the back of his neck prickle.

Brakes screeched as he cut in front of a van. Then he remembered his savior, Brian McMahon.

Eddie knew he would be dead by now by Del Condio's invisible hand if it hadn't been for that chance meeting with McMahon.

Eddie had been on the move for months by then, evading Del Condio, ever since the grab from Campbell-Beare Pharmaceuticals. Del Condio had wanted to give him only a measly ten percent. After all the risks he'd taken. He'd wanted the lion's share. He was the one who'd worked at the laboratories 'till the opportunity arose to snatch the formula for a new oral spray for those super bugs. No more ineffective antibiotics for that bug Staph aureus and whatever those other bugs were called. It was a mixture of gentian violet and some South American herbs. So he'd sold it to another eager buyer for eighteen and a half million. It was much less than the agreed price with the original buyer but it was all his. He hadn't needed to split it with anyone. After that, he'd gone into hiding, surfacing on the odd occasion to play blackjack at the back-street casinos.

He'd met Brian in Darwin at the Dry & Dusty Pub. Brian had been on the lookout for a few extra hands for his employer. Out there, there were miles of nothing but sunbaked red dirt, and bulldust so thick and even, you could fall into it before you realized; and the national parks and stations stretched out for thousands of square kilometers. It was perfect for a person who wanted to disappear for a while. So, he, Eddie, had signed up as Nick Delensky.

He hadn't counted on the dust storms and the harsh dry conditions. A shit of a place to be, but he hadn't had much choice. Nevertheless, there was plenty of solitude and that's what he'd wanted so he'd decided to stick it out for at least a year, and then surface again.

From the first time he'd met Brian, he'd noticed how similar their physical features were. That was part of the reason he'd taken the job. Here was a ready-made identity that he could take on if he needed to.

McMahon had befriended him almost right away. On their trips away from the homestead, fixing fences and doing general maintenance, Brian had talked constantly about his adoptive brother, Scott. He'd even gone so far as to take him down to spend Christmas with him.

He'd been on the station for some months, then the need to roll some dice got to him so bad he went into town with the other blokes one Saturday afternoon. A hired thug had somehow managed to track him down. The thug reminded him that he'd absconded with money that was not rightfully his.

Eddie winced at the memory of the beating.

That Del Condio had found him had been surprise enough, and he'd known that he would be made an example of if he couldn't get the dough quickly. After giving the thug most of what he still had of the original amount, he'd promised to deliver the balance with interest soon. He'd gone back to the station the next morning, half-dead from the beating, and with no idea how he'd scrape up the money. He'd spent or gambled more than a third of it away. He was ready to pack up and run.

That's when Brian had showed him the letter he'd just received from a Jean Campbell, a mother (who he'd never met), inviting him to visit. At first, Eddie had taken no notice. His head was buzzing with thoughts on how he could get his hands on some cash. However, the next time Brian talked about this Jean Campbell it had started him thinking. The company he'd stolen the formula from was Campbell-Beare Pharmaceuticals. If this lady was connected to the same Campbells…at any rate he'd had this Jean Campbell investigated, and had found out just how rich she was. He couldn't believe his luck. It must be fate, he'd thought then. Who was he to ignore its offering.

He'd filled in Del Condio's thugs in town. The word was that Giuseppe was prepared to wait for the money—only as long as it was four times the original amount.

The rest had been easy until now.

Killing Brian had been easy.

The present pushed its way back into his thoughts. A siren blared from some emergency vehicle as it passed him. The traffic had slowed as the turnoffs loomed ahead to the suburban areas of San Francisco.

He knew the way to the Bay, and he was again recalling his hated life on the station. The times when he'd gone out for days inspecting boundary fences, and then there was the fascinating job of finding stray stock. Oh yeah, and the endless days fixing fences in the hot sun. How could he forget the bitterly cold nights spent roughing it under the stars.

When Brian had packed for his trip to the States, Eddie had announced that he was leaving too and had asked him did he mind if they rode into town together.

"Glad to oblige, mate," McMahon had said at the time. "But I don't know if the boss can replace two hands at such short notice."

Eddie had made up some excuse about a very sick father and family needing him.

He laughed aloud at the thought of that father, that nonexistent family. The harsh sound filled the cabin. He didn't even know if his mother was still alive. She'd left before he'd started school. That son-of-a-bitch drunken father of his was hardly family. That bastard had beaten him for years. Beat him until he couldn't take it anymore. At fourteen, Eddie had left without a backward glance.

A driver in the next lane stared. Probably wondered what the joke was, or if he was driving next to a lunatic?

Eddie knew he'd never been saner. At last, he was going to be rich, richer than he'd ever dreamt of in his whole life.

The day he'd left the station with Brian he'd taken a last, long look at the place. He didn't know why. He'd hated it from the first day and was glad to be leaving.

Brian had even commented. "Sorry to go, huh?"

Eddie had nearly told him how he really felt. He was fucking elated to go.

It was more than a day's journey into Darwin and he used the first day of that time learning just about everything that he didn't already know about McMahon. After that, Eddie couldn't wait. He couldn't understand the feeling that gripped him; it was like a fever, a restlessness, to get it done. Get rid of the excess baggage.

He waited until they stopped for lunch at Katherine Gorge. Good old reliable Brian had packed an esky with some grub—soggy cheese and tomato sandwiches—and water. However, he took his time getting it out of the car.

"Come on. What are you doing back there?" Eddie started away from the jeep. He kicked at a gum tree in frustration for the act to be over, before he relieved himself.

"What's up? Worrying about the family are you?"

He'd stifled a laugh. "Family? Yes. I hope my dad's going to survive this heart attack," he lied. The only person that meant anything to him was Cindy back in Sydney, though he rarely wrote to her. He'd met her when he'd just arrived in the big city after walking out on his father, and had no idea where he would stay, or what he was going to do for money. Cindy, on her way home from school, had sat down next to him at the bus station. She'd taken him home and hidden him in her mum's disused garage 'till he'd found a job and somewhere else to live.

He hadn't seen her now for six months, though he'd spoken to her only the other day, he knew she still loved him. When he had his hands on the Campbell money, he might marry her. Hell, that was drastic. He would think on it some more when the time came.

When they finished lunch at the Gorge, he'd talked Brian into going to have a look over the edge.

Eddie had to admit the view was stunning. He was impressed— and that took some doing— at the stained earth and sandstone, twisted ghost gums and bushes that clung precariously to rocky ledges. The sheer drop, down to narrow rocky banks of still water that wound through the Gorge, made him retreat.

Brian was still taking in scenery when Eddie pulled out his pistol.

Brian swung around. "What's up?"

Out in the bush, guns were part of everyday life and Eddie could tell Brian wasn't concerned. Probably thought he meant to kill a snake or something.

It was not until Eddie aimed that he saw alarm in Brian's eyes. Then he'd squeezed the trigger before McMahon got any ideas. The impact flung Brian backwards, over the edge. The stunned look in Brian's eyes as he fell had made Eddie squeamish at the time. Later the feeling of power was unforgettable.

The silence in the dry scrub closed around him.

Just before Brian crashed to the ground, a honeyeater broke into song.

It was his first real kill, the other before was self-defense when that security guard had discovered him. It was just when he was about to take the formula, so it didn't count.

Even now, Eddie could hear the bird's farewell song.

CHAPTER 36

CARMEL VALLEY.

Mel Hart, sweating from the late afternoon sun, lumbered up the steps to the entrance of the neat bungalow in Carmel Valley, then rang the doorbell.

Someone peered through the blinds.

Ricardo Periuz, in jeans and white t-shirt, opened the door wide. "Come in. Thank you. You come so quickly."

Hart stepped into a small living room—fading blue painted walls, and an eclectic assortment of cheap furniture. "The message said it was urgent. What's the problem?"

Periuz's brows furrowed. "Please, you sit down. I did not know what to do? Estella is gone," Ricardo said.

"Gone where?" Hart sat on the lumpy couch, and rummaged through his jacket pockets for some gum. He popped the gum into his mouth.

"Since yesterday morning, she is missing."

"Perhaps she's visiting a friend." This was too coincidental for his liking. He'd sensed these two were holding something back when he interviewed them at the Campbell residence. He'd left another message for Amanda Blake. They had to connect soon so he could find out the details of the car accident and shoot out that happened when she returned to Australia. Why in the hell had she gone over there anyway? That woman should have stayed put instead of putting her life at risk.

"Estella would not go without tell me first. The police here, I go to them, tell them. They do nothing. Can you find my sister for me?" He went to the cluttered bookshelf, picked up a photo of his sister and gave it to Hart. "Maybe this will help. You show it to people. I am sick with worry. Has she had an accident, or what has happened? Is she lying someplace hurt? Where is my Estella? Please, you help me?"

"I'm usually only involved with homicide cases, but I'll do what I can. Where did you say she was going on the day she disappeared?"

"I already tell the police she had interview for new job. They call these people. She not go there."

"Did anyone see her leaving the house that day?"

"My neighbor. He say he see her in new sports car but he not take much notice, he was in a hurry."

"What sort of sports car?"

"My neighbor, he does not know. But, before the interview, she go to buy milk. And she not come back."

"Do you have any reason to suspect someone might want her out of the way?"

Ricardo shrugged and stared at the linoleum floor.

Hart had been in this business for too many years not to notice how tense and scared this man was. He could smell the fear emanating from him. "I can see you're reluctant. But you were worried enough to try to contact me. So if you have any information that can help us find her, tell me."

"It is very hard for us. You see we are from Mexico…and…I am much scared for Estella. She see too much."

"What are you trying to say? Do you suspect this has something to do with Jean Campbell's murder?" This case was growing by the day. Estella had missed her appointment with him the other day and he'd tried calling her a few times since then. Unfortunately, he had a bad feeling concerning her whereabouts.

Ricardo nodded. "There is something important I must tell you."

CHAPTER 37

Dusk settled slowly over Fisherman's Wharf at San Francisco Bay as Eddie Delensky stared at the dwindling throngs of sightseers and shoppers. As night closed in, the streets emptied and street actors stopped performing, and disappeared one by one.

"Listen, we thought you were a player. You told us you could handle this. Del Condio's money is on the line because of your little stunt with Beare pharmaceuticals. Don't fuck it up this time, or else you may not be around to fuck it up any more," Silvio Pozzani said, standing with his back to Eddie.

Silvio, the taller of the two men, leaned against the rail and stared at the ocean as the wind tugged with invisible fingers at his dark Armani jacket.

Eddie thrust his shaking hands into his pockets and hoped the sign of fear wasn't noticed. He waited uneasily until his partner turned to him.

"Well?" Pozzani said.

"Those guys did come with a good wrap-up. How did I know they weren't pros?"

"So how do you explain the fuck up at the hospital?"

Eddie opened his mouth to answer but Silvio cut him off.

"I don't want excuses."

"Leave Cindy Castles out of your plans for the others." Eddie could feel droplets of sweat trickle down his back.

"You have something else in mind?" Pozzani's expression was stony

"She won't talk-"

"She's trash. Forget her." Silvio pulled out a packet of cigarettes, and lit one. "The dead can't talk. It won't be long…"

"Trust me. She won't talk. I know her. Leave her alone." Cindy was someone he couldn't forget. Eddie's stomach tightened.

"Perhaps you're right." Pozzani shrugged then smiled the smile of the predator Delensky knew he was.

"I'm going in search of a little entertainment, just something to whet my appetite for later." He drew long and hard on the cigarette. The smoke he blew out quickly dissipated over the ocean.

Delensky kept his expression blank; he had no taste for the sort of games with whores this guy enjoyed. The girls he played with never worked again.

"Amanda's taken the bait. She'll be dead this time tomorrow. But not before I have my fun with her," Pozzani said.

"I thought I was going to do the job." He preferred to get it done quickly. Pozzani ground his cigarette into the low wall. "I just want to give her a real good time."

That would be messy. Eddie did not like this change in plans, but he couldn't afford to cross the bastard.

"Don't get any ideas about backing out now. We're not going to wait much longer for our dough unless you want our man to pay you a visit. You'll end up in a wheelchair but you'll wish you were dead."

Eddie nodded, not trusting himself to speak; his voice would have betrayed his fear.

The two men parted. Eddie passed a row of barrows. Some were selling hot clam chowder, and others cooked crabs and fish. The normally tempting aroma turned his stomach. He'd lost his appetite for food after Pozzani's threat.

When there was a break in the traffic, he hurried across the road. Well, he had something to be thankful for, the lure had worked, and Amanda Blake was returning to San Francisco right now, just where he and Pozzani wanted her.

He turned into a narrow side street, wiping his palms on his trousers. An empty soda can rolled towards him. He booted it away and continued up the steep incline to his sports car. The killing would not end until Amanda and Dorian were dead and then, except for the cut Pozzani and Del Condio would take, the rest of the money would be all his. He could hardly wait.

***

Silvio smiled to himself as he strode away. Del Condio had been fuming about the fuck up with the attempt to eliminate Amanda while she was in Australia. Delensky had a lot to learn. Time had run out for those hired idiots. Dead, they couldn't point the finger at Delensky or him.

He could tell Eddie was upset about the contract on Cindy. However, there was no need to tell him that his girlfriend had been whacked. Let the jerk think that she was still okay. The job was coming to its conclusion; it would not serve any purpose to upset Delensky just yet.

CHAPTER 38

Hart stared down at Dorian Campbell in the hospital bed. He wanted badly to question him, but until Campbell fully regained consciousness there was nothing he could do but wait.

Dorian, hooked up to the works, stirred again. He mumbled over the blood-filled stomach drainage tube at the corner of his mouth. "Amanda." His eyelids fluttered open, then closed.

His discordant muttering had gone on for a few hours, the nurse had told Hart.

Hart listened for a few minutes and couldn't understand a word of it. He sighed as he watched Campbell. The doctor had told him, that the new complication of a bleeding ulcer would slow his recovery. Tomorrow, the doctor had said, he would be more alert and perhaps able to answer questions.

He popped another piece of gum into his mouth. The new evidence he'd received from the Australian law enforcement guys confirmed his suspicions concerning the man who called himself Brian McMahon. He'd managed to lift Brian's prints with Rosa's cooperation and sent them off for a match. In addition, he was waiting for some more information from the police in Darwin before he could act.

The Campbell's cook, Rosa, had eventually told him she'd called the police about the new will. Just yesterday, she'd informed him that the Blake woman had called from Australia. He'd been spitting nails when he'd found out she'd gone to see McMahon over the email and that empty envelope Cohen had found in the safe. He'd done his own investigations to find out what he could about Scott McMahon. This morning he'd received an email from the Australian law enforcement authorities about a shoot-out at McMahon's home.

Then a few hours later, there had been another email....Two male cadavers found at Scott's Motors Repairs. Despite all the years he'd spend in the force and he knew that he should've been immune to this, but it had shaken him. What was going on there? Then he'd received a call from Rosa Estivariz that Amanda Blake was on her way back to San Francisco.

When he'd noticed the missed calls from Amanda on his cell, he'd tried a number of times to contact her but so far he'd been unsuccessful in actually speaking to her. At least she was still alive.

He'd left instructions with Rosa that he wanted to see Amanda as soon as she arrived. Blake had a lot of explaining to do. Maybe this Scott had sent an imposter to pose as Brian. But then how was Amanda involved? He obviously was protecting her. If Amanda was heiress to the fortune, Scott would never let her in on his scheme.

The last piece to the puzzle just did not make sense. Now with Estella missing, it complicated things even more.

When his suspect slipped up, then he would tighten the noose.

Finally, Campbell fell silent.

Hart went out. As he stumped round the corner, he met Cohen. He was visiting Dorian again. He exchanged greetings with Cohen and continued on.

***

A nurse led Cohen to a cubicle in the outpatients' section of the hospital.

"The doctor will be with you soon." She turned and left him.

Cohen took off his glasses and wiped the beads of perspiration from his forehead. He couldn't continue under this strain for much longer.

Heavy footsteps on the tiled floor announced the doctor's arrival. "How are we today?"

"Fine. Fine. Hurry up and do it. I have to get back to the office." Cohen took off his navy pinstriped jacket, business shirt and tie, and put them on the chair beside him. Now that Dorian had a bleeding ulcer, he needed more type AB blood. The sample the nurse had taken earlier from him had matched perfectly.

"Lie on the bed please." The doctor turned away from Cohen to the trolley where the nurse had laid out the necessary equipment. "You should tell Mr. Campbell when he's better. I'm sure he'll be grateful." The doctor prepared the syringe and the plastic donor bag.

Cohen stared up trying to concentrate on a crack in the ceiling while the doctor swabbed the area on his arm. A moment later, he winced as the syringe plunged in.

"No good. I'll go again."

"That hurts." It was obvious the doctor was just an intern and not very experienced.

"Sorry. It's just that you're so tense."

"Who wouldn't be? I hate this."

"You really should put your name on the blood donor register. Your particular blood type, AB, is one of the rare ones, and Mr. Campbell's so lucky that yours is a match."

"I told you this must remain between us. He must not find out. He's really a good boy."

"I'm sure he is."

"Dorian's just strayed off the track but I'm sure he'll come to his senses soon. Do you know he looks just like his mother?"

"That's nice. Now don't forget about the register. Please consider accident victims who could be in desperate need of blood."

That awful queasy feeling in Cohen's stomach started again. "Haven't you got enough yet?" He kept his eyes averted: the sight of blood, especially his own, made him feel giddy.

"Just a little more and we'll be done, Mr. Cohen. Tell me about your practice. Is it a busy one?"

"Yes." He jumped when he heard a high-pitched female voice. Felicity? His eyes flickered open. It was just some nurse standing beside the doctor. Oh…the needle, the blood going into a bag. "I feel faint." He should not have looked. He shut his eyes.

"Nearly done. Don't worry Mr. Cohen, you'll be fine. Have you heard the latest joke about blondes? Maybe not, I'll tell you."

Although the doctor's light-hearted banter made him feel less woozy, he soon stopped listening. That nurse, he dare not open his eyes again, she sounded so much like Felicity. She would not take his calls. She had been the center of his world for so long, even way back twelve months ago, when he'd entertained thoughts of asking Jean to marry him mainly because he felt sorry for her and it would have been better for Dorian to have a father figure around.

He had long admitted to himself he enjoyed her company, but it was never love. Felicity was the woman he loved. He must have been crazy not to try harder to convince Felicity of that. What was he going to do without her? He so badly needed her warmth and her understanding now.

A little while later, Cohen stood in the doorway of Dorian's room. The lawyer gripped the doorway, his knuckles white.

The plasma bag hanging above the bed was nearly empty. The hospital staff would bring the donor bag of blood soon. He averted his gaze.

Dorian stirred. "Amanda," he whispered.

Why did he call for that goddamned girl? It was Jean's fault. He'd advised her against contacting the twins but she'd refused to listen. What a stupid, foolish whim. Look what had happened because of it. She was *dead*. Moreover, his life was on a downward slide. Why couldn't she have left well enough alone? Cohen smashed his fist into the wall.

Campbell's eyes opened. "Lionel?"

Cohen walked over stiffly rubbing his knuckles. "Just called in to see how you are." He noticed they had removed the drainage tube from his mouth. It was a good sign.

Dorian's eyes shut again and he lay still.

Cohen stared down at him. Dorian had to recover. Everything had gone so wrong. He shuddered and backed up softly into the corridor. From his jacket, he pulled out a handkerchief, mopped his forehead, and then hurried to the nurses' bay.

The woman looked up from her paper work. "How can we help you?"

Even though he'd sought reassurance from the attending doctor earlier today, he had to ask again. "Mr. Campbell spoke a little before he went back to sleep. Is he going to make it?"

She flipped through pages on the folder until she found his chart. "His condition is stable."

"Tell me the truth. His parents are dead and I'm his closest family now."

"It's only the internal bleeding that's causing us any concern. But since last night, it has slowed substantially and with the donor that has come forward he'll soon be improving."

"Thank you." Cohen slid his business card across. "My home number is on the back. Please contact me if there is any change."

CHAPTER 39

At just after six in the evening San Francisco International thronged with people. Amanda, carrying her cabin bag, pushed through the crowded arrivals lounge and looked for Guy Robertson.

When she saw his head of thick black hair, she waved. He smiled as she walked towards him.

"How was…what happened…your forehead?" Guy, in tailored jacket and chinos, leaned forward to kiss Amanda.

"Just a little accident," she lied, offering him her cheek. "Thanks for meeting me."

"That's what friends are for," he said.

Friends? She was glad he'd cleared that up.

"Let me carry that." He took her bag. "Is that all you have?"

"I travel light."

He laughed. "Most women I know would find that impossible." Guy gazed at her. "Traveling suits you. Other people come off after a long flight half dead but even with that," he gestured to her wound, "you look like you're fresh out of the shower."

"What's brought this on?" She'd quickly brushed her hair and applied a touch of lipstick.

He shrugged. "You have that effect on people."

"Sure. Sure. Trying to get into my good books, huh?" She made a joke of his compliment. To take it seriously would be to acknowledge that his motive was more than friendship.

"Who me?" he said.

"Come on, let's go." For some strange reason, she felt suddenly uneasy.

She pulled out her phone and dialed Anna's number. Her friend didn't answer and the call went straight to voicemail.

"Hey Anna, just landed in California. Guy Robertson has picked me up. We're headed to the hospital. Love you!"

They rode the escalator that took them to ground level.

"Did you ask Detective Hart to meet me?" Scott had insisted he have that detective's number too, just in case.

"He's going to catch you at the hospital. I spoke to him just before I came here."

He led her through the melee of baggage handlers, travelers, welcoming parties and pickpockets out to the parking lot.

He unlocked the black Mercedes. "Where to first? The Campbell's to drop off your bag, or-"

"Take me straight to the hospital to see Dorian please." There was no way she would go near Jean's home without being sure that Eddie Delensky was behind bars. Just the thought of that murdering bastard being so close made her stomach knot in panic. She wished Hart were here.

"You're really worried about him, aren't you?"

"Dorian's been asking to see me." She did up her seatbelt.

"Then I'd better get you there." Guy drove out of the parking lot and joined the rush hour traffic going south.

The cars slowed as a fog drifted in; here and there in the thicker pockets, incandescent streetlights threw eerie distorted beams at the commuters.

Amanda prayed that Dorian wasn't another possible victim.

She jumped when her mobile bleeped. It was that detective again. She listened to his voice message. He said she should contact him as soon as she arrived. She was about to do just that when Guy turned to her.

"Who are you going to call?"

"Detective Hart."

"He's going to meet you at the hospital, remember?"

"He's left a message for me."

"You'll be there soon enough. Speak to him then."

"Okay." It would be better to have a conversation with him in private. She had a feeling that something was wrong, but she didn't know what. She glanced at her phone again and then put it in her handbag. She saw a blond-haired man driving a Toyota in the lane beside them. Through the fog, she couldn't make out the face clearly. Please no. She tensed. As the man turned to catch her gaze, she stiffened in fear.

He smiled. It wasn't Delensky; she slumped back in her seat relieved. Detective Hart probably had Delensky behind bars by now.

"What's bothering you?"

"I don't know what state I'm likely to find Dorian in. I can't understand why he'd be asking for me."

"I can't help you there." He changed lanes. "Did you find Scott?"

"Yes. But he wasn't much help," she lied. Scott. Just recalling yesterday morning with him made her hot inside; his firm body against hers. She wished she were with him now.

"What about the letter?"

"Oh that." She shrugged. "It just gave...err Brian's new address." She'd hiccupped over the name. Her twin was dead. *Dead.* Oh God. No. She closed her eyes and breathed deeply as she tried to force away those painful thoughts. Sometime, she would have to face them, but not now.

Guy slammed on the brakes as a van swerved into their path. "Stupid idiot."

Amanda gripped the seatbelt, waiting for the impact. Delensky must have set them up. "No...no...no."

She stared in horror. The van was going to smash into them. At the last moment, the driver swung away.

Car tires screeched. The van driver buzzed down his window then shook his fist at Guy, swearing. He accelerated away.

"I'm sorry. Are you all right? You've gone white."

She nodded as she let go of the seatbelt. It had been close but not that close. Her reaction was over the top. Images of that semi-trailer bearing down on the highway to Wollongong had flashed before her eyes.

Guy held the steering wheel with one hand, with the other he reached over and touched her. "What happened to you?"

"It's the fog. It frightens me." Amanda pulled away. "Concentrate on the road. The way you're driving is making me nervous." She stared out as they turned onto the freeway, more as a distraction than for any other reason. The fog was thinner here; she could see lights from rows of houses.

Guy glanced over. "Don't worry."

"What's happening with your work?"

"I'm doing pretty good, if I do say so myself. The deals here are just about all in the bag. My boss should be happy with all the new business I've picked up for him. As soon as the ink's dry on the contracts, I'm off to England. That'll probably be Saturday." He glanced at her. "What about you? Are you going to continue to freelance after this is finalized?"

"What else? The money from the estate probably won't come through for a while. Not that it would make a great deal of difference I'd be bored silly if I didn't work. I'm booked to do a spread on the Tasmanian Rivers. Zac, my partner on this job, has been moaning about the delay. So has the magazine editor. If I'm tied up here longer than two weeks I'll have to ring them both and tell them to find someone else."

An hour later, he pulled up outside St Euphemia's Private Hospital. Rows of shrubs divided it from the quiet suburban street. "Want me to come in with you?"

"Thanks for the offer, but I think I need to do this alone. Don't wait for me. I'll catch a cab."

Guy came around, and opened her door. "Are you sure? I don't mind."

"I've put you out enough."

He pulled out her bag and handed it to her. "What about dinner later then?"

"Can I have a rain check? I'm not sure how long I'll be. I'd better go and find Hart."

"He said he'd either be with Dorian or for some reason if he was held up, to wait for him outside."

He stared at her: the look in his eyes unreadable.

She felt awkward. "Thanks again."

"That's it?"

"Huh?" She puzzled over his comment for only brief seconds.

His mouth was on hers before she could stop him. Amanda pulled away. "I'd…I'd better go." Although his kiss hadn't been unpleasant, she didn't want this.

"Amanda, don't I have what it takes with you?"

"I don't want to be kissed right now. We're friends. Let's keep it that way. Anyway, all I can think about now is Dorian." It had been a mistake to ask him to pick her up from the airport. She should have caught a cab. Her life was complicated enough. However, until she was certain that Delenksy had been apprehended she had to be doubly careful.

He smiled. "Let's try that again another time. We could have some fun, you and I."

She did not respond to his innuendo

He reached over and toyed with one of her drop earrings. "Nice."

She stepped back from him. "Stop it."

He ran his finger along her jaw line. "Okay." He sighed. "Maybe later, we could-"

"I better go in and see Dorian and Hart. Thanks again for picking me up."

"See you later then?"

"I'm tired and need to catch up on some sleep," she said.

He climbed into his car and disappeared into the night.

Bright lampposts illuminated the shrubs and bushes moving in the wind, casting strange shadows on the sidewalk. She heard a scraping sound behind her. What was that? Amanda glanced back. There was a line of parked cars at the curbside; otherwise, the street was deserted. She quickened her step. The scraping sound got louder. Was someone behind the bushes? She got ready to run as her feeling of unease grew. Where in the hell was Hart? She bumped the cabin bag up the steps, not bothering with the wheels and set it down to push the glass doors to the foyer.

Subdued beige walls, potted plants, people waiting nurses walking doctors talking and the smell of antiseptic...just like it was in Australia. The dizzying rush of familiar sights and sounds assaulted her. But those pursuers were dead. Amanda froze.

A woman came towards her. She smiled at Amanda then walked past to the exit doors. For a second, Amanda had thought this female was going to attack her. She was suspicious of everyone.

Calm down, she said to herself, Hart would be waiting for her at Dorian's bedside.

"This way, ma'am." The security guard indicated for her to go through the walk-thru metal detector and into a tiled foyer. A receptionist, enclosed in a wood and glass information desk, was talking on the phone.

"Could you tell me where Dorian Campbell is please?"

The receptionist typed in the name into a computer.

A female cried out, and Amanda jumped at the sudden sound. Again, she told herself to cool it. It was a typical hospital noise. She was just too edgy. The place was abuzz with people but she felt very much alone.

The woman eyed her. "He's not allowed visitors. Are you family?"

"I must see him. He's been calling for me. I'm his sister."

"Can I see some ID?"

She pushed across her passport.

"You're on my list. But you'll have to show it again to the security officer at the door. It's Room 12B." She gave her a map marked with the route. "When you get through the doors there," she pointed, "the duty nurse will direct you to his room."

Amanda heard her mobile beep an alert. She opened the text.

'Amanda, Please meet me outside at 8:30pm. M. Hart.'

She texted him back. 'Thought u be waiting 4 me when I got here. Amanda'

'Not able to.'

She glanced at her watch. At least she had enough time to see Dorian before she would have to meet the detective.

On her way down the corridor, Amanda saw Lionel.

He seemed so deep in thought that he nearly walked past her until she spoke. "Hello. How's Dorian?" Amanda asked.

"So you're back. He's regained consciousness."

"I was shocked to hear about the accident. Have the police caught the person responsible?"

"No," he snapped.

"I'm meeting Hart later."

"Why?"

Two white coated doctors were walking along and one raised an eyebrow when Lionel asked the question.

Amanda waited as the two men moved further down the corridor before she spoke. "I've found out something important."

"The product of your overactive imagination, I've no doubt."

She didn't like or trust him. "Don't insult me. I'm not some empty-headed female. Rosa said Dorian was asking for me."

He frowned and glanced at his watch. "I'm still surprised you bothered to come."

"It's the least I could do. He did rescue me. I know you don't like me, but there's no need to get nasty."

He glared. "A good little Samaritan, are you? You hardly know Dorian."

"You pompous bastard."

"We'd have all been better off if you hadn't bothered to visit Jean in the first place."

"I was invited. What is your problem?"

"Gold digger." He spat the words.

"How dare you!" Her hand itched to slap him.

"So why else did you come except to get your hands on the Campbell's millions?"

"Is that what you think?" she demanded. "Is that what you think?"

He turned and strode away.

Amanda fumed as she watched Lionel almost knock over a man

on crutches, utter not a word of an apology, and disappear through the swinging exit doors.

Cohen visiting Dorian after office hours—perhaps he considered it his duty, one that caused him an inconvenience.

When she entered his room, Dorian was staring at the ceiling. Amanda nodded a greeting to the nurse standing beside the monitor.

"Hello. How are you feeling?"

His lips were bloodless. "Amanda, you've come at last. Come closer."

She moved to his bedside.

"I saw the driver," he whispered.

"Do you know who ran you over?"

Dorian's eyes closed.

"It's me, Amanda. Tell me."

He did not respond. She grabbed his hand. "Dorian. Wake up. Wake up!"

The nurse forced an eye open and shone a penlight into one eye then the other. "Can you hear me, Mr. Campbell?"

Dorian lay still.

"I was just talking to him...and...what's happening to him?"

The nurse gently shook him, and then pinched his arm.

Amanda stood by, shocked. "Why are you doing that?"

"It's standard procedure. Please leave. You can wait outside until his condition improves."

Dorian stirred.

"I'm staying right here." Amanda slumped into a nearby chair, and hoped this was not a setback.

He began to mumble incoherently.

The nurse checked the monitors again.

What had Dorian been on the verge of telling her?

To make doubly sure that the detective was meeting her outside, she sent a text to him. The return text didn't make sense. He didn't seem to know that he was supposed to be meeting her at all. She sent another text asking him could he be at the hospital ASAP. His reply said that he would be there in half an hour. She sighed with relief. Had Hart misunderstood Guy? What was going on? This just didn't make sense.

Finally, Dorian's eyes flickered open. "Where am I?" He tried to lift his head.

"Relax now, Mr. Campbell. Remember you've been in an accident," the nurse said, smoothing his pillows.

"Amanda? I want Amanda. Where is she?"

She jerked out of the chair. "I'm right here."

"It was him. I know it was him."

"Who?" The answer was already there in her head but it just needed confirmation.

"Hell, I thought I was gone. Someone pushed me from behind. That car was coming straight for me. I can still see his eyes. They were so cold."

"Tell me who?"

The nurse scowled at Amanda. "Don't harass him. He's still very weak."

"Brian. It was Brian," Dorian said. She had to tell Hart the full story about that impostor before he got another chance. Jesus, he'd had plenty of time to do something about Dorian while he was in a coma. She took a deep breath to try to calm down and think this through rationally. Hart should have apprehended that bastard by now. Therefore, she was safe and so was Dorian. She couldn't wait to talk with that detective and tell him all she knew.

"Amanda." Dorian stared up at her expectantly. "You must tell Hart."

She glanced at her watch. "I'm going to meet him now. She bent over and kissed his cheek. "I'll be back soon."

She left her bag in the corner beside Dorian's locker, and hurried into the corridor texting Anna. 'Arrived @ hospital seeing Dorian. Going to meet Det. Hart. lul Amanda xx.'

'Got that dirty scumbag imposter behind bars? lul Anna xx.'

'Hope so. Will no more after meeting. lul Amanda xx'

It seemed the same people were sitting in the foyer. Still talking, their voices rose and fell in a constant sound.

Amanda went to the exit, pushed through the doors and walked out into the spring night air. She stood at the top of the stairs, trying to spot the detective through the darkness. Someone locked their Buick, and proceeded across the road towards her. The glow of the streetlights illuminated the person enough, for her to see it was an overweight man. "Detective Hart?"

She ran down the steps. Thank goodness he'd come. She hurried past parked cars, toward him.

Then she realized as she approached that the man was a stranger. Now that she was closer, she could tell the car he'd climbed out of was not even a Buick. She turned back. She'd wait inside the entrance 'till he came.

The passenger door of a parked car opened, blocking her way. Funny, she hadn't noticed anyone in it when she passed before. Not that she'd been really looking.

A blond-haired man climbed out. Her mouth went dry when she saw who it was.

Delensky.

She stepped back. Her worst fears reality.

"Hello, Amanda." He smiled.

That voice filled her with dread. She steeled herself to meet his gaze with an unwavering calm stare. Her palms were clammy. "Brian. What are you doing here?" Why hadn't Hart locked this murderer up? Maybe he had done away with the detective too. She shuddered.

His look was cold, hard. "I've come to pick you up."

The back of her neck tingled with fear. "Thanks. But...but I'm going back in. I...I've got to go back in to Dorian. H...how...did you know I was here?"

Amanda retreated.

Delensky followed. "Guy rang me. The hospital's not that way." His stance was menacing.

"I...I just came out for some fresh air." She edged back some more. "Dorian's waiting for me. I…I need to get back."

She needed to get around him and surprise was her only weapon. Amanda bolted.

Delensky gave chase.

A burst of adrenalin powered her on.

She tripped over a crack in the concrete and stumbled forward. Her handbag fell from her arm.

Delensky lunged at her.

They crashed to the sidewalk, a tangle of arms and legs. The hard surface grazed her hands, her knees, and her elbows. He pinned her down. Winded, she dragged in air. His breath: became her breath. His face: at her face. She struggled under him.

Delensky pushed himself up and as he straightened, wrenched her to her feet.

"You're hurting me." Her hands stung, she wrestled against his grip.

"And where were you running off to?"

His question hung in the air like a live tension wire between them.

"You're coming with me," he said.

Her heart pounded.

She was barely aware of the ambulance, siren blaring, of a dog barking somewhere.

He tried to jerk her forward.

"Let me go. Damn you. You have no right to manhandle me like this." She twisted, trying to free herself. "Let go. What's wrong with you…Brian?"

He held on, his fingers digging into her flesh. "I think you know."

She took in panic-stricken gulps of cool night air. She screamed. He wrenched her to him, and pressed his lips to her open mouth.

The entry doors to the hospital swung open. Had someone heard her?

Voices drifted to them.

"Nice," he said.

She spat at him.

A pregnant redhead shuffled her large awkward frame down the steps toward them.

Keep him talking. He'll have wait until the woman has passed them. Time enough for her to break free and make a run for it. "It…it…must be a strain on you too. It's been terrible for you as well. What with Jean gone so suddenly and Dorian…a hit-and-run victim. God knows if he'll completely recover. Even Cohen can't seem to cope. Have you seen him? He…he looks awful." She glanced at her wrist, then up.

His eyes said it all, he was anticipating her intention. "I'm not going anywhere." Even to herself she sounded convincing.

Delensky dragged her forward. "Move."

"My handbag." She tried to pull free.

The redhead continued towards them.

"I've got a gun," he hissed into her ear. "And I'll use it if I have to."

Gun. Her stomach knotted. "Then you'd better kill me now. I'm not moving," she said with false bravado.

"If I can't convince you to come with me, I guess I'll have to find another way." He called out to the woman, now within speaking distance from them. "Can you help me? My sister's very sick."

"No. No," Amanda whispered. "Leave her." Would he take this woman as a hostage too?

"Stop fighting me and smile," he said.

"What's wrong? Should I go get a doctor?" the redhead asked.

She wanted to shout and tell this woman to get away but she dared not. The barrel dug into her ribs. She forced her lips into a half-tremulous smile and lied. "D…Don't worry. I'm fine now. The dizziness has passed."

"Are you sure, Sis?" He squeezed Amanda's forearm.

"Yes, Brian." The bitter taste of bile was in her mouth. Murdering bastard, she wanted to scream.

The woman stopped level with them and stared. "She does look a little pale. Are you sure you don't want me to go get help? It would be no trouble."

"I'm fine now. Thank you for your concern." Run from us, she wanted to urge her.

"Sorry to bother you," he said.

"You sure have a funny accent. Australian?"

"You guessed it," Amanda ground out. "Goodbye." She did not know how she could sound so calm and yet be so terrified.

"I love your koala bears and-"

"We don't want to hold you up." Delensky's smile was all artificial sweetener. The woman said goodbye and moved on.

Delensky eased his hold.

Breaking free, she made to run.

"Don't try it." He pointed a gun at the retreating redhead. "You've got one second, or she's dead."

Two lives for hers! She had no choice.

"You acted so heroically, Sis. My heart bleeds." He scooped up her handbag.

Hatred welled up inside her and she glared at him with the full force of that emotion. "Gutless bastard! If I was holding the gun I'd have used it on you."

"We understand each other perfectly. Don't we?" His lips twisted in a sardonic smile as he hustled her to his car. "I knew you'd see it my way."

The woman disappeared around the corner. The street was empty of pedestrians again. He unlocked the Lamborghini. "In. And don't get any ideas."

She maneuvered herself over the console and into the passenger seat. He climbed in after her.

He put the gun in his lap, started the ignition, and then put the car into gear.

This might be her last chance. It was now or never.

Flinging open the door, she launched herself. Delensky lunged and grabbed handfuls of her hair, and jerked her back in.

Amanda screamed in pain, her fists hammering his face, his chest.

He pulled harder. She scratched at his arms and at his cheeks.

"Bitch!"

He jerked again until her scalp burned.

"Stop," she sobbed. Hadn't anyone heard her?

"Why should I, bitch?"

She tried to push his fingers from her hair, but he held fast. "Please, I won't try again."

He gave one last yank at her hair. Then he banged her in the head with his gun. "Yeah! Just you try it."

Dizzied by the blow, she touched her scalp. Her wound above her eye throbbed too. "I won't, I promise." Her fingernails had left two vertical red welts on his cheek.

A couple strode along the sidewalk towards them; he lowered the gun below window level.

"Don't you scream again or anything stupid like that? Hear!"

Silently, she was begging the couple to call the police.

Once they had passed, he threw a scarf to her. "Blindfold your eyes with this."

Gasping for a breath, she reached into her pocket for her puffer.

"Hold it right there. What are you doing?"

"Ventolin."

He nodded and she inhaled a dose.

"Blindfold," he said.

"Bastard." Hands shaking, she put it on.

"Now turn around and hold your wrists together."

"I won't try to run again."

"Do it."

The rope was rough against her skin as he bound her arms behind her back.

"And this is just in case you get any more ideas."

He struck her at the back of her head. Pain exploded there before she spun into a black vortex.

CHAPTER 40

Hart stepped out of his Buick. "Wait," he shouted.

He was sure that was Amanda Blake who had gotten into that Lamborghini. What was going on? She had texted him to meet her here. Then he heard her scream. He started to run but the sports car took off.

"Son-of-a-bitch." He stood on the sidewalk puffing. He had to lose some weight. His heart was hammering from the exertion. He pushed himself to double back the short distance to his vehicle.

He grabbed the radio, asked for back up and described the vehicle. What he'd seen led him to believe that the Blake woman had just been abducted.

Hart slammed the door and tramped on the accelerator after that Lamborghini. The sports car couldn't have gone too far. He had the patrols on the lookout for it now.

The car was well up the street before he spotted it. He spoke into the mike. "Just turned right on Lexington." Then he told the operator the license plate number.

Hart flashed past rows of clapboard houses.

The sports car was now far ahead, over the next hill.

He put his siren on.

In this vehicle he didn't think he had a hope of catching whoever had abducted Amanda, but he had to try.

Lightening lit up the dark sky, and rain pelted the windscreen. He turned on the wipers and followed as the driver wove through the clotted evening traffic. That had gotten him entangled in another jam of vehicles and he upped the siren but it did little good.

Finally, free of the traffic, Hart careered through red lights in pursuit.

"That son-of-a-bitch is getting away." Hart accelerated through another set of red lights with horns from other vehicles blaring in his wake.

When he was within sight of the Lamborghini again, he turned off the siren and cruised, keeping one car behind.

One of the highway patrol vehicles was in the area. He snapped out the location to them. "Traveling southwest on Jackson. Could be armed. Do not approach."

On the outskirts of the city, the sports car sped off, leaving him well behind.

It started to rain and he lost sight of the vehicle.

A call came through. The car had been seen going south. Hart was going in the opposite direction. He did a U-turn and took the next left.

Then he saw the vehicle disappear around a corner. Hart swung into the street in pursuit. He sped by a neighborhood shopping mall, a bus depot and warehouses.

A container truck pulled out of a driveway. The detective braked, and blasted his horn. "Move."

The driver honked back then stuck his head out of his cabin. "What's up, pig?"

Hart leaned out and flashed his badge. "Police. Move or I'll throw the book at you for obstruction."

"No shit." The driver backed up. "Fuckin' pigs!"

Hart accelerated past, but those few minutes were enough time for the sports vehicle to have disappeared.

Hart thumped the steering wheel with the palm of his hand. "Son-of-a-bitch. Where has he gone?"

CHAPTER 41

Someone shook Amanda, and pulled off her blindfold but she couldn't see a thing.

Her head ached. "Where am I? What's going on?"

"I can't tell you that."

That voice brought her thoughts alarmingly into focus. Her eyes took a moment to adjust to the dark and see that she was still in that car. Her thoughts were roaring inside her....*oh my God...oh my God...how am I going to get out of this?*

"Brian." She had no intention of calling him Eddie, or of letting him know just how much she knew about him. Her safety might depend on it.

"Your phone." He held out his hand.

"I...I can't get it. My hands are tied."

He leaned over and retrieved it from her handbag. "Let's go."

"I can't get out like this. You'll have to untie me." She was sore all over and stiff.

"No way." He helped her out.

It was too dark to see properly but she could just make out a dilapidated bungalow surrounded by an overgrown garden.

The crunch of gravel underfoot echoed in the night. "Are we on the outskirts of San Francisco?" The road, she guessed, was at least the length of a tennis court away or more. Light, which spilled into the night from the nearest house, seemed quite a distance away.

"You think I'd tell you," he said.

"Sure."

"Shut up! Don't even think of shouting for help. You'll be dead before anyone could come." He pushed her toward the house. "Inside."

Amanda stumbled up the steps leading to the porch. "I can't see. It's too dark."

"I told you, shut up. Or else I'll have to gag you."

Once they were inside, he flicked on the lights.

The sparsely furnished interior smelt of dust and stale air. Amanda sneezed. Jesus, she didn't like the look of this place at all. Deserted...no one would hear if she screamed. "W...Why did you bring me here?"

"Let's just say you're worth a lot of money to us. Used to be that we needed you dead to collect on the money. But your persistence has changed that. Now we need you alive, for ransom. Still, what state you'll be in when they find you..." A sick smile crept across Delensky's face as he pushed her past a dirty laminated table, down the corridor, paint peeling off the ceiling and walls, to the bedroom.

It was clean. He'd prepared this room for her. Inwardly, she shuddered at the thought. "How long are you going to keep me here?"

He ignored the question as—with his foot—he pushed aside an old storage chest next to the iron four-poster bed. On it was a new mattress, partly covered by a blanket.

Eddie pressed himself against her as he retied her hands and secured them to the post, which formed part of the headboard. Then he pushed her onto the bed.

His strong musky aftershave and excited male odor made her gag.

She fought off a wave of panic as his arms brushed slowly against her breasts. His mobile rang. He answered it as he left the room.

Delensky returned with a glass of water. "I thought you might be thirsty."

"I don't want-"

Then she was choking on the liquid as he pinched her nose and poured it down her throat. Drugs...had to be was all she remembered thinking before she fell into a stupor.

***

Amanda woke suddenly.

Delensky was standing beside her with a paper bag in his hands.

"How long have I been asleep?"

He didn't answer but opened the bag and pulled out a hamburger and a drink.

She bit into the hamburger, as he held it for her, and grimaced. It was tasteless but she was famished and it had been too long since she'd eaten anything.

He watched her with a look of hunger that had nothing to do with food. She sipped her coke. "Are you going to keep staring at me?"

He didn't answer but ran his fingers down her cheek.

"I need to go," she said.

"I guess I'll have to take you." He untied her from the bedpost and led her to an old dusty bathroom. He waited outside while she went. She looked around for a window while she washed her hands in a cracked basin and saw one of those rectangular sliding windows near the ceiling. The unsteady bench top propped up on one side with a stick would never hold her weight. However, she had to try even though her hands were tied together. She was about to climb up when she heard the door handle turn.

"Hey. You finished in there?"

"I need my inhaler. It's in my handbag."

He led her to the kitchen. "I'll get it."

Delensky waited until she had a dose and then led her back to the bedroom.

"Why did you drug me?" Delensky didn't answer. He untied her hands and began to retie them behind her. She broke free and pushed him to the ground. She grabbed the key on the bed and was at the door. Frantic now, she tried to unlock it. Eddie tackled her to the ground and kicked her side. She whimpered in pain and rolled up to protect herself.

"Bitch." He tore the key from the lock.

"You're going nowhere. Get up and get over there."

Silently, she did.

"Turn round." He tied her hands behind her back and then spun her round and secured them to the bedpost, brushing his arms against her breasts again as he did so.

Then he stepped back. His breathing was heavy. Lust, there in his gaze.

She had to try to turn him from his purpose. "It's the inheritance you're after, isn't it? Let me go and I'll make sure you get my portion."

"Sure, and I'll go to jail."

"I'll tell Cohen and Hart it was my idea to give you my money," she said.

"I want all of it. I want Dorian's share too."

"Why?" Dorian's death already planned. He was the lure and she'd fallen for it. She'd been so stupid.

"I've come too far to settle for less." He raised an eyebrow. "Tempting."

Her ploy hadn't worked; she had to try something else. "So you think you're going to get away with this, Eddie?"

"Who told you my name?" he asked.

She couldn't tell him it was Scott, or he'd be on his killing list too.

"Out with it," he said.

Make it convincing, she told herself. "Remember how I found Estella going through the bin."

"Get to the point."

"In Jean's wastepaper basket was a newspaper cutting about someone called Eddie Delensky. Jean must have realized that you were an impostor. That's why the new will."

"Go on."

"The photo in the clipping kept nagging at me. When I compared it to the ones I had taken of you at the dinner table I could see they were of the same person."

"Clever, Amanda." He reached over and twirled a few strands of her hair between his fingers

"Don't. Please. It hurts."

"You forced me to do it. I didn't want to hurt you. You understand that, don't you?"

"How dare you try to justify what you've done! Go to hell." She spat in his face.

He wiped away the saliva with his sleeve. "Bitch." Delensky slapped her with the back of his hand.

Her cheek stung from the blow. "Even hell is too good a place for slime like you. You murdered Jean."

"Wrong."

"You poisoned my mother, you lying bastard." She rotated her wrists, trying to ease them from their bindings. "At first I thought Estella had killed her."

His lips curled up in a cruel smile. "She's gone."

"What do you mean?" Then she realized. "Oh my God! You didn't? Please, tell me you didn't?" However, that sadistic gleam in his eyes told her all. "You murdered Estella too." She sagged against the bedpost. First Brian…the body count kept growing. The anguish was unbearable, even in this desperate situation. You shot him too—she wanted to scream into his face—*left him to decay in a ravine.*

"It was easy." He boasted as he traced the line of her jaw. "I hadn't meant to tell you about Estella, but it doesn't matter now."

Why didn't he care that she knew? "Keep away from me."

"Feisty. I like that in a woman. Pity we couldn't have met at some other time."

Amanda shivered with fear as his breath fanned her face. She turned away.

Delensky grabbed her jaw, and forced her to look at him.

"I've already told you, I'm not going to hurt you. From the first time we met, I wanted to fuck you."

She was aware of the short hairs on the back of her neck standing on end; she knew she had to live. "Let me go, and I'll do anything you want. Please." The rope cut into her flesh as she tried to slip it from her wrists.

"Anything? You know what, I'd love that."

Then he kissed her, hard, his tongue in her mouth. She gagged, wanted him to stop. She tried not to think about his hand on her breast, kneading. She didn't want it there. Silently, she screamed against the abuse of her body.

His breathing irregular, fuelled with hunger. "Say you want me?"

Whatever was going to happen, she had to live through it. She forced a half smile.

His mouth was on hers again, his hands working their way down, down.

Her thoughts seemed to dislocate from what was happening. She was falling into an abyss.

The front door slammed and she realized that his abuse had stopped.

"Pozzani's here." He suddenly seemed very nervous. He zipped up her jeans.

Someone was moving about. "Eddie?" the man called.

"I owe him too much money. Him and Del Condio. I didn't want it to be like this for you." He backed off towards the door.

What he said didn't make sense. She would let him think she had accepted her fate; that he planned to hide her until he'd dealt with this man. It would give her time to escape.

"You're scared to death of that Pozzani aren't you? He's got you trembling. Hasn't he?"

His nostrils flared. "You don't know anything. He spoiled my plans with you yesterday ...but why am I telling you this. Goodbye, bitch," Delensky said. He slammed the door behind him as he left.

So, she'd spent one night here. The caller must have been Del Condio. Now it made sense, before he'd left to do Del Condio's bidding he'd drugged her.

Amanda looked for something within reach that she could use to cut the rope. Some duct tape and a pair of scissors lay at the bottom of the bed, but they were too far away.

The only other furniture in the room was a large old chest. Why had he left it in here? Then she had a terrifying thought. Did he plan to push her into it later and leave her to die?

She slipped off her shoe, and with her toes, tried to pry open the lid. It was so heavy that it shut on her foot before she had it up more than a few inches. Again, and again she tried, ignoring when the lid fell on her toes and bruised them, until finally, she opened it.

Empty. Empty. Empty.

Despair flared anew.

Then Amanda saw what looked like a small screwdriver in the far corner of the chest. She struggled to reach it with her toes, managed to grasp the tool only to have it clatter back. She tried again, and lifted it up and onto the mattress. As she closed the chest, the lid fell on her foot. She gritted her teeth at the sudden pain.

Amanda started on her bindings. With her earlier struggles, the rope had tightened around her left wrist, and had loosened around the other. That hand she worked against the rope, her skin burning from the effort and slippery with sweat. Suddenly she freed it, saw the bloody red welts on her wrist, and felt the throbbing pain there that earlier she'd been too preoccupied to notice.

The bloody red welts…this was her nightmare. She was living her nightmare.

The realization shook her with its accuracy. In her dream, she was a prisoner, unable to escape. She wanted to wake up as she had the other morning, and find she was safe with Scott there beside her. Tears wet her cheeks.

Shit. She was falling apart. Crying would get her nowhere. Gritting her teeth, she grasped the screwdriver with renewed vigor.

Amanda ignored the pain at her other wrist and jabbed the tool at her bindings. The knots were so tight it was useless. She pushed the screwdriver into the mattress ticking where it would be within easy reach.

That done, she grabbed the post, and tried to pull the bed across the room in an effort to barricade the door, but the heavy iron groaned and only moved a fraction. In the process, she'd cut herself on something sharp at the back of the bedpost.

She tried to pull her bound wrist to the sharp edge of the iron structure, to cut through her bindings. Was there something else she could use to free herself? For the first time, she noticed the floor covering. Why hadn't she noticed the sheets of plastic before?

Whatever was going to happen here was going to be messy.

Oh my God, she thought…she had to get away. Frantic now, she rubbed the rope backwards and forwards against the jagged edge of the bed, while listening to the muffled voices coming from the kitchen.

CHAPTER 42

Amanda didn't know how long she'd been struggling to free herself, but the setting sun slanted in through the blinds, and her arms were shaking from her efforts.

She heard a mobile ringing somewhere and knew it was hers from the Pink Panther tune it played. She wished she could answer it and get help.

Someone was coming down the hallway. Then she heard Guy Robertson's voice.

He must have overpowered Pozzani and Delensky. Somehow, he'd found her. Thank God, he was here to rescue her.

"Guy, I'm in here," she shouted. Relief flooded through her.

The door swung open.

"Untie me. Please."

"Hello, Amanda." Guy's look was deadpan. Strands of his usually immaculately combed black hair had fallen forward onto his forehead.

"Help me, Guy."

He didn't move.

Flushed, Delensky stood nervously beside him.

Something was wrong. Very wrong! Amanda's alarm spiraled.

"Surprised?" Guy's stance seemed composed and confident.

"What are you waiting for? Untie me. My wrists are going numb." She gazed at him, seeking a positive response in his face, his eyes, his soul. There was none.

"No," Guy said.

Hope shriveled and died.

"Why aren't you...you're involved with Delensky? You can't be. I don't understand. How did he talk you into this?"

Eddie spoke. "You stupid bitch! He's Silvio Po-"

Silvio interrupted. "Shut up! She doesn't need to know."

Guy an impostor too. Her heartbeat pounded with fear in her

ears.

"Y…you're Pozzani!"

"You can't keep your mouth shut can you!" Silvio snarled at his accomplice.

She could smell the tension between them, and the odors of the unused rooms. Hear every intake of breath.

"What does it matter? Who's she going to tell," Delensky said.

"Shut the fuck up. You were always too soft."

"Soft! Who fixed Brian?"

"Bastards! My brother's life was nothing…nothing to either of you."

"Shut your mouth," Pozzani warned.

"Who's she going to tell?" Delensky said.

"Didn't you hear what I said, imbecile?"

"Then let's just bag her, Silvio. It's much cleaner."

Guy…Silvio Pozzani, whatever his name was, from the way he spoke, was obviously in charge. What did Delensky mean by "bag her"? She shivered: her skin suddenly cold and clammy when the meaning became clear. The chest was there for a purpose. Then she was gasping for a breath. "P…puffer?"

Delensky held it to her mouth. But she was shaking so much she couldn't time her breath and it took a couple of goes. "J…just let me go, please. I…I won't tell anyone."

"No you won't." Silvio laughed a hollow laugh. "Leave us."

"Eddie. W…why are you listening to him? He thinks you're stupid, someone to order about."

Silvio laughed again and then stopped abruptly.

Delensky reached inside his pocket.

"Don't try it or you're a dead man." Silvio said.

"We'll see who Del Condio wants at his table when this is all over. I'll have more money than you've ever dreamt of," Delensky said. He slammed the door behind him so hard the noise echoed through the bungalow.

Silvio locked it, and then turned to her. His gaze seemed cold and calculating.

She tried to pray, but the words wouldn't come. Her terror made them a jumble in her mind.

She should have tried harder to free herself and escape, because the future was unthinkable.

He crossed the room. "Lovely, Amanda. My beautiful, Amanda who spurned my advances only yesterday."

Did he have rape in mind or was it something entirely different? He grabbed her jaw and squeezed it with his powerful fingers. The act sent pain spiraling through her face.

"We can play together, you and I. How about a rerun of that kiss that you shrank away from."

"Th...that was only because I was worried about Dorian," she said. She tried to twist her head away from his grasp but he held on.

His breath was hot on her face. Then his greedy mouth devoured hers, brutalized her on and on, his tongue thrust into her mouth; bile rose in her throat as she screamed in silence for him to stop.

When he did, Amanda gasped for a breath. Hot tears slid down her cheeks as she slumped against the bedpost.

"Your display is oh, so touching. I could almost let you go. But, it's too late for that. Besides, sympathy is a wasted emotion. Don't you think?"

She shook her head. "You dropped me at the hospital. You must have changed your mind then, otherwise you'd have taken me here yourself."

"To take you here directly from San Francisco airport when so many people had seen me with you, and you called your friend to tell her I picked you up, would have been stupid." He smiled.

She had to try to convince him to let her go. "I really do like you. But how can I respond when I'm like this. Untie me."

"Clever. But it won't work." He tugged at the bodice of her top. He eased his fingers slowly along the v-neckline.

"Don't do this, please."

"Shut up." He smoothed his hands down his face, seemingly

wiping away his uncontrolled outburst, and a dead calmness replaced it. "Can't we see a little more? Your top looks so prudish for us like this."

There was a kind of madness in him now. Why was he referring to himself as we?

"Don't talk." He pulled out a sheath knife, flicked it open to reveal a long blade.

Amanda recoiled, terrified.

"Most men like their girls tied to the bed spread-eagled. That gets boring after a while. It's a little quirk of ours to have the female standing."

Silvio jerked the lower part of her body against him.

She tried to twist away. The friction excited him more. She felt his hardness, felt her panic, felt her body stiffen and her mind try to withdraw.

A low growl came from the back of his throat. "Do that again."

"B...bastard. You...insane evil scum." she whispered.

"Don't you listen? We told you to shut the fuck up. "

He stepped back. The blade poised at her chest. She stared mesmerized at the shiny metal; then in one deft stroke, he slit her top from neckline to hem.

Her heartbeat was a galloping tattoo in her ears, her mouth dry with terror.

"Much more appropriate." He stared at the swell of her breasts captured in a white satin bra. Then his gaze traveled slowly and deliberately downwards. "Nice."

"I...I hate you." Amanda whispered.

"Now what's brought that on? Don't you want to play with us?" He unzipped her jeans, pulled them down, and cut her lace panties off. Then he thrust his hand between her legs. "Tell us how much you love this."

"I...I...." The words came out in a whimper. She wanted his hand away from that part of her. Terror burned through her veins like wildfire. When he brought the knife to her neck, pressing the flat of the blade against her skin, a shuddering ragged scream surfaced from deep inside her.

Silvio smiled.

Then she knew it would be some time before he would be finished with her.

He brought the cold metal downwards, to the cleft of her breasts. Slowly, he slit the thin white fabric holding them, and with the point of the blade flicked the satin aside.

"Lovely." His breathing deepened. "Delectable." Silvio drew the sharp blade against her breast, nicking the skin, a line of red in its wake.

Amanda took a deep shaky breath as she read that look of lust, of animal hunger, in him.

"Perfect." Distracted, he dropped the knife to cup her breasts in his hands. "So soft, so supple. Nipples… like rosebuds…made to suck. Even to bite," He murmured with reverence as he bent his head.

Amanda felt for the screwdriver concealed in the ticking while he stroked her, his tongue flicking against her skin. When he scraped of his teeth against her nipple, she knew he was about to bite it.

Gripping the screwdriver, she swung at his face.

He must have felt her movement because at that moment, he raised his head.

She jabbed at his eye. Missed.

The weapon tore a bloody gash in his left cheek as he cried out. Again, she stabbed at his face as he reached for the knife lying beside him. This time she embedded the screwdriver deeper. He fell backwards bleeding… writhing…his hands at his face…screaming in agony.

She strained to reach that knife, her toes just brushing the handle. Again, and again she tried. Each time she managed to edge it a little closer but not near enough for her to pick it up.

He seized the screwdriver, and with a gut-wrenching scream, pulled it out. A gush of blood pumped from the wound, he wiped, and wiped it until his face was a hideous mask. Silvio moaned.

He reached for the knife, the act causing him to cry out again and curl up. He moaned again as blood pooled beside him.

"No." She cried as his bloody fingers closed around the handle. He made to rise but instead, slumped to the floor like some stoned drug addict.

Finally upright, his movements were like some strange drunken dance with two steps back and one forward. The knife slid from his hand.

Frantically, she tore at the knot at her wrist and forced it a fraction.

He picked up the knife and glared at her. "Bitch. You'll wish you'd never met me."

Amanda knew he would show no mercy: no screams of pain would slow his pleasure.

He loomed closer. She balled the fingers of her free hand into a fist and punched his bloody wound as hard as she could.

He cried out and crumpled backwards. She grabbed his knife as he fell, and tried to cut through the rope.

He began to rise.

She stabbed at his shoulder but didn't connect. "Y...you keep away or I'll kill you."

He picked up the scissors that had been lying with the duct tape. "Bitch. No one will recognize your corpse when I'm finished."

Finally freeing herself, she gripped the knife with shaking hands. "K...keep away from me."

Someone was banging doors somewhere in the house.

Distracted, Silvio hesitated for a second. She swung the blade. He raised his left arm to defend himself and the steel sliced into his flesh there.

She ducked sideways when he jabbed the scissors at her chest. He got her shoulder instead. The pain stung and she felt suddenly woozy.

Many feet pounded through the house.

He listened, as if confused.

The echo of gunshots had him stumbling for the door. Then he changed direction and made for the window, pried it open, smearing the sill red.

He paused to stare at her.

"One day, Amanda, you'll look behind you and I'll be there." Then he dived through, and was gone.

CHAPTER 43

"I'm in here. Someone help me. Please help me," Amanda screamed.

"Hold on, we're going to force the door," a male shouted.

Heavy blows struck the door and the lock gave way. Two policemen and Hart, guns drawn, rushed in;

"Don't touch a thing,' Hart said.

"Silvio's escaped out the window," she said as she slumped on to the bed.

Two officers rushed over and stared out.

"Get the fingerprint team here now." Hart snapped out orders on his cell phone. "Perp's escaped out the left side window. Alert the squad searching the grounds." The detective stared hard at her as he called off. "Please, drop the knife."

She hadn't realized she was still holding it. She let go and watched him carefully pick it up with a tissue.

"Thank heaven you're alive." Hart covered her with the blanket.

The female officer leaned out into the darkness. "Can't see anyone out there."

"Then go get some flashlights and join the others outside." Hart turned to Amanda. "Silvio? Can you describe the man?"

"I...it was ...Silvio Pozzani." She took a shuddering breath. "Y...you know him as...Guy Robertson."

"The one who took you on a tour of San Francisco? The one with the Mercedes who dropped off you and Brian...I mean Delensky?" Hart said.

She nodded.

"Joe. Get a message to the chopper." Hart snapped instructions into the cell phone. "Caucasian's escaped on foot. Height's about six feet, quarterback type, black hair. No unusual marks. I want the whole area lit up like a Christmas tree. Get the squads out combing the surrounding area now. And get an ambulance here now."

"Why...didn't you meet me at the hospital?" she asked.

"What do you mean? I responded as soon as you texted me," Hart said.

"But Guy, I mean Silvio…oh wait. Maybe, the text wasn't from you….must have been a set up."

"What you are talking about?"

"I got a text from M. Hart, saying that you would be waiting for me at the hospital."

"I always sign off as Mel or Mel Hart."

"One of them must have texted me pretending to be you," she said.

"That's why I couldn't work out your text asking why I hadn't turned up," Hart said.

"I…I stabbed him in the face with a screwdriver."

"Stabbed who?" Hart asked.

"Silvio."

Hart spoke into his cell. "Caucasian's got a wound on his…" He turned to Amanda. "Left or right cheek?"

"I…can't…left," she said. "I…I don't want to think …."

"Hear that Joe? Let the squad know." He pulled out a stamped and addressed envelope from his jacket pocket. "I found it on the kitchen table. It's addressed to Lionel Cohen. They were demanding fifty million in ransom for your release."

Amanda sagged against the bed, the horror of her ordeal still raw. "I'd have been lucky to be alive when someone found me."

The female officer returned. She told Hart about the broken branches outside the window, about a trail of blood, but there was no sign of the fugitive.

The detective punched in some numbers into his cell phone. "Joe. When's the ambulance coming?"

With dismay, Amanda listened to Joe's voice as it crackled into the room. "The perp's vanished."

"Keep looking. Get the team here now. That perp's bloody prints are everywhere." Hart stared at the blood-splattered plastic covering the floor. "Holy baloney."

The female officer pulled the blanket around her further. "You're safe now. You're going to be okay."

"An officer will accompany you to hospital," Hart said.

"I'll go," the female officer said.

"I…I'm not going. After…what happened to me at that hospital in Wollongong."

"But we have to get you to a doctor."

Hart stared at the floor again. "All that blood. Are you sure Pozzani didn't hurt you anywhere else?"

"I…I stabbed him with the screwdriver."

"You had no choice," the female officer said.

"S…Silvio pulled it out." She saw the tool in the blood slick and suddenly felt very sick at the violence of her actions. Yet, she still wished that she'd been able to inflict more damage. "I…I need the bathroom." She pulled the blanket tighter around her.

"I think it's somewhere down the hall," Hart said.

She ran out with female officer trailing behind.

The officer waited outside.

After Amanda had emptied the contents of her stomach, she turned on the tap at the dirty basin, and splashed her face with cold water. The broken mirror reflected something that she didn't want to see: haunted pale features, dark-ringed eyes, and a swollen bottom lip. She turned from her reflection, and reached for the doorknob. Then she started to shake again. She pressed her forehead against the wood, and took a few deep breaths to help boost her courage: to go on, to resist the urge to retreat inwards. She opened the door.

"Better?"

"Get me out of here," she said.

As she turned to go she saw Scott coming in the front door.

"What are you doing here?" Amanda asked.

Scott pushed Amanda's hair from her face. "I was worried so I called Hart to ask if he'd apprehended Brian and about his meeting with you. He said that as he turned up at the hospital he heard a woman screaming in a Lamborghini. And he was pretty sure it was you. I was frantic. I didn't know if we'd find you in time. It was the longest plane trip of my life. I tried calling you."

"I couldn't..."

"Your shoulder's bleeding. Are you okay?" he asked.

"I will be," she said. She told him of the ordeal.

"Guy who is really someone named Silvio Pozzani. That's the man who picked you up from the airport," Scott said with disbelief.

"They had it all planned. Silvio dropped me at the hospital. I visited Dorian. Then Delensky kidnapped me. Oh God...it was horrible."

"How did Guy, or, uh, Silvio manage to get a seat beside you on your fight over to see your mother? Who *are* these people?"

"I...I don't know."

"Who did this to you? Was it Eddie?"

"E...Eddie didn't...but...Silvio...it was horrible." They had violated her in a way that was even worse. Each of them made her willing to consent to anything they might have wanted to do until.... "I stabbed him."

"Look at your wrists, your hands. We should get you to the hospital," Scott said.

"That's where we're headed," the female officer said.

Amanda stared. Silvio's wounded face loomed at her. He held a huge knife in his hand. His angry laughter echoed, louder and louder. She felt the sting of the blade on her breast. She was going to die. He was pushing his fingers.... "No. Don't," she screamed in terror. She shut her eyes. "N...no no." It was happening again. This time, Silvio wasn't going to stop. She had to fight back.

Someone shook her.

"Amanda. It's okay." Scott was holding her arms.

"What are you doing to me?" She opened her eyes. "Scott?"

"You were trying to punch me."

"Sorry," she said.

"You're safe. Hart's here too. Don't be afraid." His voice was soothing. "You're safe now."

"Sorry…I'm sorry." She shook her head. "Oh God, what's happening to me?" Her thoughts were a confused fog. Silvio wasn't here at all. She tried to stop her teeth chattering.

She folded her arms around herself, and began to shake. "Get me out of here."

He led her down the hall to the little kitchen.

Two officers were standing guard.

Delensky.

She froze. The bastard was sitting at the old blue Formica table as if he was running the show. Handcuffed and under guard, his presence was still as threatening as ever.

Delensky stared at her.

Amanda shriveled up inside, and she could feel his hands on her still. "Get him away from me."

She edged backwards, behind Scott's protective frame.

"Gutless scumbag." Scott's deep voice was thick with rage.

The officer closest to Delensky said, "Don't worry, man. He'll be looked after."

Scott lunged at Eddie.

At the same time, the officer thrust his bulk between them.

"Give me five minutes with him alone," Scott said.

Delensky jumped to his feet.

"Calm down, man," the officer said to Scott. "You…" he said to Delensky…"get your ass on that chair." Arms outstretched, he forced Eddie back.

The other officer put his hand on his holster.

"I want to put as much distance as I can between us, and that murdering bastard," Amanda said.

Her skin crawled at being in the same room as that slime. She ached to shower away the imprint of his and Pozzani's evil hands on her body.

"You killed my brother." Scott said. "You've terrorized Amanda. You're not getting away with that. If it's the last thing I do, I'm going to make sure you're put behind bars for life."

Delensky shrugged.

Something snapped inside her. She lashed out and struck Delensky across the face. "I'll cut it off if I get the chance."

Delensky's cheek reddened as he smiled at her. "You liked it. I know-"

"Scumbag," she slapped him hard again. That took the smile away.

"Step back, ma'am," the officer said.

"Gutless scum, aren't you!" Scott said.

"How can I defend myself?" Delensky raised his hands. "I'm handcuffed."

"You don't deserve a fair go. Let me at him," he said to the officer.

"I can't. Hart would have my badge if I did. Get your lady to the hospital."

Amanda wanted to see him badly hurt.

Every muscle in Scott's body corded with tension.

"Please, Scott, let's go." She added silently, *before I get a gun and fix him myself.*

Wait, what was happening here? Since when did she want to kill someone? She had to get herself together and stop these crazy thoughts.

Scott stormed past the other man to the back door, flung it open, allowed Amanda to go through, and then turned back. "If we were alone, I'd have given you the same chance you gave my brother."

They went down the steps together.

Outside, the grounds were crawling with police. Their haphazardly parked cars were everywhere.

They went past a SWAT van on the gravel driveway.

An officer standing beside an ambulance further down the drive waved them over. "Get in. I've been instructed to accompany Miss Blake to the hospital."

"I'm coming too." Scott helped her in as a dispatch came through on the officer's radio. "Chopper one. Fugitive sighted two blocks east in the South Valley Mall parking lot. Get the squad over there now."

CHAPTER 44

Two police officers were playing poker on the fifth floor of a two-roomed suite at the Albert Hotel, San Francisco.

"I'll raise you twenty dollars," Norton said as he pushed some notes across the coffee table.

The other officer stared at his cards, bent forward from his easy chair and added more cash to the small pile in the middle. "And thirty says I'll see ya."

Norton slapped his hand face up on the table. "Royal flush." He scooped up the bills, grinning. "Wanna play another hand?"

"What, and have you beat me again? No way." Schneck collected the cards, put them into his jacket pocket and rose. He edged past the double bed and crossed the stained pale-gray carpet to the connecting door of the adjoining suite. He opened the door. "You two okay in there?"

"We're fine." Scott looked over from the window.

Arms half crossed, wrists bandaged, forehead patched, Amanda sat slumped over on the sofa. She looked to be asleep. Well, at near one in the morning, most people were getting some shuteye, thought Schneck.

"Heard any news about Pozzani?" Scott asked.

"He's still on the loose. Just holler if you need anything." The cop retreated. Then he bent down to look into the bar fridge.

"I feel like something more than soda." Schneck glanced back at his friend. "Know what I mean." He pulled out a miniature bottle of Kentucky Bourbon.

"Yeah. But you know you can't," Norton said.

"But we've pulled an all-nighter. Who'll check up on us? It'll be quiet."

"You never know."

Schneck dropped the bourbon back, selected a coke, then ambled to the television, and turned it on.

"Wouldn't you know it? A Laurel and Hardy movie." He went to change the channel.

"Leave it. They're my fave. Turn up the sound."

"Okay." Schneck turned from the set and made his way back to the easy chair, slumped into it and eased his long legs onto the coffee table.

***

In the next room, Scott pulled back the drapes and stared out of the window. A few people were strolling into the hotel. The view was nothing to talk about—office buildings, their numerous windows lighting up the night sky and, further in the distance, shops, closed for the night, their signs flashing buy…buy…buy. He let go of the drapes and turned to Amanda, who was asleep on the sofa. She'd discarded that cut-up bloodied top, showered, put on a pair of hotel pajamas and robe. Her face was still pale. A doctor at the hospital had tended to her superficial injuries. They'd heal in a matter of weeks, but the psychological ones would take a lot longer.

What Delensky and Pozzani had put her through gnawed at him, made him feel guilty that he was not there fast enough to save her.

His heart constricted at the image of her in that decaying house. She was safe now and he would protect her always: if she'd let him.

The sounds from the Laurel and Hardy movie playing in the next room seemed louder now.

Amanda's eyes opened. "I must have drifted off."

"You needed it," he said as he crossed the expanse of carpet, picked up their chicken and fries containers from the coffee table, and deposited them in the waste basket nearby. The officer called Norton had brought them with him when he'd arrived. He'd said he figured they might be hungry. Somehow, with the smell of fried chicken wafting from the package, Amanda's and his appetites had returned.

Scott joined her on the sofa. He shook his head. "I have to keep looking at you to make sure you're okay. I keep seeing you the way you were back there."

She closed her eyes and shuddered.

"It's not going to be easy."

"I'll manage," she said.

"I want to help in any way I can."

"You have already. You saved my skin in Wollongong, flew over here just to help me again. I owe you."

That announcement made Scott uneasy. He didn't want her to feel like that about him. He wanted her to feel…the way he did about her. "You weren't completely defenseless with that knife."

"I can't think of anyone else who would've done as much as you." She looked into his eyes.

"I did what anyone would." He stared at those eyes the color of a blue cloudless sky and realized that he was falling for her in a big way. He wanted to feel those soft full lips against his, and to hold her again. However, she was not ready for that, she had to recover.

Amanda reached up and tentatively ran her fingers against the rough stubble of bristles on his jaw. His pulse quickened but he didn't respond.

`How did you get to San Francisco so fast? I flew out of Sydney with you on the ground, waving me off."

Scott was relieved when, moments after she'd touched his face, she'd let her hand drop. He was making it as easy as possible for her not to feel scared at any natural gesture she might make towards him. It didn't matter if it took months before he could make love to her. Those invisible wounds had to heal first. "Houdini I'm not. I caught the next flight out."

"You had it all planned?"

"No, I decided after I saw you off. I drove out of the car park, then circled back and booked the next flight. Went home, got my passport and threw some things in a bag. I was lucky, the visa was still okay to use from my racing trip nearly a month ago. I did my best to ignore the damage to the house." He shook his head.

"You have to send me the repair bill," she said.

"Some of it I'll probably fix myself. Anyway, the more I thought about you going to see Dorian, the more I was sure that you could be walking into a trap. If Delensky or What was that other thug's name?"

"Silvio Pozzani."

"Well, if they really wanted Dorian dead, they would have finished the job before you could get there. I wish I could've stopped that gutless scum from kidnapping you.

"Delensky's in jail where he can pay for taking three lives," she said.

"What?"

"My mother, Brian, and Estella, the Campbells' ex-maid. He boasted to me...about killing Estella, and I have no reason to disbelieve him. Boasted about getting rid of...of...Brian. Oh God, I wish I'd known him. Just spoken to him once." She blinked away the tears. Was it ever going to get any easier to bear?

"Killing means nothing to Delensky." Scott thumped the cushion in anger.

"I...I...could've been next." Her voice quivered.

"It's over."

"It isn't for me yet."

"You're safe now. He...they can't get you. That scum's behind bars and there's two policemen outside protecting us 'till they find Pozzani."

She looked up. "I know. I just can't help it."

He wanted to take her into his arms but didn't. "It's going to take time."

"I keep thinking about the way I spoke to Estella before I left to see you. Maybe if I'd believed her, if I'd listened."

"You didn't know. Don't blame yourself, blame him." He sucked in a breath. "That twisted pyscho murdered my brother in cold blood. I'll never forget. I have to live with that."

"So do I." She wiped away a tear.

"Sorry." He squeezed her hand. "We won't talk about it."

"One day soon, I want you to tell me all about him," Amanda said.

"By the morning they should have caught Pozzani, then we can be free of these cops."

He jumped up. "I'm feeling a little caged up in here." He shoved his hands into his pockets and strode past one of the two single beds to the window, pulled aside the drapes and stared, past the twinkling lights from offices, shops and cars, into himself. His short stint in the Army; like the other blokes he'd had a girl near the base, then when he left for civilian life, there'd been a few more. However, none of them had affected him this way and there'd been a few in his thirty-two years of living.

Then Amanda was there behind him, kneading his shoulders. "You're so tense. Is that better?"

How did she creep up so quickly? His breathing quickened. "Thanks. Enough."

"Scott."

He let go of the drapes and swung round. She was a step away. "What?" His pulse thrummed.

"Talk to me."

"I need to go for a walk." However, he didn't move. He just stared back knowing he was drowning.

She leaned forward.

But he stepped back.

Amanda stared at him. "What's wrong?"

"You've been through a lot," he said. "I guess I need some sleep and so do you. It's been a long day."

He wanted her, and he thought he might love her, and he was willing to wait for as long as it took for her sake.

"Goodnight, Scott," she said.

CHAPTER 45

Morning sunlight slanted through the window as Amanda stared at the gift that the two officers had brought with them at the start of their shift only moments ago. The inscription on the tag read… *Dear Amanda, Hope you're okay now. Dorian.*

They told her a courier had left it at the station a couple of hours ago. The officer said that it had been opened and checked there first. She slipped off the paper and bow that were already hanging loose. "Chocolates."

"Aren't you going to have one?" Scott said as she replaced the lid.

"Normally you can't stop me. But I don't have much of an appetite today. You have one." She was too uptight with Silvio still on the loose.

"Maybe later."

She put them down on the bed, as her phone beeped.

It was a text from Anna.

'Hi, Funny face. What u been up 2? No speak too long. lul Anna xx.

She texted her best friend. 'Hi Anna. Got KIDNAPPED. Bastards in jail. Safe now but pretty shaken up. Speak soon. lul Amanda xx'

'Shit. Give me a heart attack. R u hurt? What happened? Glad to hear bastards in jail. Hope ur ok. Give me a call soon. Sending u hugs. lul Anna xx.'

Amanda would speak with Anna when she was up to talking about what had happened. She put down her mobile and paced to the interconnecting rooms and back. The police officers were drinking coffee in the other room. "Can you tell me what's happening? Has Silvio Pozzani been caught yet?"

The square-shouldered female officer leaned forward from the sofa. "We've circulated descriptions of him at all the exit points to the country, ma'am."

The next time Amanda paced in, she said, "I wish they'd let us know what's happening."

The officer's cell erupted with a sharp trill.

Amanda jumped, her nerves still on edge.

"Hey," the male officer said. "Yeah. Nothing's happening here. Yeah. Yeah. Look can you put the lady in the picture. She's getting restless."

Scott walked through the connecting door and stood, hands in pockets, next to Amanda. "Who's on the-"

"Hart." The officer handed the cell to Amanda.

"Has Delensky confessed to the murders?"

"You mean of Mrs. Campbell and Ms. Periuz? Our investigations are still continuing in both cases."

"What do you mean? You've got Jean's killer now."

"Perhaps we have."

"Why aren't you certain?"

"I didn't indicate that. I'm sorry. I can't discuss it."

Amanda watched the officer pour himself another coffee. "Have you found Pozzani?"

"We've got zilch on him, and we've pulled out all the stops on this one. He's either gone to ground or already left the country. I asked Delensky and-"

"What did he say?"

Hart sighed. "He's not talking."

"I don't even have a photograph of Silvio I can give you. He saw to that." She told him how Pozzani had, accidentally on purpose, dropped her camera and it was crushed under the wheel of a car.

"Sure was a smart move on his part. Anyway, I told Delensky I'd throw the book at him if he didn't cooperate but that still didn't work. I know he's protecting Pozzani. We can't make him talk."

She gripped the receiver. "Let me try."

"After what Delensky put you through? You're out of your goddamned mind."

"I want more than anything else to see Pozzani behind bars. The man's evil."

"I think you'll be wasting your time with Delensky. And putting yourself through needless pain. We're bound by the law to protect you. I don't think we can let you do this."

She persisted.

Hart's tone seemed to be full of reluctance. "Release forms will need to be signed. And Delensky may not want to do this."

"I want to see him put away for a long time."

"Let me see if it can be done."

CHAPTER 46

Hart trudged into the hospital room, two faces turned to him. Campbell—his color had returned—was sitting up, the tubes and machines were gone. Cohen was perched on a chair at his bedside. Hart was pleased the lawyer was here. It would save him a visit to his office.

"Good morning, I was notified that Mr. Campbell is well enough to make a statement today."

"The security guard told me you'd be coming," Dorian said.

"I'll record this interview then it'll be typed up and presented to you for your signature." Hart unwrapped a stick of gum, and popped it into his mouth. He pulled out his voice recorder, placed it on the bedside table, and stated the time and date. "Now tell me what you remember of the accident."

Ten minutes later Hart had enough to charge Delensky with attempted murder. Then there were the other charges he would slap on that son-of-a-bitch—kidnapping, fraud and the murder of that security guard at the Campbell-Beare Pharmaceutical Company last year, the theft along with it— and the list of crimes the Australian authorities had waiting for him when he finally left the confines of the US jails.

In addition, there was the murder of the Campbell maid. However, they had yet to find her body.

Amanda Blake told him how blatantly Delensky had boasted— probably thought Blake would not live long enough to tell anyone— and that psychopath had not admitted to any of it so far. Ricardo Periuz had been right to be alarmed about his sister's disappearance. He'd informed Ricardo about their suspicions concerning Ms. Periuz. One of the duties he dreaded. "So that's it. That's all you can remember?"

"Yes. I don't think I've left anything out. Is that enough to charge him?" Dorian asked.

"Don't worry. He's going to prison for a long time, with your evidence and Miss Blake's."

"But she wasn't there," Dorian said.

"No. She was kidnapped by Eddie Delensky," Hart said.

"Who? Why?" Dorian and Cohen said in puzzled unison.

The detective told them that the police had found Brian's body in Darwin, about Delensky assuming his identity.

"That's why Bri...Delensky tried to run me down."

"So the body was positively identified as Brian McMahon? Cohen asked.

Hart nodded.

"I never liked that mother-fucking imposter from the start." Dorian leaned forward, his blankets slipping sideways. "What happened to Amanda?"

Hart told them briefly about the abduction, of Delensky's capture, the real identity of Guy Robertson, Silvio Pozzani. In addition, of Pozzani's escape.

"Where is she now? Is she going to be okay?" Campbell asked.

"She's under guard until Pozzani's found and apprehended."

"So why haven't you questioned Delensky about him?" Lionel asked.

"He won't talk."

"Jean died thinking this Delensky guy was Brian," Dorian said.

"I don't believe Mrs. Campbell was completely fooled. That's why she wrote to Scott McMahon, to find out certain things about Brian. Then she probably tripped up Delensky with the information. I'm reasonably sure now that's why Mrs. Campbell drafted a new will."

Ashen-faced, Cohen blustered, "That's not possible. It can't be the reason."

"Delensky nearly succeeded with his deception, but for Amanda Blake's persistence to search for the truth."

Dorian's eyebrows drew together. "My half-sister's one hell of a girl."

"Now you have the person who murdered Jean and you can wrap

up the case," Cohen said.

"Maybe, and maybe not." He stared at Cohen. "You see. The cyanide could have been in that bottle of mouthwash for days. There are two things that lead me to believe Delensky may not have killed Jean, it could have been someone with another motive. You wouldn't have any ideas of who it might be, would you?"

Cohen jumped from his chair, nearly tipping it over. "Why would I?"

"Dorian. Did you find out who donated their blood to you?"

"I was told the person insisted on remaining anonymous."

Cohen was not quick enough to disguise the fleeting signs of alarm in his eyes.

"Strange, isn't it, how quickly a donor was found," Hart said.

Cohen jerkily shoved his hands into his trouser pockets. "What are you going on about? All this baloney over a blood donor. Does it really matter? The important thing is that it saved Dorian's life."

"How well did you know Dorian's mother?" Hart asked.

Cohen's forehead glistened with nervous sweat. "She died a long time ago. What does it matter?"

Dorian glanced at Cohen, puzzled.

"Please answer the question."

"But I don't see what it has to do with this case," the lawyer said.

Hart smiled. "I'm tidying up loose ends. Housekeeping, you might call it. I can visit you at your office if you prefer."

"Eh. Well, Murray was the one who engaged my services while she was still alive."

"Didn't you and his first wife attend the same university?"

"But I hardly knew her then."

"Thank you, Mr. Campbell." Hart raised his hand as a goodbye gesture. "It was a pleasure to see you here today, Mr. Cohen. It's saved me considerable time."

Cohen's forehead creased with worry. "I did?"

"More than you'll ever know."

***

The two wardens and Hart led Amanda through to the room where a pretext call had been set up.

She shivered as she entered, as if an arctic wind had blown in—but the late morning sun filled every corner with its warmth, and summer was only weeks away—it couldn't have been possible.

"Any time you want to end this, all you have to do is hang up," Hart said as he sat beside her.

She pulled out the chair. The sound of its legs scraping on the tiled floor echoed against the walls. She sank onto it. There was nothing to do but wait until the allotted time, which added to her nervousness. The urge to go now before she had to speak to him again almost overtook her and she jumped up and strode to the small barred window.

"You okay?" the detective asked.

"Yes!" Amanda stared at the golden elm outside, its apple green leaves glowing in the warm afternoon sun.

He looked at his watch. "It's time," he said as the phone rang.

He nodded which indicated that she should pick up. The call was being taped so she didn't have to worry about remembering what he said.

She took a few deep breaths. Even though walls separated them, the thought that he was so near scared her so much that she wanted to run from the building. Her mouth went dry as she tried to speak.

"Hello, Amanda," Eddie said.

This was the man that, in Scott's words, so closely resembled Brian. The Brian she would never know. The living, breathing human Delensky had extinguished, her brother, her twin.

"Do you want to talk to me or not?"

Torn between love for the brother she'd lost and loathing for this person speaking to her, she hesitated for a moment. This devil had taken her mother's life, as well…oh God. Sickened at being in the same space as him, she gripped the armrest, her knees knocking. Her fear overshadowed her hatred for him and combusted inside her.

Over and over, she told herself that he could not hurt her here.

"Are you there, Amanda?"

She took another deep breath, to allow time for the inner turmoil to ease. "Eddie."

The name burst out from her as if it was a vile thing of which she had to rid herself.

"They told me you wanted to speak with me. After what I did, I can't understand why. What do you want? An apology? Is this some stupid idea of yours to make everything better?" he asked.

His words thudded at her. The smart-assed answer was just the impetus she needed. Her fear subsided. Hate rose and welled inside her. "You rob people of their lives and you think one word can mend that? You destroyed my family. I'll never forgive you. Apologize!" she took a steadying breath. "That's a useless word for you."

"Look, I was caught up in trying to get enough cash to pay back what I owed to Pozzani and...his boss," he said.

"Shit, I'd hate to imagine what you'd do if you were in a real fix."

"I was."

.She expelled a pent up breath. "Who is Pozzani really? Besides trying to kill me, what else was he doing in San Francisco?"

"You're more stupid than I thought if you think I'll tell you anything."

"Scared of Pozzani, are you?"

"I didn't say that," he said. However, the confident note in his voice had gone.

Amanda settled back. "If you can't tell me what he was doing here at least tell me where he is?"

"I'm hanging up."

"You're interested only in saving your own selfish skin. He could be still after me. I can't go anywhere without a guard."

"So that's all you're worried about."

"Was it you and Silvio that organized to have that semi-trailer try to run me down?"

He was silent.

"I suppose that nurse and the thug who tried to kill me at the hospital were also hired by both of you."

"Are you finished? Because I am. Take me back." He said to someone.

It must have been him. He didn't ask any questions, because he already knew. "Who organized the murder of that nurse?"

"What? What nurse? What murder?"

"That blonde Cindy…Cindy someone: the nurse at the hospital who attended to my cuts and bruises. There was a news flash on the TV while I was in Sydney. Channel Seven I think it was…something about her body being found."

"No. No. Not Cindy," he cried. "It can't be. Tell me. I want to know now. Tell me!"

Got him, she thought with surprise. "She was found in Sydney harbor. Her throat had been cut." Could she use this to her advantage? Cindy must be the only person he cared for.

"No…no." He moaned. "Not Cindy my Cindy! I told him to leave her alone. Pozzani didn't listen, he didn't listen."

She could hear a noise. It sounded like he was scraping back a chair. At last, Amanda knew she had the upper hand.

"I'll tell you where you can find Pozzani. He's…No…I can't do it."

"Don't you want to get Pozzani for what he did to Cindy? He used you. He had Cindy's throat cut."

"Shut-up. Shut-up."

"She's dead because of him."

"Stop it!" He screamed. "Stop."

"That scum had her dumped in the harbor. She was the only person that cared about you." She was amazed at the emotion he was showing for this woman.

"Cindy...Cindy," he sobbed.

When he'd calmed down he spoke, his voice, flat. "I'll tell you. What have I got to live for anymore? The only woman I've ever loved is gone. Silvio's got connections with the Hands of Luck Casino in Las Vegas. That's the only place he'd head for."

Her stomach tightened at what she had to ask next. "What about the letters in the safe from Jean for Brian and me?"

"I went looking for the will and found them as well. That lawyer was so careless. I barely even had to hide to get a good look at the combination for the safe. I couldn't let you see those letters. Jean had added stuff about me in yours. Stuff that would have told you just how suspicious she was of me."

"Did she…?" Amanda paused unable to say the words. "Did she write about her feelings for me?"

"Yeah. I can't remember what."

Amanda wanted to scream abuse at him. That letter which meant so little to him meant so much to her.

Disgusted, she rose. "What about Estella? Are you going to tell them where her body is? Ricardo would want to give her a decent burial."

"I don't know what you're talking about. No one can pin that one on me."

"But you-"

"Like I said, she's got nothing to do with me."

Eddie must have moved his chair again. "Life's a shit anyway."

"You scumbag." She stared down at the table, spent from her efforts.

CHAPTER 47

Cohen had gone from the hospital straight to his office. He now sat motionless at his desk. He stared past the highly polished wood, the expensively carpeted room, the two Picassos on the walls. They were the trappings of his successful practice. All this was choking, stifling, him. He pulled his silk tie from his collar. The appointment book lay open at today's date.

Appointments and more appointments; the first was due in half an hour. He buzzed his assistant. "Cancel everything for today and the rest of the week. I'm going away."

He heard a swift intake of breath at the other end. "But, Mr. Cohen, your client is due in soon. He'll be most upset."

Lionel switched off the intercom without answering.

Five years. Five of the best years of his life, he'd had with Felicity, and now she had deserted him.

Last night when sleep didn't come, which was nothing unusual, since…since…he did not want to think about that, never wanted to think about it. Instead, he had reflected about his mistakes with Felicity. He should have seen it coming. The past months, she'd been more demanding sexually, and he had been more pathetically flaccid. In the beginning, she'd been very understanding. He had thought the love they had for each other would endure and eventually he would overcome that limp problem. She was not willing to wait, was she? In the early hours, he realized something that had been there but he had not wanted to acknowledge. Felicity had never loved him the way he loved her.

Above all, his son was the most important person in his life, after him, Felicity. Neither of them really cared about him. He'd made a mess of everything. No one loved him. No one wanted him. No one cared.

CHAPTER 48

"Mel Hart?" the heavier of the two suited men asked. The other was standing easy, eyes taking in everything. They had just flashed some ID's at the officer at the front desk, walked down the narrow corridor and into the heart of the Monterey City Police Department, crossed the desk-cluttered expanse of worn carpet then stopped beside Hart's seated figure.

Heads turned.

Hart slammed down the phone next to the crowded tray on his battered desk and looked up.

"Good afternoon," the other one with a round face said. "We need to speak to you about a case you're on."

"Where did you say you're from?"

"FBI," he said, flashing his card with the name Brian Tarpan. "We're pleased you invited us in on this one."

"I didn't." Hart frowned. They were adding to the clutter already in the room, and he wasn't fond of this clutter.

They smiled benignly.

Three detectives walked past glancing curiously at the interlopers. The afternoon crew was buzzing around; and if they weren't before, they were now. A printer somewhere began its mechanical whine.

The heavier one extended a hand, which Hart ignored. Then the man introduced himself as McCreedie.

"Can I see your file on the Campbell woman?" Tarpan asked.

"Jeez. It's here somewhere." Hart shuffled the papers and folders around on his desk, some slipped to the floor and he scooped them up. "Can't seem to locate them, boys. Can you come back some other time when I'm not so busy?"

Round face leaned over the desk. "Are you trying to obstruct the course of justice? Because if you are-"

"Hold it. I didn't say you couldn't have them. I just can't locate them." He'd started this and he was going to finish it. No one was going to march in and swipe this case from under his nose.

Hart caught the guarded glance from his partner across the room.

"Why haven't you put it into the computer files yet?" Tarpan asked.

"Computers. Goddamned contraptions. Anyway, I haven't had time." That was partly true; which was just as well, they wouldn't be taking over without them.

"Well from here on we're taking over the case," McCreedie said.

"I was doing just fine."

"What with that felon Silvio Pozzani on the run, murder, and the Delensky fraud. And we have reason to believe that Delensky and Pozzani were linked to the robbery at Campbell-Beare Pharmaceuticals in Denver last year."

"Time. I need just a little more time."

Tarpan glared. "The files!"

"I'll let you know just as soon as I find them."

"You'd better," round face said. Then they left.

Hart picked up the phone and dialed Las Vegas. "Hi Danny. How are you? Gee I miss those card nights we used to have."

"Still trying to make me feel guilty about moving away after all these years, huh?"

"Nah. I've moved away myself. Down to Monterey, cause the wife wants to take it easy. How's your boy? Still playing Little League?"

"He's the team captain now."

"Great. What have you got for me?"

"That bulletin you sent out to all the hospitals from San Francisco to here drew a result. This morning a doctor in Barstow reported seeing a patient with the sort of facial wound you described. By the time we got there, he was long gone. One of the plain-clothes boys we had hanging around the casino spotted Pozzani in the connecting shopping mall only an hour ago. They almost had him, but Pozzani just vanished."

"I'm on my way to the airport now."

"We've got enough men to cover it here."

"I know, but I want to be there when you catch him."

"What's this about the FBI taking over the case?" Danny asked.

"Have they been to see you too?"

"Not yet. But I hear things."

"Well, I'm a bit hard of hearing myself, as it turns out."

Their conversation over, Hart replaced the receiver and pulled out two files from under the pile of papers in his tray. He scanned the room. Everyone looked busy, or at least tried to. Hart slipped the files into his bag, and left the building.

***

"Paging Mr. Melvin Hart." The public address system at San Francisco International could barely be heard above the cacophony of voices, trolleys and other noises.

Hart shoved his ticket back into his rain jacket pocket, grabbed his overnight bag, picked his way through a group of basketball players—their jackets and bags piled beside them—and crossed the floor to the courtesy phone.

He picked up the handset.

"Can I help you, sir?" a female voice asked.

"Mel Hart. I'm being paged."

"Ah yes, just a moment. Go ahead, sir."

"Hello," Mel said.

"Have you got your cell phone on? I've been trying to ring you."

"Oh hell. It's switched off. So what's the problem?"

"There's no need for you to come," Danny said. "That goddamned slippery son-of-a-bitch has skipped. He flew out of a private airstrip in a twin engine plane heading towards Mexico over an hour ago."

"He what?" Flat-palmed, Hart hit the counter in frustration. People turned to stare.

"He'll be over the border by now. It was only through a tip-off that we found out at all."

"Thanks for letting me know. I'll call you back later."

"I'm sending you a full report."

"I'll need it." He hung up the phone.

CHAPTER 49

"Aren't you going to finish your meal?" Scott was sitting opposite Amanda.

The room service waiter had wheeled into their hotel suite a white-linen-covered table laden with their three-course lunch, their celebratory meal. Pozzani had left the country, and the officers had gone back to the station.

Amanda pushed the meat around on her plate, and shook her head. "I'm not really that hungry."

"But you've hardly touched it."

"I'm still upset about Delensky saying that he had nothing to do with Estella's death." After Amanda had come back from the call with that twisted psycho, she'd showered and changed into a red dress. However, nothing had lifted her spirits, not the meal, not Scott's attention.

"Hart'll keep digging. They'll have plenty of time to find more dirt on him. He's going to be behind bars forever. Between attempted murder and kidnapping, that's a life sentence right there." Scott poured another glass of Cabernet Sauvignon for himself. "Would you like a top up?"

"Yes." She pushed away her half-eaten plate of grilled steak and vegetables. "I just can't enjoy this food knowing Pozzani's slipped out of the country when he should be behind bars."

He reached across the table and touched her hand.

"I won't feel secure ever again knowing that he could still come after me." As his parting words echoed through her head, she repeated them to Scott. "He said... One day, Amanda, you'll look behind you and I'll be there... I don't want to spend the rest of my life watching my back." She shuddered.

"Nor would I."

"I wish...I'd never met Silvio." She would be wary of trusting people so quickly. It had cost Brian his life and very nearly her own.

269

"Tell me about Brian." Even if it still hurt, she had to start somewhere. By knowing more about him, it might ease her pain.

He sat contemplating for a moment. "Where do you want me to start?"

"Tell me what was special about him."

"Let me think…as a kid, he was always bringing strays home. If it wasn't a dog, it would be a cat. One time he snuck a duck into the house. He loved animals. Another time it was a joey he'd found on his way to school. He used to keep it in an old cotton sack 'till it was old enough to fend for itself."

"Anyway, he'd run home from school at lunchtimes to bottle feed it. When it was old enough, it hopped into the bush and we never saw it again. Mum had a hell of a time trying to keep the numbers down, giving the cats and dogs away to neighbors," he said.

"I have a soft spot for strays too. But I didn't dare bring any home." She stood, and took a deep breath as sadness welled up inside her. "Did you two fight?"

He went to the window. "Hell. We never stopped fighting. That is, until mum and dad died. That's what made us so close."

"At least you had someone to fight with. I never did. I grew up wishing I had a brother or sister." Her brother had lived and died, and she'd not shared a single moment with him. He might have been there for her when she'd broken her leg on the first day in high school. He might have been there congratulating her when the photo she'd entered in an international competition won first prize for best wildlife shot. She buried her head in her hands.

He turned to her. "Talking about Brian is tearing you apart."

She shook her head and tried to smile.

"Amanda, it's me, Scott, you're trying to convince, not some stranger who doesn't know you. Okay, I know we haven't known each other for years, but after all that we've been through, it seems like we have.

"I have a stack of family photos. I'll show them to you when we're back home."

"I can't wait to get back to normal."

"In small ways he is you. Certain gestures, your smile."

"How can you stand it? It's hard enough for me," she said.

Scott stepped closer. "It's you I see here now. And I know what you've been through. I won't make any demands."

"Kiss me. I want you to make me feel real again."

The seconds ticked by. Scott seemed frozen. Then he pulled her into his arms. "I just don't want scare you."

"Just kiss me."

"God you're impatient." Then he drew her against the full length of him, pushing his fingers into her hair.

The image of Silvio momentarily intruded, and then was gone, as Scott kissed her hair, her neck, and her mouth.

She abandoned herself in the sensation of his lips against hers, her hands exploring his wide shoulders, his thick auburn hair.

He groaned as they parted. He trailed kisses from her earlobe, and along her neck then back to her waiting lips.

Her heartbeat kept time with his as his hands caressed her breasts through the fabric. His thumbs drew lazy circles against her nipples.

"I want more of you. You're sending me crazy." He ran his hands over her shoulders and down her arms. "Are you sure about this?"

"Don't stop."

Scott closed the curtains and then unzipped her dress. She stepped back and allowed it to slide to the floor.

His arms enfolded her. When he kissed on her neck and her shoulders a quicksilver of feelings coursed through her. He picked her up, and carried her to the bed. Then he slipped off his jeans and t-shirt, and joined her.

He whispered to her. "Amanda, touch me."

His hair was springy on his chest, and it felt right. At the same time, his fingers traced lines along the edges of her bra. Then he pulled gently at the fabric.

"Don't do that." She froze, her desire gone. She did not like him doing that. It was what Pozzani's had done. She pushed him away.

The memory of that night swamped her. The smells of that decaying house returned with an intensity. His evil face loomed, his hands pawed, his repulsive body ground against hers. "No. Get away from me. Don't hurt me." She tried to fight him off, her arms flailing. Harder, she struggled. "Stop it. Let me go," she screamed.

Minutes passed before she came back to reality.

Scott stared at her. She was in the Albert Hotel suite.

"Amanda, I'm so sorry."

Breathing hard, as if she'd run a marathon, she doubled over. "It's me. It's not your fault. I can't...I can't help it." Tears welled up and spilled over. She reached out to him.

He cradled her in his arms. "It's okay. You're safe. Delensky's in jail. Pozzani's gone for good."

"I feel stupid." She blew her nose.

"You're only human, and after what you've been through. Jeez, I don't know how I would be, probably worse."

"Keep holding me, please."

Scott drew in a breath. "The trouble is I don't want to stop. Get your dress on."

Why did she have to go and spoil it all? Scott was the best thing she'd come across. More than that, she wanted him, but the horror at that place haunted her. She did not want to spend all of her nights alone.

Early this morning she'd woken up screaming. Scott had been there to comfort her. She needed him for all those reasons and more. Independence was great, but it was empty. She realized now that she wanted someone to share her highs and lows. She needed someone to help pull her through the cycle of anorexia that was taking over her life again. She was scared that she couldn't stop it.

She stretched out and kissed his shoulder. "Sorry."

"It's not your fault."

"I really want to. I just don't think I'm ready yet. Can we try again sometime?" She trembled, fearing rejection.

He didn't answer.

She half expected he would jump up, and leave. He sat so silent and still, it was as if he'd turned to stone.

Amanda kissed him, a tentative soft press of her lips against his.

When it was over he said, "I know it's difficult for you."

"Please."

He swung around and captured her to him. "I've got to be mad or in love. I can't work out which."

Her heart somersaulted. Love? Did he mean it? She did not want to ask and spoil this moment. She smiled and ruffled his auburn hair as he pulled her down, and rolled against her.

"I'll get over this eventually."

"Let's not worry about it today."

He held her until they both fell asleep.

CHAPTER 50

After speaking to the owner of the Hands of Luck Casino, Silvio Pozzani hung up the phone in the fifth floor suite of the Mitchell Hotel. He'd guessed that Delensky would tell the cops about his connection with the casino and his plan had worked. The cops had already interviewed that doctor in Barstow, who was on the take, and had swarmed around the casino after they'd received a tip-off that he was supposed to be there. Too bad for them that he hadn't gone near the place. Nor had he left the country. The casino owner didn't like the heat, but he owed Del Condio and him a few favors.

He picked up his binoculars, then walked to the window, edged them through the slit in the heavy drapes, and stared across the street to the fifth floor window of the Albert Hotel. It was Amanda and Scott's suite.

The box of chocolates had worked. They'd led him to Amanda.

She'd been pacing the room before. Then he'd seen her talking on the phone.

He'd been worried when he saw her leave with the cops later that morning. He'd thought that she wouldn't return. But a hunch had made him wait; he hadn't seen Scott leave. He figured while that imbecile was here she'd be back. He'd been right.

Silvio glanced down at the entrance to the Albert. Earlier, the two cops had left; none had come to take their place. He guessed they'd been called off after they'd been told he'd left the country.

Now Scott was caressing her. Bitch. He could almost taste her mouth against his own. She had never kissed him like that. Bitch.

He was getting hard just thinking about what he'd do to her. It would be nice and slow, and she'd cater to his every fantasy before he killed her.

He saw Scott draw the curtains. The asshole was going to lay her.

Pozzani touched his wound. Stitched and covered with gauze, it wasn't throbbing so much now. She wasn't going to get away with doing this to him. "I'll have you yet, Amanda," he rasped.

CHAPTER 51

Hart, shoulders hunched, clutching two sandwiches, trudged past the interrogation room. Inside the perpetrator's voice rose, fell, and cajoled as he tried to leverage his way out of his predicament. Most perps never learned and they were back again all too soon.

His stomach grumbled and the gum he was chewing did nothing about solving that problem. It was way past his normal lunchtime. Damn, that son-of-a-bitch Pozzani. At least they had Delensky.

"Hi, Mel," Shulton said from somewhere behind him.

Hart waited from him to catch up.

"That Blake dame we were minding was surprised to receive the box of chocolates from Dorian Campbell."

"What are you talking about?" He continued along the corridor, nodding a greeting to workmates he passed.

Shulton slowed his stride to keep level with the detective. "The gift-wrapped chocolates were delivered by a courier to our front desk first thing this morning. The note said they were for Amanda Blake."

Hart stopped abruptly in the doorway to the squad room and stared at the man. "What?"

"The morning shift took them over when they came to relieve us. Don't be so alarmed. They'd already opened the box first even though it was from family."

"Did you check with Dorian Campbell that he'd actually sent them?"

"No."

"You should have! Or at least checked with me before you took them over." He had to stop himself from grabbing the man by the shoulders, and shaking some sense into him. "Campbell couldn't have sent them. He didn't find out about her being kidnapped or that she was being guarded 'till much later this morning. I know that because I was the one who told him."

"How was I to know?"

"You ask! Now we have to find out if the Blake woman and McMahon ate any." His midsection tightened.

"Poison?"

Hart nodded. "Or someone wanted to find out where Blake was holed up. Either way, I'm goddamned uneasy."

For a heavyset man Hart moved quickly when he wanted to. He crossed the desk-cluttered room to his workplace, and called the Albert Hotel.

"So who do you think sent them?" Shulton asked.

"My guess is they're a parting gift from Pozzani." The phone kept ringing.

"Oh, if you're wanting that Blake woman, the last I heard, she was planning to go shopping with Scott McMahon," Shulton said.

Hart slammed down the receiver. "Where?"

"I don't know."

It was all Hart could do to stop himself from screaming at Shulton. He redialed. The bell desk told him that they were holding luggage for Ms. Blake and Mr. McMahon. He called off.

"Get back to the hotel and find those chocolates. Get them sent to the lab. Then try to find Blake and McMahon. And let's hope they haven't eaten any."

CHAPTER 52

Gina Carouso stepped off the Carmel bus and pushed up her umbrella against heavy drops of rain, which had started to splash the sidewalk. When there was a pause in traffic, she hurried across to a metal gate set back from the street

She stopped and searched her purse for the keys. When she found them, she unlocked the gate and walked into a small paved courtyard at the front of Mr. Cohen's house.

She shook off her wet umbrella and put it beside the door. She unlocked the door and then paused to listen for any sign that Mr. Cohen was home. He didn't usually come home for lunch, but only last week he'd been here. And since he hated her to make any noise while he was around, she'd had to make herself a coffee and wait until he'd left.

The house was still, so Gina changed from her tennis shoes into slippers, and put her bag beside the narrow curiosity table by the door. She stared at the two envelopes on it and then picked them up. One was addressed to Dorian Campbell and the other to a Detective Hart at the Monterey City Police Department. Strange that Mr. Cohen had forgotten to take them. It was so unlike the well-organized employer she knew. She wondered if she should mail them for him. Perhaps he had left them there for a reason. She put them back and continued along the plush carpeted hallway to the cupboard that contained the long hose for the built-in vacuum system.

Gina pulled out the hose connections, some cloth dusters and a mop, but couldn't find the bucket. It didn't matter; Mr. Cohen had a couple of fishing buckets in the garage. She'd get one from there when she got around to mopping the kitchen and bathroom floors.

Two hours later, with the vacuuming and dusting done, she went in search of a bucket. She padded across the terrazzo tiles in the cedar-paneled kitchen to the family room, skirted the glass-topped table, and tut-tutted at the pile of legal folders strewn across it. Even the leather couch had folders on it. What had happened to the meticulous man for whom she cleaned? Now that her employer wasn't seeing that woman anymore, he was always working.

The internal door to the garage was tight. She put her mop against the wall and gave the handle an extra hard yank. She went down the two steps into the garage.

Then she saw him.

Mr. Cohen's body hung from a thick rope secured to the wooden framework in the ceiling.

Somewhere someone screamed. The noise disturbed her thoughts so much that she couldn't clear her mind. Then through the fog in her brain she realized, that she was making that noise.

She clamped her mouth shut and covered her eyes to shield her gaze from the sight of his purple engorged face, his staring eyes and his dangling suited body.

Backing off, she repeatedly made the sign of the cross. Beads of sweat formed on her skin. Gina bolted back into the family room.

Where was the phone? She'd been cleaning this house for four years now, but in her panic she couldn't think. She scanned the room.

Then she saw it on the kitchen bench. She rushed over, and with a shaking hand, picked up the phone. Numbed with shock, Gina stared at the buttons.

Moments later, without being aware if she'd punched in a number or not, a voice was talking to her.

"...help you? This is 911. What is your emergency?"

"Mr. Cohen. Please hurry. Hanging. Garage... Carmel." She began sobbing and slid to the floor.

CHAPTER 53

Hart stared at the cadaver in the body bag as the officer zipped it up. There was no need to investigate any further. The note from Cohen, addressed to him, said it all. Its contents hadn't been a surprise. He'd guessed as much days ago. Still, he couldn't fathom why someone would commit suicide. Even after all these years in this job. He slipped the letter into his pocket beside the one addressed to Dorian Campbell. That one, he'd personally deliver later.

"There's a call for you on the radio," the officer from the Carmel Police Department said.

"Thanks for calling me. I'm finished here." He threw back as he hurried outside to the Buick, popping some gum into his mouth on the way.

He eased his bulk into the cabin. "Hart here."

"Sent the chocolates to the lab. A few are missing," Shulton said.

"Did you find out where Blake and McMahon are?"

"Yeah. A department store…Golds Sixth Avenue. The Campbell chauffeur is picking them up about six from the hotel."

"Get over there now and find them. I'll meet you there."

CHAPTER 54

After the rain stopped, the sun seared the San Francisco sidewalks, drying up any puddles. The afternoon would have been even hotter if it hadn't been for the sea breeze racing up the hilly streets.

Amanda and Scott entered San Francisco's Golds Sixth Avenue. The department store was having a May Day sale and was abuzz with shoppers. In the cool of the air conditioning, women jostled each other at perfume counters and jewelry stands.

Amanda grimaced. "I hate crowds, but I do need some clothes. Let's go upstairs," she said to Scott. "We've got three hours before Ricardo picks us up."

They rode up the escalator. It was not as busy on this floor.

Amanda browsed along the racks. She picked out a couple of dresses, a top, two pairs of pants and a jacket.

She turned to Scott and held an Anne Klein dress against her. "What do you think?"

A woman stared enviously. "I wish I could fit into that."

Scott held another in his hand. "Try this one on."

"How about this?" She held up cream halter-neck dress. "It reminds me of Marilyn Monroe when she stood over that air vent."

"Very sexy." He handed her some more. "Try all these on too."

"What will I do with that many dresses, and pants? Most of the time I live in boots, jeans and tee shirts."

"Any other girl wouldn't need any encouragement."

Amanda laughed. "You win." With a dozen items over her arm, she went to the dressing rooms.

Scott waited outside.

She slipped off her dress and tried on a deep-blue one. Perfect. She'd parade this one for Scott.

Then she heard a siren. Amanda stepped from the cubicle.

***

Hart, now on his way to Golds, took a bite of his sandwich while at the traffic lights, and listened to the code 10 alert—a bomb threat—at the department store on the police scanner.

The detective threw down his sandwich, whipped out the magnetized flashing siren unit from under the seat, set it on the roof, and floored the accelerator.

Now he knew what Pozzani had planned.

The chocolates were a kind of Trojan horse. He had to get to the department store fast.

***

Amanda listened to an announcement over Golds' public address system asked shoppers to make their way to the exits. With no time to change, she grabbed her own dress. She would send the store the money for the one she was wearing.

Scott burst in. "Let's go. I heard someone say it could be a bomb threat."

They ran towards the stairs. People pushed past them. Shop staff had positioned themselves at the exits, and shouted above the noise for customers to remain calm.

Scott and Amanda joined the descending tide of customers in the airless hot stairwell.

"You okay?" Scott gave her hand a reassuring squeeze as they came out at the ground floor.

"I'll be better when we get outside."

More people spilled from the elevators. Despite the staff and security guards' efforts, people fell, others pushed, and babies cried.

"Get out of my way," a man screamed. "We're all going to die."

"Let me outtahere," a woman shouted as she shoved an earring stand out of her way.

The air conditioning was off and the place was a large airless box. Someone fainted near Amanda.

"Give him air," a man shouted.

"We should help him," she said.

Scott shook his head as sirens wailed in the distance. He held her hand as they edged past overturned cosmetic displays and perfume counters.

Suddenly pulled apart as the chaos of bodies surged toward the entrance, Amanda stood on her tiptoes to see if she could spot Scott in the sea of would be shoppers.

"Joanne? Maryjane? Where are you?" a woman shouted.

A lost child cried out for its mother. Another baby started to scream.

Policemen had cordoned off the area to traffic.

Pedestrians screamed in fear. Hampered by the barricades, they felled them and fled in every direction.

"Scott." Amanda cried.

Someone grabbed her arm. Relieved that Scott had found her, Amanda turned.

The cold eyes of a killer stared back at her.

Silvio Pozzani. A bandage covered the wound on his cheek.

Stunned by the sight of him, she let her dress fall.

"L…let go of me!" She tried to wrench herself free but the crush of people slammed her against him.

Pozzani smiled. "Keep struggling. I like it," he whispered into her hair, as he jerked her even closer to his body.

"Let go." She shoved him away. "Help me! Someone please. He's a murderer!"

He jabbed the barrel of a gun in her side.

"Shut up," he hissed into her ear. "Or you die."

She couldn't breathe. She reached for her inhaler as she slumped forwards.

Silvio wrenched her to her feet. "Don't pull any tricks. Hear!"

"I've got asthma." She drew in the medication.

One, then another person stared at her, but they hurried away. "*Help me,*" she mouthed.

Pozzani pushed her. Another male glanced at her and she hoped he would see how distressed she was, but he too hurried away.

"Where are you taking me?" She spoke with a calm she didn't feel.

"I nearly lost you in the crowd back there," he said.

"Jesus, you were stalking me."

"Yep," he said.

"You were supposed to have left the U.S." She noticed the crowd was thinning as they moved further away from the department store.

He smiled again.

"Why come back?" As soon as she'd uttered the question, she wished she'd kept silent. The not knowing would have been more comfort.

"I want the kisses you gave Scott. They were mine. You shouldn't have let him touch you."

"What?" Amanda asked.

"I watched you with him from the hotel across the road."

"You're a psycho. A real psycho!" Amanda felt violated again.

"You won't be kissing anyone after I'm finished with you. You'll be begging me to kill you."

His hand gripping her arm was suddenly more than imprisoning it was lascivious. The horror of that bedroom, trussed up like live slaughterhouse meat; he wouldn't get the chance this time. "You made that bomb threat."

He laughed a self-satisfied laugh.

That was answer enough. "You think you can get away with anything."

"Yep," he said.

Police were putting up more barricades. Loudspeakers were directing people to a safe area.

Anger at what he had done and what he might try to do bubbled away inside her.

They were a block and a half away from Golds now, the crowd was dispersing.

She slowed her pace deliberately as she looked for an opportunity to escape.

"Move 'till I say stop," he snarled, as his hand shackled her.

"You're hurting me."

A policeman stared at her for a moment and she mouthed the word, "help." The cop screwed up his face in query before he moved on. He hadn't understood her.

The spark of hope that swelled inside her, shriveled. Her body sagged in bitter disappointment.

"Don't get any ideas," he said to her as he jabbed her side with the barrel.

As they neared a crossing, she saw Scott on the opposite side, scanning the area for her.

The lights flashed WALK as they went by.

Scott stepped onto the road with the rest of the pedestrians. She prayed he would see her. "Scott," she shouted.

"Told you, bitch."

He jerked her so hard that she stumbled and nearly fell except that he had hold of her arm. She was gasping now as her lungs tightened. Pozzani dragged her by a newsstand, her face plastered on the front page of all the newspapers—the heading—Heiress abducted and kept in a shack.

"Keep moving."

She reached for her puffer.

He jammed the barrel hard at her side again. "Don't get smart again."

They turned into a side street. She stumbled up the incline, past a cafe, then a florist. Flowers from barrows, seemingly spilling onto the street, but the only scent she could smell was her own fear.

"Where are you taking me?"

He shoved her towards a parked Mercedes Benz. "On a holiday, you stupid bitch."

"Amanda!"

Scott's voice came from somewhere behind them.

Amanda glanced back and saw Scott more than half a block away and the detective farther back.

Scott broke into a run. "Let her go!"

In the seconds that Silvio was distracted, Amanda jerked away.

Pozzani lunged for her.

Hart shouted something but she couldn't make out what it was.

"Help!" She fell between two parked cars.

Silvio tried to wrench her to her feet.

"Get off of me." She tore free. With one hand she lashed out with her nails at his face—with the other, she threw a handful of gutter dirt into his eyes. Blinded, he fired: the bullet whistled past her cheek. She jabbed upwards at his gun and knocked it from his grasp. It fell onto the road and cars ran over the weapon.

"Bitch." Blinking dust from his eyes Pozzani pushed her toward the oncoming cars. Amanda punched his wounded arm. He cried out as he fell, grabbing for her. She stumbled backwards screaming and crashing to the ground with him.

"Mandy," Scott cried.

Amanda didn't look to see where Scott was. She shoved Silvio hard and he rolled further onto the road, and started to rise.

Then Scott was there lifting her to safety.

A Ford slammed into Silvio, lifting him like a rag doll onto the hood. The car skidded to a halt. Her would-be abductor tumbled onto the road, horns blared, cars screeched, the air smelt of hot rubber.

Silvio, sprawled in the middle of the road, lay very still.

CHAPTER 55

Scott cradled Amanda's shaking body in his arms. "It's over."

"Hold me. Just hold me." Amanda glanced up. Two paramedics were carrying Pozzani, his face covered by an oxygen mask, to the ambulance.

Hart was snapping out orders to a couple of officers who were guarding Pozzani. The officers followed the stretcher into the ambulance.

"I thought he was dead. I wanted him dead. I wanted him dead," she said.

"So did I," Scott said. "If he'd hurt you, I'd have hunted him down." Then he took her hand in his. "I love you. I think I've known since the first time we met."

Words she needed to hear. Before Amanda could respond, Hart joined them. She touched Scott's arm instead.

"Pozzani will be charged as soon as he regains consciousness, that's if he survives. There's something else I have to tell you."

His tone implied it was unpleasant. She tensed.

"Estella Periuz's body has been found in the Los Padres National Forest."

Amanda had believed Delensky's boast from the start, but the confirmation of Estella's death shocked her all over again. "Jesus."

"We're waiting on the report from ballistics. It should prove the bullet that killed the Periuz woman was fired from Delensky's gun."

"It's got to," Amanda said. "Delensky deserves everything the courts can throw at him."

Hart nodded. "There's more than enough to lock him away for life."

"Who found her?" Amanda asked.

"A hiker. The body was covered by broken branches and leaves."

"Does Ricardo know?" she asked.

"He was in earlier today to make a positive ID. Can I offer you both a lift to the hospital?"

"I'm fine. I'm more shaken than anything else." She was still reluctant to step inside a hospital again.

A few police officers were holding back a growing crowd of curious spectators.

"You need those cuts seen to," Scott said.

"They're nothing a dab of iodine won't fix."

"Scott will be with you when the doctors at St. Euphemia's attend to you," Hart said. "I'll be there too. Then we'll go and see Dorian Campbell. I have a letter from Cohen I need to deliver to him."

"What's this all about?" Amanda asked.

"I'll explain when we're with Campbell. I think you may want to be there when he opens the letter. He'll need the support."

CHAPTER 56

Eddie walked into the day room; its walls that were once white were now gray. Two men were playing chess at the metal table and chairs screwed to the floor and two others in the far corner were playing ping-pong. He was glad to leave behind, even if it was for a short while, that drug-addled roommate and the Spanish idiot who never shut up opposite him. He was in a two-man cell but there were two metal double bunk beds, pushed up against opposite walls. There was hardly room to walk between them.

Four men, of various ages, were watching another rerun of "I Love Lucy." He sat on a metal chair, a little away from them, preferring to be alone. The gangs that permeated every inch of this place made him nervous.

Lucille Ball never stopped being funny. It would be good to have a laugh and release some of tension building inside him but the noise of the bouncing ping-pong ball was driving him nuts and he knew he couldn't tell them to quit.

Finally, the inmates packed up the paddles and he relaxed a little and enjoyed the show.

When he got up to leave, three men were waiting just inside the doorway. He hadn't noticed them enter. Where had the other prisoners gone? His stomach tightened when he saw the way two of the men slouched against the doorway and the third had something clutched in his hand.

"Let me pass," he said more softly than he intended.

"Now aren't you a pretty boy," the one with tattoos down body-builder arms said. "It gets lonely in here."

He wished that he'd been quicker to go. "I'm in for murder and kidnapping so don't mess with me."

"I'm real scared," the shortest one— who had part of a tattoo visible at the base of his neck—said as he straightened.

"What are your names?" he asked.

289

"Call me Shorty," he said as he pushed something into his pocket.

"Blondie," the third one said, still against the door jam.

He'd have to tough this out. Never show fear. He knew that from his time on the streets in Sydney when he was a teenager. Stealing and selling drugs kept him in food and somewhere to stay after he'd left Cindy's. He'd never used except for the once; he was too smart for that. And he'd never pimped; he hated the thought of it. He walked closer to the doorway, where they stood.

Tattooed Arms flexed his muscles.

Eddie tensed. "Don't you try no shit with me!"

The three men shared a glance. Shorty stepped forwards and Blondie shut the door.

Fuck. He'd been in more than a few fights over the years. He got ready for the first attack but it didn't come. They were playing with him. Blondie stepped towards the TV but Eddie didn't want to turn his head to watch him. He kept his gaze on the other two and listened hard for Blondie.

As Shorty lunged, he ducked. Then the other two moved. Blondie came from his left side, kicking. Eddie leaped sideways and went to grab a chair to steady himself but Shorty knocked him off his feet with a powerful side-kick to his knee. He tried to jump back up but Tattooed Arms went in low and slammed a fist into his stomach. Eddie groaned and sucked in air. Shorty landed a blow on his jaw but not hard enough to do any real damage. Still, the blows were adding up. Eddie punched him right back and swung round, landed a right hook to the side of Blondie's head. Blondie went down to the concrete.

Eddie lunged for the door, wrenching it open. A guard was passing and he shouted out, caught his gaze for a split second, but the guard ignored him as Shorty and Tattooed Arms grabbed him. One from the back with a headlock and the other twisted his arms painfully behind his back.

He tried to fishtail free, kicked, and shouted, but they held tight. Dragging him back in, they kicked the door closed for the second time.

Blondie got to his feet. "Son-of-a-bitch." He spat blood. "I'll make you fucking sorry you did that."

"Let's do a deal. I can make all of you rich," Eddie said, breathing hard. There had to be security cameras in here. Peripherally, he saw someone had smashed the only two in the room.

Shorty laughed and released him, and went to stand against the door. "How am I going to spend the money when I'm in here?"

"I'll give you a million to share between yourselves if you leave me alone and warn off the other prisoners." He still had four million left that he hadn't gambled or wasted of the eighteen that he'd stolen from Del Condio. He'd told Del Condio's thugs he was giving them all he had. He'd split the money into separate accounts in different banks, in Switzerland, the Cayman Islands and Austria.

Shorty said, "So where you keeping it? Buried somewhere?"

He expelled a slow breath. Maybe, this would go his way after all. "Bank. I can give you the account number. No signature needed."

"Give it up then." Tattooed Arms bent his knee and put the heel of his foot against the wall, as if he was casually waiting for someone.

"Let me pass and I'll tell you."

"Hey. We got no paper to write it down," Blondie said.

"You know where to find me if I don't come through. You can look after your family."

Blondie spat. "Got none. Stop wasting our time. We got to get back to our cells." He exchanged a glance with the other two.

They came for Eddie all at once with him kicking and punching. Eddie threw a left hook but Shorty blocked and bloodied his nose. Tattooed Arms went for his stomach again but he sidestepped and evaded the worst of the blow. Then Shorty came back with a right then a left. Eddie fell....tried to rise but Shorty punched him in the liver and he went down.

They flipped him on his stomach and Tattooed Arms started ripping and cutting off his prison blues with something sharp while the other two held him and spread his legs. He heard the opening credits of a James Bond movie on the TV.

Tattooed Arms trailed the piece of sharpened metal along his arm and then jerked it against his neck. "Keep still, hear!"

He heard a fly being unzipped and he closed his eyes.

He screamed when the first one did it and after than he just lay there trying to block out the grunting and focused on the sounds of 007 in a shoot-out.

After Shorty zipped himself up, he took over holding the metal.

He thought they'd never stop and when finally they did, he took some small solace that the rape was over.

007 was in bed with a beautiful busty brunette. He gritted his teeth with anger at the injustice of what had just happened to him.

"By the way, I have a message for you." Shorty's breath stank.

"Huh?" He went to move but Shorty still held the metal to his windpipe.

"Cindy's dead."

"Who told you this?" Eddie was glad they didn't see the tears in his eyes. Losing the only woman he'd ever loved had crushed his spirit more than he thought possible. He remembered Cindy's smile, the scent of her and the way she walked with that slight wiggle.

"Del Condio."

"Fuck." There was no escape from Del Condio's tentacles.

"Del Condio said you fucked up. No more chances."

Eddie went cold all over.

As Shorty slashed Eddie's throat he whispered, "Too bad we couldn't take your money, Del Condio would find out and then we'd be dead too."

They left him after that and he put his hands to his throat but he knew he had only moments to live. With bloody fingers, he wrote Del Condio's name on the concrete.

CHAPTER 57

Day had given way to night but in St. Euphemia's, nurses still hurried down corridors and patients buzzed for attention; a constant flux of visitors wandered in and out.

After a doctor had attended to Amanda's superficial wounds, she went with Scott and Hart to see Dorian.

When they entered he was sitting up in bed reading a magazine.

He put the magazine aside. "Hi Amanda, Hart." He glanced at Scott but didn't say anything.

"How are you feeling?" Amanda asked.

"Getting better."

She bent over and kissed him on the cheek. "This is Scott McMahon."

They exchanged greetings.

Amanda explained to Dorian what had happened to her, and that Pozzani was hospitalized and under guard. "But the best thing is Pozzani isn't expected to live."

"Just what that goddamned killer deserves," Dorian said.

Hart cleared his throat. "I have some news I have to break to the both of you." He told them about Cohen's suicide.

Dorian stared at him dumbfounded. "What? I can't believe that."

"He was rude to me the last time I saw him," Amanda said. "Was he depressed?"

Hart pulled out the letter from Cohen addressed to Dorian. "I think this will explain everything."

Dorian tore open the envelope. His hand trembled as he began to read the contents. "Fuck. This can't be true! Did you know about this, Amanda?"

"I've no idea what you're talking about."

He gave it to her. "Read it to me, please. I can't..." He slumped back against the pillow.

"It's hard to know how best to tell you something you deserved to know a long

time ago. While Murray was alive, it was difficult especially since I would have had to tell him too. Afterwards, I did not know how to approach the subject. I know these are only excuses and I am ashamed that I let them stop me from telling you. It is time you knew what your mother and I kept secret for far too long.

I only wish things could have been more amicable between us. Perhaps it might have been easier. Here I am making excuses for my failings.

You are my son.

I love you more than you will ever know.

As your father, I always wanted the best for you."

"I suspected this but then thought I was crazy to even think it," Amanda said.

"It can't be true," Dorian said.

"It is. He addressed a letter to me too," Hart said.

"Oh God. Why didn't he just tell me? Why?" Dorian thumped the bed. "I can't get my head around this. My father wasn't really my father? Son-of-a-bitch. Do you have any idea how it feels to be lied to?"

"Only too well," Amanda said.

His angry features softened a little. "Sorry, I'm completely stupid. I wasn't thinking. This has thrown me. Lionel screwed my mom. I'd put her memory on a pedestal. I thought she was better than Jean. And now...son-of-a-bitch."

Amanda continued to read aloud from the letter.

"I poisoned Jean."

"What the hell? What did he do that for?" Dorian cried.

For Amanda, this was the final blow. Bitter tears coursed down her cheeks. "I...I thought that it was Delensky who'd...killed Jean."

As she brushed away her tears, Amanda looked up at Hart. He was the only one who hadn't expressed surprise. "You knew, didn't you? You knew!" Her voice rose with pent-up fury. "For God's sake, why didn't you do something? Put him away...something?"

"I didn't have any proof...nothing that would stand up in court. I was waiting for Cohen to incriminate himself," Hart said.

"Amanda, it's not Hart's fault," Scott said, standing beside her. "Like me to read the rest?"

In agitation, Dorian jiggled his foot, which made the bed shake. "I've heard enough. Just throw the thing in the trash. I didn't think I'd care about Jean being gone but God, somehow, I do."

She wiped her eyes, and turned away from them. After a few deep calming breaths, she turned back. "We might as well know the rest."

"It was to protect you, my son, from losing your inheritance. Jean's new will would have left you so little, it should have been all yours. Upon her death, I could not trust some stranger, Amanda Blake, to be generous enough to share the estate with you. In so many ways, I justified the deed beforehand, but afterwards I was tormented. I did not know that taking someone's life would be so hard to live with. How stupid of me. Jean had trusted me and I had betrayed that trust. I'm sorry–"

Amanda folded the letter unable to finish it.

"It won't bring her back." She ignored the tears that slipped down her cheeks.

Dorian squeezed her hand. "I've been so selfish. I'm sorry."

She couldn't answer, sadness welled in her throat.

"I can't get my head around that Lionel did this for me." Dorian's voice faded to a whisper. "He must have been the anonymous blood donor?"

Hart's phone rang as he confirmed Dorian's suspicions. "Let me take this in the other room." Five minutes later, Hart returned. "Eddie Delensky is dead."

"What? How?" asked Amanda. She'd prepared herself for a long trial, years of appeals and having to look that scumbag in the face. Now she wasn't sure of what she felt. Had justice been served?

"They think this Del Condio man is behind it. It seems like Eddie owed him a lot of money."

CHAPTER 58

After Hart's departure, the trio in the hospital room had fallen silent.

Though Amanda knew she would eventually forgive Lionel, she wanted to scream obscenities at him now. No matter how Lionel had justified his action, it didn't make it any easier to accept that she no longer had a mother. Murdering bastard!

She glanced at Dorian, certain he'd heard her scream the words. He stared at his bed coverings with a stony expression.

Scott, his brow furrowed, was gazing out of the window at the starless night sky.

No one had heard her. She hadn't uttered the words at all.

Alone, she would curse, scream, and hope that would help get this frustration out of her system. Not here. Not now.

She brushed a twig from the sleeve of her new dress that looked far from new now. There were stains on the front and a tear at the side. They were a reminder of events she'd rather forget. She would never wear it again.

"It's taken a long time, but I think I get why Jean decided to cut my inheritance. She could see what I couldn't," Dorian said.

"What do you mean?" Amanda asked.

"I was an idiot to demand my trust fund money from Jean and Lionel. It was for Garth's medical expenses. He said he had AIDS. I called him earlier today and asked why he hadn't come to see me. He said...the son-of-a-bitch said he's too busy getting on with his life. He's just married some millionairess. He's twenty-five, she's sixty."

"A real gold digger."

"Garth has red patches all over his arms and legs. One of my real friends called in this morning and told me what he really had. The son-of-a-bitch has some rare form of psoriasis." His eyes glistened with humiliation as he bunched the sheet in his fist. "Blind and stupid, that's what I've been!"

Gone was the carefree arrogance he'd had when she first met him.

"He did you a favor," she said.

"You've got that right."

"You're better off without someone like that. We all make mistakes. I did with Guy...Silvio I mean."

A nurse's footsteps echoed in the corridor.

Dorian's depression seeped between the trio like a mist and clung in every corner.

"When do they let you out of this hotel?" Scott asked.

"Tomorrow afternoon." Dorian rearranged the pillows, and then leaned against them.

"Are you well enough?" Amanda asked.

"The doctor's hired some nurse to baby-sit me."

Dorian gave her a half smile and it was gone so quickly, she could have imagined it.

"I'm sure she'll be just fine." Amanda forced a smile, trying to look cheerful.

"Can I call you sister?"

"You know I hated when Bri...Eddie called me "Sis" but you can call me sister anytime." Gratitude welled in her chest. She had to get used to wearing her emotions, instead of hiding and suppressing them.

"You and Scott will be staying on for a while at the house, won't you?"

"Sorry. We're...Scott and I are leaving for Sydney after lunch tomorrow," she said.

"Why so soon?"

"Work." Scott said. "I own a car repairs workshop." He caught Amanda's hand, and squeezed it gently.

His touch sent tingles all over. "I've got an assignment waiting on the Tasmanian Rivers. The bloke supposed to be assisting me will be off on another job if I don't show up soon."

"Job? But you don't need the money now."

"I've never done this for the money. Not that I didn't need it, but I just love to get away in the wilderness. Breathe the unpolluted air.

Lose myself watching animals. I'll get off my soap box now."

"I got the picture." Dorian rolled his eyes.

Scott said. "You've got that faraway look."

"Have I?" She smiled at him and squeezed his hand before she went to sit at Dorian's bedside.

"Yeah. I'm going to be old fashioned..." Scott put his hands in his pockets.

What was going on, she thought?

"Since you're the closest thing to a brother to Amanda, is it okay if-"

"This sounds serious. Amanda hardly knows you," Dorian said.

"You haven't asked me," she was a little peeved that he had thought to tell Dorian first.

"I've made a complete mess of this. I was hoping you'd agree to be my girlfriend," Scott said.

Dorian raised an eyebrow. "This is sudden."

Amanda's cheeks were burning. "Let's not define what's between us yet. I need time to get over everything."

Scott looked crestfallen. "If that's what you want."

"Amanda's going to be very wealthy and- " Dorian said.

"I'm not after money if that's what you think. I'll back off," Scott said.

"That's right you will. I'm going to do the brother thing and advise you to take care, Amanda," he said. "I don't want to see you get hurt."

She'd ached for a brother for as long as she could remember, although he would never replace Brian. Now, tears spilled over and she was sobbing.

Scott opened his arms and she fell into them.

After a few moments, she'd composed herself enough to look up. "I'm a mess. Sorry."

"Don't apologize. You have a right to be. I'm sort of that way myself," Dorian said.

"I'm the one who should be apologizing, Amanda. I'm a complete insensitive idiot. I shouldn't have spoken about this right now," Scott said.

"Forget it," she said.

Scott glanced at her. "We should go."

She nodded, and went over and hugged her brother.

Dorian shook hands with Scott. "My sister is very dear to me. Look after her or you'll have to deal with me."

"I'll be back for the inquest. I think Cohen's partner said it was scheduled for six weeks' time. See you then," Amanda said.

"Jean's place is yours too. I'll expect you to stay with me."

"I'll go find a cab. See you, Dorian. I'll wait outside for you, Amanda."

Her brother smiled. "You're all the family I have now. I don't want to lose touch with you."

"We can email, or skype. And you can to visit me in Sydney anytime."

"I've been thinking maybe I should change courses at the end of the semester and major in economics. I want to be more involved in the running of Campbell-Beare Pharmaceuticals. What do you think?"

"If you're sure."

He shrugged. "I've been bumming around for too long."

"You've got nothing to lose by trying." She gave him a sisterly hug. His warmth and concern for her felt strange, but somehow comforting.

"Scott seems like a nice guy but now that you're worth squillions…all I'm saying is be extra careful. Bye, Amanda"

She was sorry to leave him. He had tears in his eyes. This was really doing her in. She was tearing up again herself. She went back and gave him another hug. "Bye."

"Don't forget me, please."

"No way," she said as she left.

Her life would never be the same. She wanted to forget all the ugliness, remember the few precious moments she shared with her mother, a hug, her touch when she wiped away her lipstick from Amanda's cheek. It was all she had.

She walked outside and down the steps, past the shadowy bushes, lit by low garden lights and moonlight. The noise of branches rubbing against each other in the breeze didn't frighten her now. Scott was waiting on the sidewalk.

"When I rang about our luggage I found out that Ricardo had it picked up. I can't believe that man is still on the job. He must be devastated by the news of his sister's death."

"What would I do without you? Thanks." The breeze fanned her blonde hair. She studied his face, at that mop of auburn hair, the way it fell over his forehead; the fine lines at the corners of slate-blue eyes.

Hand in hand, they waited while he flagged down a cab.

Thank you for reading to the end. I hope you enjoyed this story. If you did, please leave a review on Amazon, Goodreads, Booklikes, Pinterest and anywhere else you can.

My next mystery/thriller will be coming out mid-2015. Please like my Facebook page if you want to be notified when it comes out or contact me at olga990@yahoo.com.au. I love to connect with my readers.

LINKS:

AMAZON KINDLE: http://www.getBook.at/B00I0DI0MY

FACEBOOK https://www.facebook.com/pages/The-Deadly-Caress/543137822419408

GOODREADS:https://www.goodreads.com/book/show/20967943-the-deadly-caress

PINTEREST: https://www.pinterest.com/olgaolha/the-deadly-caress/

TWITTER: https://twitter.com/olgaolha

Thank you for reading my story.

ABOUT THE AUTHOR

Someone asked me why I wrote The Deadly Caress. It's what captured my attention at one time from a newspaper article and I started to get the what ifs going. What if a person was to discover that the woman she thought was her mother wasn't. How would she feel? What if this mother was murdered? What would this person do?

Then there's a scary scene with Amanda driving down a mountainside and that comes from my memory banks. I grew up across the road from a very bad intersection and every weekend there would be at least one horrific accident. Some of these were youths speeding or chasing each other. Others were drunks or drivers who had miscalculated the sharp turn and careered into an oncoming car or the nearby light post. My dad would run over to see if an ambulance needed to be called as we were the only family in the street to have a phone. He'd take blankets over if the person/people was badly injured and I would help him. My sister and my mother would be too upset to be of help and didn't go.

Once a car overtook another and miscalculated. He caught the side of the vehicle and the side panel was peeled away like a giant orange peel. This I have included in one of my scenes.

I find my characters everywhere and nowhere.